BOOK ONE

Heart Sick

International Bestselling Author
MONICA JAMES

Cover Model: Luke Eisner
Photographer: Michelle Lancaster
Editing: My Brother's Editor
Formatting: E.M. Tippetts Book Designs

Follow me on:
authormonicajames.com

Other Books By
MONICA JAMES

THE I SURRENDER SERIES
I Surrender
Surrender to Me
Surrendered
White

SOMETHING LIKE NORMAL SERIES
Something like Normal
Something like Redemption
Something like Love

A HARD LOVE ROMANCE
Dirty Dix
Wicked Dix
The Hunt

MEMORIES FROM YESTERDAY DUET
Forgetting You, Forgetting Me
Forgetting You, Remembering Me

SINS OF THE HEART DUET
Absinthe of the Heart
Defiance of the Heart

ALL THE PRETTY THINGS TRILOGY

Bad Saint

Fallen Saint

Forever My Saint

The Devil's Crown-Part One (Spin-Off)

The Devil's Crown-Part Two (Spin-Off)

THE MONSTERS WITHIN DUET

Bullseye

Blowback

DELIVER US FROM EVIL TRILOGY

Thy Kingdom Come

Into Temptation

Deliver Us From Evil

IN LOVE AND WAR

North of the Stars

Fall of the Stars

REVENGE IS SWEET SERIES

Crybaby

HEART MEMORY TRANSFER DUET

Heart Sick

STANDALONE

Mr. Write

Chase the Butterflies

Beyond the Roses

Someone Else's Shadow

Author's Note

HEART SICK is a **DARK ROMANCE** containing mature themes that might make some readers uncomfortable. It contains violence, attempted suicide, death, drug use, medical procedures, psychological treatments, misuse of a corpse, blood gore, and some dark and disturbing scenes. In no way, shape, or form is the author glorifying any of the situations or circumstances in this book.

There is no cruelty to animals.

You've been warned…

Luna

"Sweetie, he's gone."

Those words play on a loop—over and over again.

But they can't be real, because what sort of world would cut short the life of a twenty-three-year-old man who had his whole future ahead of him?

A cruel fucking world I want to burn to the ground.

When I feel the gentle hands of my best friend, Joy McNelly, attempting to pry me away, my body switches to fight or flight mode, but at the forefront is fight because no one, *no one* is taking me away from my…son.

My son who lies in this sterile hospital bed…brain dead at age twenty-three.

"No!" I scream over and over again. This has to be a bad dream.

"Mom, it'll be okay. I've got you. It'll be okay." That's what

1

Misha would say. He always knows what to say to calm me down.

It's only been us since Misha was born, as his father left the day I told him I was pregnant.

I was fifteen, almost sixteen. A young girl who shamed her devout Catholic family by having a baby out of wedlock. But it was even more shameful having an abortion. I was sent away to reform school for deviant girls like me to have Misha in secrecy.

The moment he was born, I lovingly counted his ten fingers. I kissed his ten perfect toes. I knew then and there what my purpose was, and that was to be his mother. I didn't care that my family would disown me because it was decided by them that I was to put Misha up for adoption.

But the moment I saw him, I knew I had met the love of my life, and I would do everything in my power to protect and love him unconditionally.

I brought Misha home and thought my parents would also fall in love. How couldn't they? He was perfect with his blond hair, blue eyes, and cherub cheeks. He was an angel sent from God.

But when my father dropped dead from a heart attack the moment he set eyes on his grandson, my mother only saw Misha as a punishment sent from the heavens to chasten her for raising a daughter with loose morals.

She threw Misha and me out, convinced this is what her God would want. This was her atoning for her sins, and it was from that day forward that I renounced religion because what sort of God would be so cruel?

Is this my punishment for turning my back on a God which has never shown me any mercy?

"I'll get your medication. You rest," Misha had said as he kissed my forehead before grabbing my car keys from the coffee table.

I was sick with the flu and needed the medication my doctor prescribed me. Misha offered to get them for me. If only I insisted he didn't go, none of this would be happening. If only he stayed home…

He had his whole life ahead of him, and I know he would have accomplished great things.

He was playing college football and the scouts saw that he was something special. But I already knew that. My Misha would have changed the world.

But he never got to reach his full potential, thanks to a driver who veered onto the wrong side of the road. Misha didn't stand a chance. The driver fled, while here he is…my beautiful boy, kept "alive" by these machines where each beep taunts me with everything that I've lost.

I link my fingers through Misha's. He's still warm.

"Ms. Huxley, I'm Dr. Sterling. My colleague and I have looked at Misha's scans, and I'm afraid the swelling in his brain has just worsened. These machines are the only things keeping him alive. His brain activity is—"

I go to a better place, a place where Misha is alive and well, where he is playing professional football, where he is everyone's hero and not just mine. I see his children. A boy and a girl with blue eyes just like their daddy.

I hold my grandchildren with love and pride because family is the only thing that matters. I've not spoken to my family in years because if they didn't accept my son, then they didn't accept me. And we didn't need them anyway.

Misha lived on campus, but he often visited as our home wasn't far from school. We lived in an expensive neighborhood and could afford lavish things because I busted my ass to provide for my son. But I didn't mind.

I learned early on that men would do almost anything for a damsel in distress. And a young damsel in distress, well, she could get anything she wanted. I was a homeless, teenage, single mom. Desperate times called for desperate measures and I don't regret a thing.

I learned that women are the superior sex, and I used that to provide for me and Misha.

I worked as an exotic dancer, or as most would say, a stripper, until one photographer who was thirty years my senior asked if he could take photos. I agreed, for the right price, of course. It turns out he was a photographer for a popular men's magazine and that was when I was "discovered."

Before I knew it, I was the most popular centerfold girl in all of America. But I never forgot why I was doing this—everything I did was for Misha.

I now work for that men's magazine, recruiting models. My modeling days are over. But I offer my experience to newbies who were just like me. Most times, there are no magical potions. Just pure luck.

But I refuse to believe that in this circumstance because there is no luck, no silver lining in Misha being unresponsive and relying on machines to breathe.

"Ms. Huxley, your son is an organ donor and we were wondering—"

"Don't you touch him!" I cry, covering Misha with my body as I glare at the doctor. "You will not touch a hair on his head!"

A guttural sob breaks free, grating my throat raw. But my heart, my heart suffers in the worst possible way. It isn't just broken; it is destroyed. I doubt it'll ever beat the same way ever again.

"Luna, if he can help another person live—" Joy softly says.

"I said no!" I bellow, clutching Misha tightly. "He is my son, and I promised, I promised to keep him s-safe. You can't…you just can't. I won't allow you to desecrate his body. You vultures! Keep away!"

I bury my face in Misha's chest, my cries echoing into his lethargic heart.

"I won't let them hurt you, baby boy. I promised to protect you and I will do so with my very last breath."

I run my fingers over Misha's face. His arms. I close my eyes and become in sync with the gentle lull of his breathing. I refuse to believe this is the end.

"Take these tubes out. He can't breathe." A panic overcomes me as I frantically scramble to take the tubes out of his mouth and nose.

"Ms. Huxley! Stop."

But I will not.

The doctors and nurses don't know my son better than me. He was born a fighter. He doesn't die this way.

Strong arms pull me away, but I am stronger and fight with all my might. I may be slender, but that's never stopped me in the past. I kick, scream and bite, but in the end, I am yanked away from Misha as doctors and nurses attempt to restrain me in a brown leather chair.

Spittle dribbles from my chin as I am a rabid momma protecting her cub.

Dr. Sterling crouches low as I thrash wildly. "I know this is very painful for you. I can't even begin to imagine your pain. But we have a match for Misha's...heart. Don't let his death be in vain. Your son can live on by saving the life of another. Please, Ms. Huxley, honor your son as I know he would want."

His *heart*?

Vomit rises and I turn my face, expelling nothing but bile onto the polished linoleum.

"You want to take his...heart?" I ask, horrified, my voice quaking when I can construct a coherent sentence. "You monster!"

The doctor doesn't take offense. "Only with your approval."

I know protocol is that the hospital can proceed even over family objection, and I am objecting very damn hard. But Dr. Sterling is trying to reason with me. She wants me to see this is the right thing to do.

But there is no right.

Why does this person deserve to live while Misha dies?

He walks around with the heart that is as much a part of me as it is my son's. No, that isn't fair. That is a cruel reminder that I will never get back the only person who I ever loved in this world.

"*Think if it was me, Mom. If I had the chance to live...*" Misha's words ring loudly and I cover my ears, blocking out what I know is the truth.

"If I do that, that means you d-die," I whimper, squeezing my eyes shut.

"Who are you talking to?" Joy asks, her concern clear.

"*I'm already gone. But I can live on. Every beat of my heart helps another live.*"

Misha has always been selfless, and it seems even in death, it's no different.

But how do I say yes? How can I live knowing I said yes to ending my son's life so another can live?

"We don't have much time," the doctor says softly.

"Who is it?"

"We are not at liberty to—"

"If I am giving you my son's fucking heart, then I want to know it's going to someone who deserves it!" I remove my hands and blink back my tears.

The doctor peers around the room to ensure no one can hear. "It's a young man, a little older than your son, and I can assure you...he will look after Misha's heart."

"What's his n-name?"

The doctor appears torn whether to reveal this information to me, but she knows this will make all the difference. If I can humanize this match as not merely a number but a person, she knows I will say yes.

"Dutch."

"What sort of name is that?" I ask abruptly, sniffing away my tears.

"It's a unique name for a very unique man. He will honor Misha because his heart is theirs. It's because of Misha that Dutch can live. Please."

Peering over at Misha, I can't help but think he would actually like Dutch's strange name because Misha never judged. He accepted everyone.

I watch the rise and fall of his chest and memorize every single breath. But this won't be the last memory I have of my son.

I come to a shaky stand and forget where I am as I climb onto the hospital bed and press my ear to Misha's chest. I listen to the tender rhythm of his heart, the heart which was always too big for this world.

Wrapping my arms around him, I sob quietly. I don't think I'll ever run out of tears. "I'm sorry, Misha. I'm so sorry. You don't deserve this. You deserve to live. If I could give you my life, I would, because I am nothing without you. Please forgive me. This is my fault."

Clutching Misha, I remember his smell, the softness of his skin. I remember that no matter what happens, in life or death, he will always, always be my son.

"Okay," I whisper, choking back my tears. "You can have his heart because mine is fucking broken."

And those are the last words uttered as I succumb to the darkness, wishing to never see the light again.

Dutch

This is fucked up.

There is something incredibly morbid about being excited to accept the heart of another to help you live because you know for that to happen—they have to die.

But here I am, in an Uber, on the way to the hospital because I got "the call."

When Dr. Norton called, it was apparent she was more enthusiastic than me. She explained the donor was a healthy male and was on life support. She didn't give me any other details. With her colleague, Dr. Sterling, they had run the tests and he was a perfect match.

But that seems like the wrong phrase to use when speaking of taking someone's heart and making it your own.

I hate that I need it. I wish we both could live and if this were a perfect world, that's what the outcome would be.

I think of his family, how they probably hate me for doing something their loved one can't—live.

I was born with a congenital heart defect, a hole in the heart which should have closed over, but didn't. I had surgery which "fixed" it. For a little while, anyway.

I lived a relatively normal life, doing all the things a kid with a normal heart can do. But the doctors told my parents I wasn't to do anything too strenuous. I stayed away from sports as my overprotective parents were worried I would overdo it and undo the surgery. Not possible, but lucky for me, I didn't like sports.

But music…music was my calling.

I was six the first time I heard Beethoven and fell in love. I then listened to every piece of music I could get my hands on. My fondest memories are laying on my bedroom floor with my dad's oversized headphones as I listened to the classics on vinyl.

I loved every instrument as each one has the ability to transport you to another world, but I soon learned that piano was my soulmate.

I never got lessons. I just…knew how to play. I read books or watched instructional videos. And that was how I learned how to play.

I was gifted, everyone would say. But I never saw it that way. Playing piano was almost an extension of who I was. The moment I placed my fingers on those keys, life just drifted away and I existed in a world where it was just music and me.

I didn't have many friends which was fine. I didn't like many people. No one seemed to understand why I would choose piano over getting wasted or getting laid.

But music was my drug. It was the only mistress I needed.

However, my mom wouldn't hear of it and sent a video of me playing piano without my consent to some musical scout and before I knew it, Juilliard was calling, offering me a place at their school. I found it strange that one would get schooled on playing piano, so I politely declined.

But when I saw the disappointment on my parents' faces, I changed my mind because all they ever wanted was for me to live a full, happy life.

Juilliard was better than I expected. I kept to myself, but was surprised that word spread so quickly about my playing. I was told the competition was tough, but I never saw it that way. We all were there to excel at something we loved.

But being "top of your class" didn't do me any favors. I was seen as arrogant or rude because I didn't talk to anyone. I was neither of those things. My entire life, I let the music speak for me, so I often forgot actually engaging in conversation was what most people do.

I was considered a freak and loner most of my life, but at Juilliard, that seemed to make me intriguing and a mystery most wanted to decipher.

I was never the popular jock at school. Spending hours in front of the piano meant I wasn't gym-obsessed like most guys my age. But late at night, when my parents were fast asleep, I would slip on my headphones and get lost in my favorite songs as I ran the streets.

It was in the darkness where I wanted to belong. It was where I thrived.

My mother was worried about how much time I spent alone. She suggested I see a doctor who said I was depressed. I wasn't depressed. I just didn't want to socialize with people who had no substance. I wanted to connect to someone how I did with music.

But I never did.

At Juilliard, there was no shortage of attention from the opposite sex, which surprised me. I never knew what was "cool" because it never mattered to me. But when every girl I dated passionately tugged on my long dirty blond hair during sex, or told me they could come just by looking into my blue eyes, I realized they saw something I didn't and that was because I didn't care.

What is on the outside means nothing if you're ugly on the inside, and this world is filled with much ugliness.

I casually dated, but no one came close to stirring anything in me like music did. I began to think maybe everyone was right—maybe I was a freak.

And I was so okay with that fact.

My teachers offered me an opportunity that I couldn't pass up. I was to go on tour and play piano in Europe for three months. It was my dream come true.

But that soon turned into a nightmare when I had to undergo some physicals and it was discovered that both of my ventricles weren't functioning how they should be. Dr. Norton read over my long-ass file and took me on as her patient. She explained the ventricular failure happened because of a long-standing valve obstruction.

This then led to irreversible heart failure.

She asked if I had any issues with my heart and I confessed that lately, it was getting harder to do small things. I was often out of breath and light-headed, but I ignored it and just got lost in the music because I always felt better after that.

But truth be told, I always knew my heart would fail me one day. It was what made me different. It was what made me want to write a masterpiece to leave behind as my legacy because I never anticipated living a long life.

My parents blamed themselves, seeing my defect as something they did, but I didn't see it that way. I just felt lucky to have lived, and I lived an extraordinary life.

I left Juilliard as I didn't want to be looked at as "that poor guy." The guy who was a prodigy in his prime, only to be dead a year later because that's what Dr. Norton predicted.

She prescribed an arsenal of drugs and at first, I took them as it gave my parents hope. But they made things fuzzy. They may be helping my heart, but they interfered with my brain and when I sat at my Steinway grand piano and couldn't play a single note, I knew what I had to do.

If I couldn't play, I may as well be dead. So I stopped taking the medication.

I got sicker and sicker. Weaker and weaker, but the music never stopped, and that's all I ever cared about because if that was what I was born to achieve, then I would happily succumb to death.

I was sitting at my piano when I got Dr. Norton's call.

At first, I didn't know what to think. She had mentioned a heart transplant as the only way to live, but the odds of that happening were slim.

But it seems life isn't done with me yet. Maybe my masterpiece is yet to come.

I haven't called my parents because I didn't want to wake them. They've been through enough.

The driver pulls up at the hospital, glancing with curiosity over his shoulder and appearing to wonder why I would need to come here in the dead of night. I look like the perfect pillar of health. But it's what's on the inside that fails me.

I often wondered if maybe that was why I couldn't love how others do. Was my heart broken in every sense of the word?

I close the car door, but don't enter the hospital right away. I lift my chin, close my eyes, and listen to the heavens. The universe speaks at night and the sounds are utterly beautiful.

The soothing rustle of the wind. The occasional hoot of an owl. Music is all around us—we just need to feel it.

"Dutch, the doctors are ready for you."

Opening my eyes, I bid the stars farewell and hope to see them again soon.

I follow the nurse into the hospital, the sterility hurting my eyes. It's quiet, eerily so. But I suppose hospitals aren't usually associated with happiness. My Doc Martens pound on the polished floor and I suddenly feel so undeserving.

I am nothing special.

Why do I get this chance when others don't?

The nurse ushers me into a room where she runs some tests and asks some questions. I answer on autopilot because this is all surreal. I understand time is of the essence.

"Please remove all jewelry and here is a gown and a hat. Please tuck all your hair under it." She leaves the room to give me some privacy.

I do as she asks and change into the scratchy hospital gown.

I wear a lot of jewelry, I always have, so I start with my leather cuff and silver bracelets. I then remove my silver rings which feels weird. I never take them off, even when playing. I place everything in the plastic bag on the dresser. I then remove my silver necklaces but leave the one with a black crucifix till last.

I'm not a devout Catholic, but my family are and this necklace was given to me by my grandmother. She said it would protect me and God knows, I need all the protection I can get right now. I feel incomplete without it.

My hair is long enough to tie back, so it takes me a while to tuck it all under the mesh hat.

Once I'm done, I lie in the hospital bed and two orderlies then push me toward the operating room. They try to make conversation, but all I can focus on are the wheels on the bed turning and the fluorescents above buzzing, making their own sound.

In my head, I commence writing a piece of music, my fingers moving on the invisible keys as I use the surrounding sounds as my inspiration. I hear it clearly. I connect with the music as it courses through my body, thrumming in sync with the irregular concerto of my heart.

"Dutch Atwood," a nurse with a clipboard says, turning over my ID bracelet to ensure I am who I say I am. "We're all set."

She continues talking but as I'm wheeled into the operating room, all I hear are the hypnotic pulses of the endless machines. They too inspire the piece I write in my head. Some may say this is a coping mechanism, but this is how my brain is wired.

I don't know how to exist any other way. I see…hear…feel music everywhere.

I am poked and prodded, and when Dr. Norton's face comes into view, I know it's time to rest because when I wake, I have a masterpiece to finish.

But now, now I must silence the sounds and surrender to the quiet.

What a strange place to be.

Dutch

T*hump.*
    Thump.
     …Thump.

That foreign pattern plays over in my head, but my brain is too heavy to formulate any lucid notes. I don't like it.

My eyes aren't ready to open, but I force them to take in my surroundings because I've been incoherent for long enough. I blink past the blurry veil to see the apprehensive face of my mother.

"Oh, thank God," she says on a rushed breath. "If you didn't just have surgery, I would slap you for not telling us."

I try to shift, but everything feels heavy.

"Your father is just getting a coffee." From the looks of her, I dare say either of them haven't slept.

"How long have I been out of it?"

"A very long time."

No timeline means it's been days? Maybe weeks?

No wonder I feel like a zombie. But regardless of how fuzzy things are, the one thing which sounds steady is…*his* heart which is in my chest. It's funny, the first thing I think is, what did Dr. Norton do with my heart?

It's a reject, so I'm sure it's sent with all the other reject parts. But I can't help but feel somewhat sad that it wasn't given a nicer send-off. I mean, it did try its best for thirty years. To just discard it because it was no longer needed seems somewhat cruel.

I would have liked to keep it, as macabre as that is. It was the epicenter of who I was, and now, I have someone else's heart beating within my chest.

"How are you feeling, Dutch?" Dr. Norton asks as she enters my room. She reaches for my chart off the end of the bed and begins reading over my vitals.

I owe her a lot. Not only has she tried to help me cope with this ordeal, she just gave me a new heart.

"Feeling okay. My brain is a little cloudy, though. That will go away, right?"

Dr. Norton nods as she knows why I've asked. I would rather not have a healthy heart if my brain remains plagued by this weight, which stunts my music. I am anxious that I cannot hear the notes in my head.

"Yes, that's completely normal," she replies, peering at me over the rim of her designer black-framed glasses. "The transplant was a complete success."

My mother sighs in relief. But I know we aren't in the clear just yet.

"But we have to be prepared that your immune system may reject the new heart. This is your body's normal response to a foreign object. Your immune system sees the organ as a foreign threat and will attack it."

"What does that mean?" my mom asks, hand over her throat, horrified.

"It just means Dutch will need to take medications to trick the immune system into accepting the transplant and stop the body from attacking it."

"For how long?"

She doesn't need to answer. I know how long by the look on her face.

"If they fuck with my head, then no, absolutely not."

"Dutch!"

But my mom knows my stance on this.

"If I can't compose, then I may as well be dead." And I'm not being melodramatic.

"There is more to life than music."

But that's where she's wrong. If I don't have music running through my veins, then I don't want this heart because music *is* my heart.

"We can talk about this later. For now, I just want you to rest. The next forty-eight hours are imperative. We will monitor you very closely. No strenuous activity, nothing that will get your heart rate going. And especially, under no circumstances, are you to play music."

"That's a little hard, Doc, as I don't see a grand piano laying around, do you?" I swiftly sweep my hand around the cramped room, the IV pole almost careening into the plastic chair.

I already feel the walls closing in on me and when this

happens, I would sit in front of my piano and play my worries away.

"Diana, can I speak to you outside?"

My mom looks at the doctor apprehensively, but nods.

I know she wants her to be on board with whatever decision I make, but she will fight me if I decide to stop taking the medication. But this is my choice and she knows I always get what I want.

A young nurse enters and I throw her a flirty smile because although she is really beautiful, there is something I need, and it's not her number. She goes to check my vitals, leaning in close. She smells of ripened strawberries on a spring day.

The hospital gown sags low and she doesn't make it a secret that she's looking down the front of it, no doubt attempting to work out what my tattoos are. My body is randomly inked with sheet music from my favorite pieces. Some are just a bar of music, but each note means something to me; it helped shape me into who I am today.

My favorite is down the side of my neck, starting under my ear—I have the opening musical notes of my favorite classical piece—Moonlight Sonata.

She tilts her head to take in the piano keys tattooed on the outside of my forearm. "I take it you like music then?"

"What gave it away?" I quip, throwing her a flirty smile.

She nervously brushes a strand of hair behind her ear.

"I don't suppose I can borrow your pen?"

Before she can object, I reach for the pen which is clipped to the collar of her scrubs. A shudder of breath leaves her.

"And some paper?"

She appears confused by my request, but doesn't see the

harm in it and she digs into her pocket. She tears off a few sheets from her small notepad.

I position the movable tray in front of me and shift to sit upright, ignoring the pain in my entire body. "Thank you."

She places the sheets of paper onto the tray and watches with interest as I organize them in a line. Pen in left hand, I begin to draw the keys of a piano, lost in that world I go to whenever music is near. When I am done, I look at the sight before me and a sense of peace overcomes me.

My fingers twitch just as they always do and this to me, this is foreplay. This is what gets me hard. I place my fingers on the makeshift keys and close my eyes, familiarizing myself with my mistress because all I want to do is make her scream.

I decide to play a piece I already know, something a little upbeat—Franz Liszt's Hungarian Rhapsody No. 2 seems like the perfect choice.

I wait for the music to kick-start in my brain, but all I hear is white noise. I give it a minute because Dr. Norton said this was normal, but when all I hear is…nothing, a heaviness kicks me in the chest. I am aware of his heart beginning to trounce wildly, but I ignore it because that sound is the only thing I can hear.

It is drowning out all other noise and I want it to stop.

I move my fingers to the keys I've memorized by heart, but I hear nothing.

"Dutch, your heart rate—"

But I ignore the nurse.

I push aside her voice filled with concern and every other sound which is drowning out the music and focus. However, the harder I concentrate, the foggier things become.

20

No fucking way will I surrender.

I vaguely hear the sudden commotion of machines beeping and a flurry of panicked voices swarming around me because the faster his heart beats and the harder it is to breathe, the music begins to breed. It's small at first, a flicker of light, but as the pain heightens and I struggle for air...I hear it.

Music flows through me and my fingers move.

The soothing sounds of the notes are all I need because the harder I play, the faster his heart beats. I ignore it, however, and let the music consume me, surrendering to the melodies which flood my brain.

Finally, I am home.

"Dutch! Can you hear me?" Dr. Norton screams. Her voice amalgamates with the music and it feeds the beast.

I only play harder.

"Nurse, get me the defibrillator. Now! He is about to go into cardiac arrest!"

His heart gets faster and faster. Louder and louder. And unfamiliar images begin to flick before me; memories that aren't mine. They make me want to vomit—blood, so much blood.

There is only one thing I can do to make it go away.

Blindly reaching for the pen, I violently stab it into my chest, scissoring it along the fresh wound. Blood coats me and the warmth fills me with such joy. I dig my fingers into the wound, desperate to pull out the heart with my bare hands.

"Dutch, no, please no. Please, God, no!" My mom's guttural sobs are the perfect transition into a somber chord.

I can hear it loudly. It's beautiful and I never want it to end.

But when his heart suddenly stops, the hollow echo ceasing to deafen me, I realize that is what I need to finish this masterpiece. This foreign alien within my chest needs to stop beating for me to exist.

Ironic, this was supposed to save me, but it looks like I am beyond saving.

DC al Coda...

Three

Luna

"Do you want me to get the car?"

Voices echo around me, but I don't really hear them. I can't. All I can focus on is the mahogany coffin in front of me because inside it is my son.

I think the service was beautiful. I don't know for certain as it felt like I was viewing it through the eyes of a stranger. How can I accept this reality, a reality where Misha doesn't exist?

A sob gets caught in my throat and fresh tears fall down my cheeks. I don't think they'll ever stop.

Joy organized this simple, yet tasteful funeral for Misha. He wouldn't want a fuss. It didn't surprise me the chapel was overflowing with people. Everyone loved Misha. His friends gave a beautiful account of who my son was.

He touched so many people. But now, he won't be able to touch anybody ever again because he's inside that fucking coffin. And it's my fault. I should have been in that car, not him. I should have told him to stay home and get the medication in the morning. It was so wet and cold out. He should have stayed home.

I measure my breaths as I know I'm on the cusp of hyperventilating—again.

When I was asked if Misha's wishes were to be buried or cremated, I answered neither, as his wishes were to be alive and well. But as that will never be an option ever again, I decided for cremation as the only way to hug my son from here on in will be in the white ceramic vase I chose his ashes to be in.

I thump my clenched fists against my legs, angered life would be such a cruel, sadistic bitch. It gave me a son I loved with everything I was, only for him to be taken away before he even got the chance to live.

The day Misha died, I died too, and this person now, is just a shell of her former self as I will never heal. I don't want to as life has lost all meaning for me. I have nothing to live for anymore.

Joy has been a great support. She has taken on the burden of organizing all of this because all I want to do is close the curtains, lie in bed, and sleep away this pain. But I doubt it'll ever go away.

"People will be arriving at my house for the wake, sweetie. Are you ready to go?"

Looking at the coffin, I feel myself about to break and it's not going to be pretty. "Can you take me home?"

"Of course, but do you think that's a good idea? You shouldn't be alone."

"That's all I want to be. Please take me home."

I know this is highly impolite to not attend my son's wake, but the thought of watching people eating, talking and… breathing twists my stomach into knots. If I am on the verge of a messy breakdown, I prefer it to be alone, and not with people looking at me with those faces filled with pity.

I don't want their pity. I just want my son.

Joy eventually agrees to take me home as she knows my mind is made up. Just as we are about to exit the chapel, Trista, Misha's girlfriend, meets us at the door. She throws her arms around me, sobbing into my shoulder.

I stand rigid because she was only dating Misha for six months. What right does she have to cry? But I know this is just my grief talking. But I can't help but feel numb to this all.

"I am so so-sorry," she cries loudly.

"Thank you." It's all I can muster, as I am not here to console anyone. No one understands the loss of a mother losing her child.

"We were talking about getting a place together. And we often spoke about the future. He wanted to have a big family. We had so many plans. But now…now he's gone."

Every part of my body begins to scorch. I envision pushing Trista off me and slamming her lovely face into the stone wall— over and over again. Or better still, ramming her head through the stained glass window and seeing it shatter around her. It would rain so many pretty colors, interspersed with her blood.

A giggle bubbles from me and both Trista and Joy look at me as this is hardly an appropriate time to be laughing. But how dare she think she knows my son better than me. From what Misha told me, Trista was just someone to have fun with.

She was a little on the possessive side and Misha was

thinking of breaking it off.

So to hear her say they were something serious when I know he never saw a future with her, has me wishing to gauge out her eyeballs and to rip out her deceitful tongue.

This violence frightens me, but when I suddenly see a flicker behind Trista, a flicker of Misha in his football gear, I wonder if maybe that's what I need to deal with this insufferable pain.

"Trista, I'm taking Luna home." It appears Joy is sick of Trista's theatrics too.

"Oh? You're not attending the wake? That's probably a good idea. I will let everyone know."

Of course, she sees this as her opportunity to shine and brag about her time with Misha, hoping to gain whatever sympathy she can. I don't know who died and left her in charge. I suddenly wish I used a different phrase.

What is the matter with me?

I am suddenly so fucking angry. The sadness has subsided and made room for…this.

"When you're feeling…better—" I try not to scoff as there is no better in this scenario. "I was wondering if I could talk to you about Misha. He was…"

But she never gets to finish as Joy cuts Trista off. "This can wait. We *are* at her son's funeral."

Trista nods, appearing genuinely sorry for bringing up whatever she wanted to say.

Joy senses my shift in demeanor and quickly ushers us from the chapel and toward her black Mercedes which is parked out front. People watch me closely and I hate it. I don't know what they expect to see.

Joy takes off while I sigh in relief. Thank God that freak

show is over with. I do wonder what Trista wanted to say.

Joy tries to make conversation, but eventually gives up when I simply stare out the passenger window, silent. The landscape passes me by and the dismal gray weather is a perfect reflection of how I am feeling inside.

I trace the raindrops on the window with my finger, leaving a pattern in the condensation. I know Joy is watching me closely, concerned by my behavior.

When we pull up at my house, I open the door and without a word, I take off my heels and make my way toward the front door. Joy's quickened footsteps behind me reveal her worries, but I just want to be alone. I unlock the door and make clear I don't want Joy to come in.

"Luna, are you going to be okay?"

Turning to look at her, I smile. It's strained, but I don't want to worry her any more than I have. "I just want to go to sleep. Thank you for everything."

She chews on her pink stained bottom lip. The shade looks striking on her. But Joy is beautiful in whatever shade she wears. She's been my rock in more ways than one. We met when her son, Kyle, and Misha were in the same class together.

She never judged me for being a young, single mother who took off her clothes to care for her family. She opened her home and heart to me and made sure Misha and I were fed. She is older than me and I think in some ways, she took on the mother role toward me. God knows where I would be without her.

I owe her so much. She is the only family I know, which is why if I die and Misha was no longer here, I left everything to her, which is a hefty fortune. She insisted she didn't want a dime, but it's the least I can do.

Her bastard husband took off with his secretary, leaving her a divorcee at forty-five. She doesn't work, so I know she's doing it tough. But what is mine is hers because she took me in when no one else did.

She treated Misha like her own son and I know she loved him dearly. He also loved her. I often found them cooking dinner together when I was working late. I loved that they were as close as we are.

"I will call you later. I'm sorry I couldn't—"

"Shh, don't you worry. I'll take care of it. You just look after yourself. I will check in tonight. But I'm worried about you. You were talking to yourself again during the service."

Joy has mentioned this a few times. I don't see anything wrong in talking to my dead son. But she clearly does. I know she's very worried about my mental health. So I try to put on a happy face.

"Are you going to be all right?"

All I can do is nod and hold back the tears. When will they end?

Joy gives me a warm hug and I try to return the gesture, but I just feel so numb. She doesn't take offense and eventually leaves, but not before looking over her shoulder at me at least a dozen times as she walks toward her car.

I know she doesn't want to leave me alone, but she won't push as she knows how stubborn I am. I stand in the doorway, waving goodbye, watching her car become a small dot in the distance. When I can no longer see her, I step inside, close the door and press my back toward it.

The house is so quiet.

The marble staircase in front of me used to be one of my

favorite things. I close my eyes and clearly see Misha running up and down the stairs, his innocent laugh filling the hollowed void. He loved this house. We came from nothing to this lavish home in the suburbs.

It was something we were both proud of because the sacrifices made were to better our lives, and it was better.

Pushing off the door, I amble up the stairs, the cool marble against my bare feet sending a chill through me. However, I doubt I'll ever feel any warmth ever again.

The hallways are decorated with expensive artwork, but it all seems so pointless now. This home is now just a house without Misha in it.

My heart begins to quicken and each beat is a silent fuck you, reminding me that someone else has Misha's heart inside their chest.

"Dutch," I whisper to myself in almost disgust.

That's the name of the young man who got a second chance at life. I shouldn't feel animosity toward him, but I do.

Everything feels heavy and each step suddenly feels like ten. I walk past my room and slowly open the door to Misha's bedroom. Everything is the way he left it.

His football trophies line the shelves above his bed, and I remember how proud I was when he received each one. But even if he didn't excel, I would have been proud. He was such a good son.

"I can't do this without you." I lean against the doorjamb, unable to step inside because I am afraid I'll never resurface if I do. "I'm so sorry. This is my fault."

"Yes, you can. You're strong. Look what you did for me."

His voice suddenly tackles me from behind and I grip on to

the doorframe to stop from falling to my knees.

"Misha?" I cry, turning around so quickly, the room spins.

In a perfect world, he would be standing behind me with that gorgeous smile, telling me it was just a bad dream. But all I see is nothing.

All I feel is nothing.

"I was only strong for you. But I have nothing left to live for."

The tears I've kept so hard to keep at bay threaten to break past the floodgates, and I know this time, it won't be pretty. A thought suddenly collides into me, and it scares me. Even when times were unbearable, I never once thought that ending it would be so much easier than living.

But I look over the railing of the staircase and know it would be so easy to end this pain.

"Don't you dare."

"Why not? I've lost my reason to live." I stagger toward the railing, gripping the cool balustrade in both hands.

Peering at the white polished floor below, I know the mess I'd make if I jumped would be horrific. I don't wish for my cleaner, Lucinda, to have to clean blood and brain matter off the walls.

"Too messy."

Overcome with purpose, something I haven't felt in days, I make my way down the red carpeted hallway and enter my bathroom. I look at the extravagant claw-foot bathtub in my en suite.

"Too cliché."

And besides, I don't fancy being found naked, floating in my own blood from the slits I carved into my wrists.

"Please, Mom, don't do this."

As each morbid idea surfaces, Misha's voice gets louder and louder. It comforts me which is why I race into the en suite and open my vanity mirror cabinet above the sink. Small orange bottles litter the shelves and I frantically turn the labels around so I can read what each one is.

My doctor prescribed me anti-depression pills because lately, things have been getting too much. And everything has been cloudy. He also thought some sleeping pills would help. And now seems like the perfect time to catch up on sleep…only to never rise.

"Mom! No! There's no going back."

"That's the point. I don't want to go back," I say into thin air, replying to the voice which isn't there.

"You don't want to do this."

But I ignore Misha because he isn't here. He never will be again.

However, as I flip off the white lid of the bottle and peer in the mirror and see him standing behind me, I know a way that I can see him again.

"If I die too, then I can find you. I don't believe in heaven, but I know there is more to life…than this."

Misha shakes his head desperately, begging me with those poignant eyes that I don't do this.

But it's too late.

I throw back my head and empty the entire bottle of pills into my mouth. Cupping a handful of water, I swallow it, sending the pills down into my empty stomach.

Once I've ingested them all, I open the other bottle, which is another medication to help me sleep. They have dangerous consequences if mixed, that's what the doctor told me, which is why I repeat the same action as I did with the first bottle.

Once it's empty, I drop it into the sink, and it skates around the porcelain until it comes to rest in the drain.

I peer at my reflection in the mirror, gripping the basin to stop from falling because things become a little blurry.

"There's still time. Throw them up."

"No," I stubbornly argue into the mirror.

"Mom, please."

It seems the closer I come to death, the more vivid Misha's voice sounds. It's like music. A lullaby I wish to get lost in.

I stagger out of the en suite and crash into the wall as I attempt to navigate my way out the door. The hallway becomes a spinning tunnel and I smile as I know it's almost time.

"I won't let you do this!"

But this isn't Misha's choice.

I stumble into his bedroom because there is no other place I wish to be than in here. My stomach churns and my heart begins to race. My body wants me to expel the drugs, but there is no way. As each moment blurs in time, the pain subsides as everything is moving in slow motion.

"Mom, please, no…forgive me."

I collapse face-first onto Misha's bed. His scent engulfs me and wraps me into a tight embrace. I inhale deeply and sigh contently.

The silence is welcomed as I close my eyes and transport myself to happier times—when Misha was alive. I start from the beginning, from when I first held him in my arms.

Moving pictures flicker in and out of focus, cataloging my life with Misha. This is where I want to be forever. I may not have had any control over Misha's death, but I do over mine. And this is what I choose.

"I love you. Please live…live for me."

As I feel the bed dip beside me and Misha's arms wrapping around me, I let go of the sadness and embrace this fate.

Tears are heavy in my eyes as, with my final breath, I whisper, "I love you too."

Bright lights blind me.

Is this the proverbial light at the end of the tunnel most speak of?

Am I dead?

Have I been wrong this entire time and heaven does, in fact, exist?

But when I hear a voice, I realize hell exists on earth, a place I still inhabit. "Ms. Huxley, can you hear me? I'm an ER doctor. You took a lot of pills. Can you remember?"

Surely life isn't this cruel?

Opening my eyes slowly, I see that it, in fact, is.

I'm in a hospital ER with a cannula stuck in my arm, pumping me full of drugs to clear out the others I took. But I don't want that.

"No!" I tug at the tube, desperate to pull it out.

Nurses dive on top of me to stop me. "Ms. Huxley! Please. We are trying to help."

"I don't want your help!" I reply, eyeing the nurse angrily. I feel terrible because it isn't her fault. "I thought taking the endless pills I did made that very clear."

"Your friend Joy found you. If she hadn't…"

If she hadn't, I would be in a better place. But here I am, once again burdened with this pain. It was gone for a moment, when I embraced death. I want it back.

"I don't want to be here!" I thrash wildly, desperate to break free.

"We need to sedate her."

Before I can object, the nurse injects a clear fluid into my IV and the darkness drags me under…for a little while at least.

I feel like I've been run over—twice. But I will my eyes to open.

When I realize I am still in the hospital, I sigh and sink into the pillows. I try to move, but peer down and see I am restrained to the bed by my wrists and ankles with tan leather straps.

"What the hell? Nurse!"

I would push the call button, but can't, seeing as I'm restrained.

"Ms. Huxley, you're awake. Are you feeling better?"

The young nurse enters, her scrubs are a lovely pale yellow. My stomach suddenly drops. "Am I in the fucking psych ward?"

"Just for observation," she replies, her soothing monotone no doubt learned to keep "crazy people" like me calm. "You took a lot of pills. Why would you do that?"

I open and close my mouth before a maniacal laugh spills from me. "I think it's fairly obvious."

When she blinks once, I realize she needs me to draw a diagram.

"Because I was trying to kill myself," I whisper sarcastically.

She shakes her head, writing something in my chart. I crane my neck in hopes of catching what she wrote, but when a doctor hobbles into the room, it's clear it doesn't matter. I am stuck in here.

"Ms. Huxley—"

"Luna," I correct over the top of him.

He nods once. "Luna. Do you know why you're here?"

Has the world gone mad? Why are they talking to me like I'm the crazy one?

When I don't reply, he continues. "You're very lucky to be alive."

A cackle gets caught in my throat and tears leak from the corners of my eyes. "Lucky? In case you missed the memo, I don't want to be alive. Hence, the pills. You're wasting a hospital bed, Doctor. Let me go, and give it to someone who needs it."

"*You* need it," he stresses, not appreciating my aloof behavior. "You're in here just for observation. And when you're no longer a threat to yourself—"

"How long?" His pep talk isn't wanted. I just want to know when I can get out of this—when I look at the bars on the window—I realize this isn't a hospital, it's a prison.

"There isn't a timeframe for emotional healing."

"Oh, for fuck's sake, cut the bullshit. When can I leave?"

"That remains to be determined."

"What the hell does that mean?"

A frustrated sigh leaves him. "It means that when we believe you are no longer a threat to yourself."

This is some horseshit. "I want to speak to my lawyer. I do not agree to be in here. This is a violation of my civil rights!"

"We weren't the ones who had you committed."

I know who did and never have I felt more betrayed in my life than I do now.

"Joy was only trying to help."

"Oh, Misha, shut up."

The doctor pauses from writing something down. "Do you hear voices often, Ms. Huxley?"

"It's Luna," I correct again through clenched teeth.

"Misha was your son?"

"*Is* my son," I amend with venom.

He writes something else down, peering at me with a pursed mouth. "Is he talking to you right now?"

"No, but you are, and I wish you'd stop. Suicide doesn't seem like such a bad thing now because it would mean I wouldn't have to listen to you!"

I have no idea where this anger has come from, but it does feel good, just as it did when I envisioned using Trista's head as a bowling ball.

A husky chuckle sounds just outside my door, inciting an unexpected riot within. I tilt my head to the left to look around the doctor as he is blocking the doorway, but I can't see anything. I wish that I did because I want to see who the owner of that gravelly laugh is.

"We will administer a light sedative to help you relax. It'll help you sleep."

"Are you serious?" I taunt with a smirk. "You shouldn't have pumped my stomach if you wanted me to sleep. Seems like a waste."

"Ms. Huxley, making jokes about your attempted suicide concerns me."

"Well, your shoes concern me."

"My shoes?" he asks, puzzled as he peers down at the brown leather monstrosities on his feet. "What about my shoes?"

"They're ugly, and offer no arch support. That probably explains why you hobbled in here. You should look at getting orthotics. Or at the very least, better shoes."

He looks at me with nothing but confusion. But is quick to compose himself. "I will see to your medication."

I would wave him goodbye, but seeing as I'm restrained, I smile—it's sickly sweet. The doctor is in a hurry to leave. I do, however, notice he seems to exit with a little more grace this time.

A laugh erupts from me because if I don't laugh, I'll cry. And I have done enough of that.

I peruse my bleak surroundings—it's everything you'd expect from a psych ward. I can't believe I'm in here.

A plastic white chair is positioned near the bed and I focus on it, wishing to materialize the only visitor I want. He is there a moment later.

"Misha."

He's clearer than ever before. *"Mom, why did you do this?"*

"To be with you," I reply with a smile.

He looks so handsome. He's wearing his favorite football jersey and blue jeans. *"I don't want that. I don't want you to live the rest of your life like this."*

"Well, I don't want you to be dead," I counter, proud he is just as stubborn as me.

He leans back in his seat, giving me that look. He was always so concerned about me. He wanted me to find a man who would treat me well and settle down. I knew that was because he didn't want me to be alone when he eventually made a family of his own.

I wasn't lonely. Nor did I lack male suitors. I had money, brains, and was blessed with looks. But I am incredibly fussy, and I didn't need a man to complete me.

I complete myself.

"I am dead. But I won't allow that fate be for the both of us."

"Misha—"

"Who you talking to?" The moment I hear a deep voice, a chill racks me from head to toe.

A young orderly with large silver-rimmed glasses and dark brown hair enters and my immediate response is to shrink away. He has no expression behind his dark eyes and my skin instantly crawls. I want to dissolve into this bed, but can't, thanks to the restraints. And when he examines them with a slanted smirk, I come to realize how vulnerable I am.

"I'm here to help. My name is Noah." I glance at his name tag, which says Hayden.

He notices me looking at the name tag. "We have a little policy here; we don't use our real names."

"Why?" I'm almost afraid to ask.

"Because it's better not to know one another on a personal level. Things get too…messy otherwise."

I have no idea what that means, but when he visually undresses me, I understand perfectly. If he was to relate to me, to humanize me, then he couldn't do the deplorable things I am certain he intends to do.

"Open up for the airplane," he mocks, sweeping the clear medicine cup through the air.

He is speaking to me like a child, and that shit won't stick with me. "Fuck you. Don't speak to me like that. I—"

I never get to finish my sentence because Noah launches forward and seizes my cheeks between his fingers. I try to pull away, but he only grips me harder, puckering my lips.

"This is how things work around here," he snarls, inches from my face. His breath is cigarette laden. "I give the orders. You obey. We clear, crazy bitch?"

I am horrified he would speak to anyone this way.

"Nod if you understand me because your mouth has other uses." He doesn't give me a choice when he forces me to move my head up and down as he's still holding my face prisoner. "Good girl. I can be your best friend. Or, I can be your worst enemy. You take care of me, I take care of you."

My stomach drops because I can read between the lines.

"Understood?"

I fake surrender, which appeases Noah who stupidly lets me go, but the moment he does, I rear forward and bite his nose and don't let go. I am like a dog, tearing at a bone as I shake my head from side to side.

"You fucking bitch!" he cries, but doesn't call for help.

And I know why. I am in so much trouble.

Noah punches me in the ribs, winding me. I gasp for air, letting go of his nose. I can't do anything because of these fucking restraints, but I don't show weakness. I can't.

An imprint of my teeth is indented in Noah's skin, which pleases me, but the reason he won't report this is because he doesn't want any issues to arise because that would mean he can't do whatever he pleases. He wishes to fly under the radar, not drawing any attention to himself and the disgusting acts he commits.

"That wasn't very nice." He pulls his hand away from his

nose to see if he's bleeding. He's not. Shame, that. "It's always the hot ones who are the craziest. But that's okay, I like crazy."

He tongues his cheek, his heated eyes revealing all the nasty things he's currently thinking.

Before I can tell him to fuck off, he stuffs the pills down my throat, forcing me to swallow them as he pinches my nose. Eventually, I have no other choice as I gasp for air.

Noah slaps my cheek playfully. "Good girl. I'll be seeing you really soon. The boys and I have a little initiation late at night for the newbies. See you soon, crazy bitch."

I watch as he exits coolly, while I wonder how being in here is better than death.

Dutch

Weeks Later...

"I really can't," says Monique, my nurse and the only hope of me getting what I want. I know she uses a pseudonym as the policy here is that we are not to know any of the staff or other patients by their real names, but she looks like a Monique.

It worked last time, but I suppose word spreads quickly about the man who tried to cut the donor heart from his chest with a ballpoint.

I haven't heard a single note since. All I can hear is this deafening asshole, sounding strongly in my chest.

When they asked me if I would try to remove my heart again and I said hell to the fuck yes, my mom had no other choice and on the advice of Dr. Norton, had me committed.

And here I am.

I suppose it does sound a little crazy trying to cut out your heart, but not being able to play music is crazier. This has never happened before. Regardless of the bullshit in my life, I have always been able to play. But now that that's stopped, it feels like a porn star in his prime losing his hard-on right before he's about to perform.

I am impotent.

"I promise I won't tell if you don't." I'm currently trying to coax Monique into giving me a real fork, and not this plastic one which I'm expected to use.

But she's been given the direct order by Dr. Norton to keep me away from anything sharp that could be used as a weapon—a weapon against myself, that is, because the moment I do, I am carving this motherfucker from my chest and playing soccer with it.

I don't like it. I want my old heart back.

Monique simply smiles and goes back to reading her magazine.

I can't even eat unsupervised. Not sure why. The only risk I have is choking on this slop they call food.

Pushing the tray away, I peer out the window, the silence greeting me, as usual. The view is of a rose garden. But it may as well be a brick wall. The universe sings to me no more.

"All done?"

I nod.

She presses the call button for someone to collect my tray. Another order from Dr. Norton is that I am to never be alone. And if I am, then I am to be restrained.

They tell me it's for my own good, but what good is being held captive, your spirit dying with each passing day. All because this motherfucker in my chest beats strong.

"Did you want to take a walk in the garden?"

I can't help but laugh as "walk" translates to her pushing me around in a wheelchair like an invalid. Again, Dr. Norton said the flight risk is too high. I'm in good shape, regardless of the operation I just underwent, and could outrun any of these assholes.

She has every right to be worried.

I know both she and my mom think they are doing this for my own good, but they are killing me, and killing me softly.

On any other day, I would hear Roberta Flack's haunting voice singing her famous hit, but nope, not today, or any other day.

Monique is waiting for my reply, so I nod.

Dr. Norton is one shrewd woman as she has only assigned women to look after me. Seems a little sexist, but she knows I would never hit a woman. I would never hit a man either, but if my knee happened to accidentally on purpose connect with their dick, then it's survival of the fittest.

Monique wheels over my chair and smiles. I envision it on fire as I climb out of bed and sit into it. Monique straps me in, before placing the gray blanket over my legs, and away we are. I do feel better the moment we exit my room.

I do hope she wheels me past the room of the woman I heard cussing out the doctor yesterday. I couldn't see her, but heard her, and dare I say by her sarcasm alone, we're destined to become great friends.

But she doesn't.

She wheels me down the hallway and the starkness, the absence of color, just adds to the depressing vibe this place embodies. This establishment is supposed to make people better, but I can't imagine any healing could be done in an institution such as this.

The hospital has different wards, but this ward is for the people, who, like me, don't want to exist. Seems unfair we are forced to be here. It is *our* lives.

I don't look into the rooms of others because who am I to judge? Why they're here is none of my business. What is my business is trying to end this silence. I see the irony in that as I assume most are in here to silence the noise.

While me, I want it to deafen me.

It's fucking cold out and with any luck, I'll die of phenomena. But Monique steers me toward the wooden pergola and parks my chair underneath. I'm not sure what I'm supposed to do because I can look at this view from my room, but here we are.

She sits near me and opens a magazine. A nurse walks past a moment later and whispers something into Monique's ear, looking at me with a smile.

"Wow."

I doubt Monique is using that phrase to describe the miserable view, so I turn my cheek to look at her, but am taken aback to catch her staring at me. She's given me a sponge bath, so I literally have nothing to hide. I wonder what she's looking at then.

The other nurse throws me a wink before walking away.

"You're like famous."

I arch a brow. "I'm really not. If I was, would I be strapped to a wheelchair, being spoon-fed by your lovely self?"

Her cheeks turn a bright shade of red. "One of the other nurses said you went to Juilliard. All the music tattoos now make sense."

I'm honored they'd take the time to look me up, but I hate to be the bearer of bad news. "They may as well be balloon animals because none of them make any sense to me anymore."

"What do you mean?"

Clearly, the other nurse failed to explain why I tried to carve my heart out with a pen. "It means I used to live and breathe music, and now…now I can't hear a single thing."

Her eyes soften. "That's so sad. Is that why you're in here?"

"I guess so."

"You've been neutered," she says, which is not exactly the word I would use.

But when she comes to a stand and peers around to ensure no one is watching, I soon understand why she opted to use such a phrase. When she is content we're alone, she drops to her knees before me and subtly places her hands under the blanket.

To anyone looking on, it would appear she is just making me comfortable and, I suppose, in a way she is as she runs her fingers over my dick. The thin hospital gown leaves nothing to the imagination, but she's seen it all regardless.

I watch with interest as she licks her bottom lip. "Maybe you just need to find a muse? Someone who can inspire a work of art from you. Isn't that how artists work?"

I'm only half listening to her because her hand on my dick is very distracting. I don't want it to feel good, but it does.

"I don't work that way," I reply, trying to keep my shit together because this shouldn't be happening. This isn't going to inspire anything other than regret when I come in her hand, which will happen very soon as she bypasses the gown and commences jerking me off.

"How do you work then?"

I like that she gives me eye contact, that she is owning her actions. She knows what this means if we get caught, but it seems she doesn't care as she begins to stroke me faster.

"Life is my muse," I explain, trying to measure my breaths. "I would be inspired by being alive."

"That's deep," she says, and just when I think I've misjudged her, she reveals why the only thing I could ever connect with was music. "I want you balls deep in me. You're so fucking hot. All the other nurses are going to be so jealous when I tell them about this. You have no idea how sexy you are, do you? It took every ounce of willpower not to do this sooner."

Life is fucking weird.

I know I should probably be flattered, but I just feel so numb…and fucking alone.

But suddenly, something happens, something which has the air becoming thick and electric, as it would just before a thunderstorm. The heavens are about to open and drown us all. But I welcome it. I want to catch the raindrops with my tongue.

I peer off into the distance, over Monique's head, when the doors slide open and a flicker of warm honey catches my eye. I feel…something, but it's more than that. It's the motherfucker in my chest which skips a beat.

On any other day, I would be hoping it wouldn't restart, but today, that doesn't happen. I am desperate for it to return to normal rhythm so I can take in the woman who comes into view.

Who is she?

She is strapped to a chair and pushed by the disgusting creep, Noah. I hope he isn't assigned to take care of her because he's a filthy asshole. All the nurses have mentioned this. I'm surprised Dr. Norton hasn't fired his ass.

A sudden possession overtakes me and I envision ripping off Noah's scrawny arms and beating him to death with them. I've never felt this before.

I can't take my eyes off her. It feels almost sacrilegious to do so. Her hair is a beautiful golden brown and I imagine the summer sun highlighting the blonde throughout. Her face is utterly enchanting. I literally can't look away.

The infernal bastard in my chest begins to beat stronger, a joyous tune because it seems to have found its home. How does this make any sense?

She looks small, but I don't allow her size to fool me because I get the feeling if she wasn't strapped to the chair, drugged out of her mind, she would be kicking Noah's ass. I want to see her up close, but I suddenly remember Monique's hand is still around my cock.

"Oh, you're so hard."

Yes, I am, but that has nothing to do with Monique.

Noah wheels the woman away and parks her chair under the other pergola across from us. She is far away now, but it doesn't matter. I can smell her cherry blossom perfume. I can hear her jovial laughter. I want to know her, but I feel like I already do.

Images once again flash before me, but I don't recognize a single one.

Suddenly, everything quietens, akin to the calm before a storm. I beg her to look at me.

I need it.

I want it.

And on cue, she lifts her chin and although a field of roses separates us, I feel it. We lock eyes and everything shifts and she becomes my focal point. The epicenter to why I am here.

My mouth parts as I'm about to come, and I can feel her watching me closely because she knows, she knows what is happening beneath this blanket. Even though I can't see her clearly, I see her in my mind. My mind, my body…his heart recognizes her.

And in my mind, I see her rolling her eyes and smirking, and if that isn't the hottest thing I have ever seen, then take my eyeballs because I don't need them anymore.

And only when she leans down, her soft lips tickling my ear as she gives me permission, whispering, "Come," do I do as she says.

I come so hard, but it's still not enough because it's not Monique's hand I want. I feel like a bastard, but to Monique, I'm only someone to brag about. This isn't going to inspire sonnets anywhere.

When I return to the now, the woman is staring off into space and I wonder if maybe I imagined the whole thing. Is that how fucked up I am?

Monique stands and reaches into her pocket for some tissues to clean herself off.

She stands in the way, and I don't hide my displeasure that she's blocking my view. She turns over her shoulder to see who I'm looking at.

"Oh, gosh, not you too." She rolls her eyes in annoyance.

It seems I'm not the only one who is enchanted.

"What's her name?"

"You know the hospital's policy," she scolds, appearing

jealous. I suppose she did just have her hand around my cock.

"You know my name," I remind her because she and the other nurse had no qualms looking me up.

I suspect this rule is in place to protect the privacy of patients so the Moniques of this world can't look their patients up. I do wonder how they know who we all are? By number? Seems fitting in an institution such as this.

"And besides, I think we've bypassed all hospital protocol."

She smirks and I know this comes with a price, a price I will happily pay because when she says, "Luna," something happens…I hear it.

Music.

It's just a flicker, but I welcome it after being lost in the silence for days.

Monique wheels me inside, but when we pass Luna, I realize that maybe she was right, after all. Maybe I needed an inspiration to fight my way through the darkness, because I think I just found my muse…and her name is Luna.

His heart beats loudly, and it seems we finally agree.

Five

Luna

I'm aware of two things.

The first is that therapy isn't for me.

And the second is that the man with the most intense blue eyes who is sitting across from me hasn't stopped watching me since I entered the room.

I have no idea what he's looking at.

I'm not creeped out like I am with Noah who, so far, has left me alone. With this handsome stranger, I feel…curious, I guess. He looks to be in his late twenties and on the "outside," I'm sure he doesn't lack admirers.

With that dirty blond hair which falls in just the right way that accents his sharp jaw and luscious mouth, and a body which looks toned, and covered in some tattoos, I know he would probably just look at someone with those inquisitive eyes and game over.

But not me.

Even though I was drugged out of my mind yesterday, I'm pretty sure I saw the pretty brunette nurse give him a hand job under the blanket. I don't judge, but it's in poor taste for both him and her. And besides, I'm not here to get to know anyone. I'm here to get the hell out.

Whatever I have to say or do, I will do.

This place has me wishing I was successful in my suicide attempt. Ironic, considering that's the complete opposite of why anyone is committed. But Parkfields Hospital would have anyone wishing they were anywhere but here.

"At Parkfields, our policy is that everyone is equal," explains our therapist, "Jade," in a soothing, soft voice. "Which is why we believe it's better not to know people by their names because we are all here to escape who that person is. We are here for new beginnings."

I can't help but scoff and it's clearly louder than I thought because the circle turns to look at me.

Jade purses her lips, addressing me, peering at the name tag in my lap. "Let's start with you."

Our first get to know you exercise was to pick a name we wanted to be called by. I actually can't believe they think this is a good idea, that being known by another name is supposed to help one heal.

What a fucking joke.

But when Jade makes it clear she is waiting for an answer, I turn the name tag over and show my fellow circle members the name I chose.

"Misha," Jade says, and I try to conceal the pain I feel at hearing his name.

51

But that's why I chose it. If I'm to be known by another alias, then there was none that I wanted than that of my son. If I'm here to "heal," then the first step is being able to hear Misha's name without wanting to slit my wrists.

I'm clearly a long way off, however.

"Let us welcome Misha into our safe, happy place."

"Welcome, Misha," the group sings, while Jade nods, indicating I'm to attach the name tag on my gown for all to see.

I don't bother arguing because the sooner I get this over with, the sooner I can return to my room because being around this many people makes me miss the comfort of solitude.

Once the name tag is affixed firmly, the attention is thankfully diverted off me, all but the handsome stranger, who still watches me closely.

I lift my eyes and meet his, and I like that he doesn't shy away. He doesn't smile, however. The expression on his face is one I can't quite place. If this were the "real world," I would guess he's interested, regardless of our age differences, but I don't know what the rules are inside here.

So I simply stare back.

I make it a point to examine him and I can't deny he is striking. The thing I find most appealing, though, is that I don't think he realizes how attractive he is. He is arrogant, yes, but conceited, I don't think that he is.

The way he holds himself, he commands the attention of the entire room just by walking into it. He is confident and has something about him that draws people in. I know I'm not the only one who seems to be just as intrigued by him.

Jade smiles, leaning forward so the collar of her silk shirt opens just enough to reveal the top of her breasts. "And what name have you chosen?"

She is talking to my stranger, but he doesn't pay her any attention because he is still watching me. I should be concerned, but I'm not. I like that he seems intrigued because there is something about him which…comforts me.

For the briefest moment when we lock eyes, the pain of missing Misha shifts and I feel…warm. I almost forget that he's gone because being in the stranger's presence makes it feel like Misha is right here with me.

When Jade clears her throat, I bite my bottom lip to stop from grinning. The stranger follows the movement and I suddenly feel hot. All over.

The man next to the stranger nudges him in the ribs, but he still doesn't break eye contact with me as he turns his name tag over to reveal his alias. When I see what it is, I almost stop breathing.

"Let's welcome Bowie into our circle."

The room does as Jade says while I remember to breathe.

This is a coincidence, but my stomach still drops because, what are the odds that this stranger would choose Bowie—mine and Misha's favorite musician? I always felt like I could escape to a different place whenever his music was on.

My love for Bowie passed onto Misha, and I have such fond memories of us listening to his music in the car, at home while I was making us dinner, or just as background noise. David Bowie was always playing.

So, to see that the stranger has chosen that name has thrown me for a loop. It unsettles me.

He seems to read my apprehension and frowns. He appears troubled that he has upset me.

"Bowie, would you like to talk about why you're here?" Jade coaxes, while he leans back in his chair, crossing his ankles.

An image of Misha crashes into me, and I grip the edge of my chair to stop myself from fainting. The image is stenciled over Bowie and it's a perfect match because his mannerism is just how Misha's was.

I often reminded Misha to sit upright because his posture was terrible. And he would tease me for my impeccable posture, which was thanks to wearing those stilettos when dancing. We teased one another every day. I miss that so much.

But looking at Bowie, I can't deny that the similarities don't just stop at the name.

They have the same tousled dirty blond hair. The same intense blue eyes. Both are blessed with a sharp jawline. Both are slim yet muscular and tall.

And now to witness Bowie behave the way Misha would, it's too much.

"I lost something and I want it back," are the words which stop me from crumpling into a mess.

Breathing through the impending hysteria, I focus on Bowie because his confession touches me deeply.

"And how does that make you feel?"

He tongues his cheek, deep in concentration. "Angry."

I listen closely because I can relate.

"And why is that?" Each time Jade prompts him, he appears to grow madder.

"Because I never asked for this!" he snaps, the blue to his eyes swimming in black. "And I can't change it."

"Everything can be changed. You just need to ask the right questions. You are the decider of your own fate."

Did she get that from a fortune cookie because, what in the actual hell?

I roll my eyes because that doesn't help. Nor is it right. I can't change the fact Misha is dead. Sure, I can change my response to the situation, but the situation itself is permanent.

What a thoughtless comment, no wonder Bowie scoffs, losing his temper. "That is just fucking stupid," he retorts, shaking his head. "Did you learn that in your crash psychology course because a trained specialist wouldn't say such a dumb-ass thing?"

Jade clears her throat, her cheeks turning red. "I have been a practicing therapist for ten years. There is no room for hostility in the circle. This is a safe place for everyone."

"Again, something learned from your shrink handbook?"

He is baiting her and I guess she's not used to it because she is accustomed to getting what she wants, thanks to her good looks. But Bowie is immune to her charms, it appears.

"I don't feel very safe with you telling me I can change something which is really fucking permanent. How about you?" Bowie looks at the middle-aged guy, two seats down from him, and grins, drawing attention to the fact he has his hand down his pants, jerking off frantically and using Jade as inspiration.

Some gasp, horrified, while most laugh. Jade doesn't see the funny side in this, however. "Merlin, what did we discuss about that? That is something you do in private."

"Looks like Merlin's fondness for jerking off in public is another thing which can't be changed. Isn't that right?" Bowie extends his wrist toward Merlin, who fist bumps him, thankfully with the hand which is not down his pants.

"Did Jade ask you the right questions, Merlin?"

A maniacal laugh erupts from Merlin as his actions grow faster. "No! No! No!" he singsongs, bouncing in his seat.

"Merlin, that is enough!" Jade declares, finally losing her cool. "If you do not stop, I will have you taken away and restrained to your bed for a week!"

"I thought this was a safe place, Doc?" Bowie counters, arching a challenging brow. "I thought anything can be changed by asking the right questions?"

His tenancy, it reminds me so much of Misha. I can't help but feel I am looking at him right now.

"Merlin is being punished because he likes pussy...pussy which should probably wear a bra to therapy."

Jade's mouth falls open and I don't know if she's insulted by Bowie's comment, or the fact he isn't jerking off to her like Merlin is.

A laugh suddenly escapes me, and it surprises me because it's the first time I've laughed since Misha died.

I attempt to quash my laughter, but the harder I try, the more difficult it is to contain. My cheeks hollow from trying so hard to stop, but I soon give up and burst into uncontrollable laughter. Soon, the entire room bursts in, and when some patients jump on their chairs, their hilarity akin to feeding hyenas, I know the session is over.

I look at Bowie, who sits back, proudly watching the mayhem he created.

Orderlies come running into the room, attempting to subdue the frenzied patients. But it soon turns into a game of chase as the patients run and the orderlies run after them, all except for Bowie and I, as we remain seated, watching one another.

His confidence is sexy, as are his convictions because it's apparent he stands up for what he believes in.

The pandemonium lashes around us, but everything soon fades into the background because it's just Bowie and I. We openly take the other in, appearing just as mesmerized by the other. I don't know, but he looks and feels so…familiar.

It feels as if we have met before.

My heart begins a deafening staccato and it's bittersweet as it's a reminder that Misha's heart beats within the chest of another.

Dutch…

When Bowie looks at me, it feels like he can see me, the real me. It's scary and exhilarating, all in the same breath.

"Come with me." Noah latches on to Bowie's arm, yanking him up, breaking our almost trancelike exchange.

Bowie rises casually, a slanted smirk slapped on his handsome face.

"You won't be smiling when I throw your ass into the vault."

I don't know where or what that is, but it doesn't sound good. "No! Let him go."

On instinct, I jump up and run to where Noah is leading a very composed Bowie away. When I am a few feet away, I come to an abrupt stop, however, because now that I am up close and personal with the man who I've merely exchanged looks with from across the room, I realize those looks were in vain.

He watches me with interest.

Being this close to him, I am able to appreciate his good looks because he is the most handsome man I have ever seen. His eyes remind me of an ocean, so blue, so clear, one can see the bottom beneath them. His nose is strong, slightly upturned, giving him a look of arrogance which I have seen him embrace.

His mouth is full. His jaw sharp.

His dirty blond hair frames his gorgeous face. I see he has musical notes tattooed on the left side of his neck. His shoulders are broad, and I guess underneath that hospital gown is a body carved of granite. I suddenly want to see it more than I need air to breathe.

But all fantasies are shattered when Noah grins, revealing his large teeth which has him on par with a rat. Goose bumps spread from head to toe.

"Can't stay away? Don't worry your pretty face, I'll be seeing you real soon."

A feral snarl leaves Bowie and I like his possessiveness. But I can look after myself.

There is promise to Noah's words and it stirs the beast within. The only way he can beat me is if I'm tied to my bed or sedated, thanks to the drugs he forces down my throat. I am neither of those things at the moment.

Sucks to be him.

I don't give him the satisfaction of replying because actions speak a lot louder than words and right now, those actions involve me ripping out his heart. Without warning, I jump onto him and cling on tightly with my arms around his neck and legs around his waist.

He is taken off guard, which is the perfect time for me to attack.

Before he has a chance to speak, I bite down on his nose—again—but this time, I do draw blood and I don't let go. I tear off a hunk of flesh and spit it out, it splattering against the wall, before sliding to the floor. The sight inspires more violence because it's in the depraved I feel alive.

I claw at his face, his eyes with my long fingernails, and when he attempts to throw me off, I headbutt him. Both our skulls crunch under the impact and I see stars, but there is no way I'm letting him go.

He loses his balance and very ungracefully tumbles onto the floor, taking me with him. But he breaks my fall. He's winded, while I get a second lease of life and commence slapping his face. I make a closed fist and am about to punch him, but he gets in first and punches me in the nose.

I instantly taste blood.

"Payback's a bitch. I am going to destroy you!"

A delirious laugh mixes with the blood as it seeps into my mouth before dribbling down my chin. Noah bucks me off and just as he attempts to punch me again, I am pushed aside. I am startled, not sure what is happening, that is, until I see Bowie diving on top of him and connecting with his face, over and over again, beating him without mercy.

A shrill alarm blares over the speakers and the room flashes red, but Bowie doesn't stop. His hard hits drown out the alarm and it's music to my ears—a concert played solely for me.

I watch in excitement as Noah is being beaten to death. Bowie shows no mercy. He is slathered in the enemy's blood all because of me. Droplets of blood somersault into the air, and I watch them, mesmerized by the almost hypnotic rhythm.

The swirling red light complements Bowie's bloodied fist and I stare at him, under some sort of spell because the longer I look at him, the more intense these inexplicable feelings grow.

I have felt…dead since Misha's passing, but now, I feel alive. I almost feel guilty for the fact.

But all guilt is soon replaced with rage as two men rip Bowie off Noah and begin beating him senseless.

With an animalistic roar, I dive on top of them, biting and scratching. "Don't touch him!"

They fling me off like I weigh nothing at all and I crash into the hard brick wall. I am about to get back up, but sadly, this fight is over—for now.

"Stay down!" Jade orders and before I can tell her to go to hell, the red room is eclipsed into darkness and silence.

I jolt awake, unsure where I am. The last I remember is… the memory instantly triggers the headache, thanks to being knocked out cold.

It's dark and dank, and I suspect I am in the place Noah mentioned—the vault.

There is a silver toilet and basin attached to the wall and a small simple wooden base on short legs which I'm guessing is supposed to be a bed.

The walls are brick.

Rubbing my arms does nothing to keep out the cold. This place is a fucking prison.

Storming over to the door, I pound my fists against the solid wood. "You can't keep me locked up like some animal! The moment I get out of here, I'm calling my lawyer!"

I'm greeted with silence.

"Fuckers!" I scream, kicking and pounding on the door. "This is so wrong! Let me out! You can't treat people this way! This is fucking unethical!"

I kick and scream until I tire because it's evident no one is coming.

Breathless, I press my back to the door and slide down it, accepting defeat. Wiping my nose, I feel the dry blood caked underneath. Peering at my hospital gown, I see it is slathered in deep red blood.

"At least Merlin had a good time."

I dare not to breathe, almost afraid I imagined his voice.

"Bowie?" I softly ask into thin air, unsure if or where I heard his hoarse voice.

"Are you okay?"

A thankful sigh leaves me. He really is here.

My heart begins to quicken. "I'd be better if I were soaking in a bubble bath, using Noah's head as a pillow."

"Ooh, vicious." A husky chuckle follows.

"Where are you?" I strain my eyes in the darkness, but can't see anything.

"I'm under your bed."

I arch a brow, confused.

Please don't let the only person I trust in this place be insane.

"Look under the bed," he instructs when I don't reply.

With apprehension, I do so, plagued with images of Bowie jumping out and scaring me like a bad horror movie. But when I see a small vent in the wall, I sag, relieved.

I scamper over on hands and knees and try to move the wooden base, but of course it's bolted to the floor. With no other choice, I lay on my side and slide as close as I can to the vent.

The dim lighting passing through the holes in the vent makes a hexagon pattern on the dirty floor. Reaching my arm out, I trace over the shape, counting each line. It transforms into a running horse before my eyes.

"We need to get out of here," I say, realizing more time spent here will surely drive me insane.

"Yes, we really do." His voice is smooth, like a neat scotch. It comforts me when all I've felt lately is desolation.

"How?"

Silence, and I know that's because he is thinking of a plan.

"Who had you committed?"

Bowie has guessed me being here isn't voluntary.

"My best friend. She thought it was for my own good."

"How about you?"

"My parents," he replies, and although I am desperate to know the reason why he's here, I won't ask. And I know he will do the same with me.

"You're thinking if we can talk to them, they might be able to help?"

"My parents will make a decision on the advice of my doctor," he shares blankly. "But if you can talk to your friend, and convince her being in here is worse than being out there, then maybe."

I wish I could see him.

I stretch my arm out, almost yanking it from the socket in hopes of touching the vent as it makes me feel somewhat closer to him. But I can't reach.

"What about you?"

A heavy sigh leaves him. "I don't have anything of worth waiting for me out there."

His confession saddens me because I, too, am in the same predicament. "I suppose I don't either."

"So why are we trying so hard to leave?" he asks, laughing

lightly.

The sound makes me smile.

"I don't know. I guess I'm no sadder in here than I was out there."

But that's not entirely true.

Being in here, being with Bowie, completes me in a way I don't understand. I feel guilty for it.

"I was happy once, but I'll never feel that again."

Bowie is quiet and I wonder if I've shared too much.

"I can relate to that. So we plan a jailbreak, only to be miserable on the outside? Doesn't sound like a very good plan to me."

I smile, his sense of humor similar to mine.

"At least I don't feel so crazy being in here," he shares, his humor giving way to his thoughts. "I don't know what will happen once I get out."

And here we are, caught at a crossroad.

"I lost my reason to live," I confess softly, hoping I don't sound melodramatic because it's the truth.

But when he replies, I understand why we've connected.

"I did too. It was ripped from my chest."

"So was mine." I think of Misha, sadness dragging me under. "How do you fill that hole? Where your heart once beat?"

A shadow soon dances in front of my eyes and I realize it's Bowie's hand pressed to the vent. My heart swells at the gesture, but I wish I could feel his hand against mine.

"I don't know, but I'll die trying." There is promise to his words and I know that's the reason we're all in here.

"I suppose that's what got my crazy ass thrown into here," I say, needing to lighten the mood with my dark humor.

Misha would laugh, but I realize Bowie may not appreciate the quip.

However, what he says next has me bursting into very inappropriate laughter. "We clearly should have tried harder."

"Clearly," I agree, unable to wipe my smile clean.

"I like your laugh," he says, catching me off guard.

"Well, it's nice to laugh. I didn't think I would again." And the truth is, I don't think anyone else will ever be able to. But Bowie isn't just anyone.

I hear a gentle tapping against the vent and it transports me to a different plane. It's a piece of music only our ears can hear.

"Moonlight Sonata is your favorite?"

"How did you know?" he asks, his surprise clear.

"Your tattoo," I explain, revealing I've been paying close attention to him.

"And you recognize it from the notes?"

"Yes, I love music. I—" But I stop myself from sharing how music was something both Misha and I loved.

"Just another reason to like you."

His confession once again leaves me speechless. It pleases me he feels this way.

"Do you play?" I ask, wanting to know more about him.

"Not anymore." The heaviness to his tone has a sadness weighing heavily within my heart. I guess that is the reason he's here.

"It'll come back," I say, unsure what I mean, but it feels like the right thing to say.

I can't explain what this is with Bowie, but I feel in sync with him somehow.

"I wish for that every day. Until then…"

"Until then what?" I wait with bated breath.

"Let's fuck shit up until we both find what we've lost."

I decide not to tell him I'll never be able to find that again. But with Bowie, anything seems possible, and that scares me. I accepted my life was to be lived in darkness, but being in literal darkness right now, I have only focused on the light because that's what Bowie has brought into my world.

And I have no idea why.

Dutch

"Rise and shine, princess."

Groaning, my entire body protests as I attempt to move. I suppose that's what I get for falling asleep on this fucking hard floor. But I couldn't move, not when I could hear the gentle breaths of Luna as she surrendered to sleep.

I know I'm breaking the hospital's cardinal rule by knowing her real name, but I don't want to call her Misha. His heart suddenly feels like it's running laps.

Rubbing over it, I sit upright and look at the old timer standing in the open doorway. "Don't even think about it," he warns, reading my thoughts. "You run, they throw your ass in here for another night. And who will protect your new friend then?"

"Where is she?" I ask, narrowing my eyes and prepared to draw blood—again.

"Oh, calm down. They took her to her room this morning. She's fine. The same can't be said about you. You want to survive in this place, you gotta learn how to play the game."

"I appreciate the pep talk, but no." I stand, stretching my arms overhead.

He shrugs. "Fine, suit yourself, but don't be surprised if they separate you."

"What?" I ask as he now has my attention.

"They won't want another scene like yesterday, so they'll make sure you're kept apart."

His heart begins lashing against my chest, rattling the invisible bars in protest. "So how do I ensure that doesn't happen?"

The old timer grins a toothless smile. "You need friends in here."

"Do you want to be my friend, old timer?" I tease with a smirk.

"You help me. I help you."

"What's the catch?"

He enters the room, which means whatever he's about to say he doesn't want anyone else to hear. "You give me the only currency which talks in here," he explains while I arch a brow. "Your pills."

On the outside, money talks. But in here, it's the red and blue pills that get you what you want. "I don't want them. So you'd be doing me a favor. But how do I do that without them finding out?"

The last time I was given my medication, the nurse pretty much gave my mouth a strip search to ensure I swallowed my pills. Our drugs are administered from the nurses' station in the sunroom, where we are monitored closely to make sure everyone is sedated well before bedtime.

We stand in an orderly line and are told to take our drugs as it'll make everything "better." So far, I feel fucking worse, and the only drug which seems to be working is Luna. Speaking to her last night, I heard it again.

Music.

It was soft, a dull sound rattling around in my head, but it was there.

During therapy, I couldn't stop watching her because I feel like I'm looking at her through familiar eyes. She incites warmth inside of me, but she also has a blanket of sadness dragging me under. It makes no sense, but I suppose none of it does. One would be thankful to get a second chance at life, but not me.

I can't shake the feeling that I need to tell Luna something, but I don't know what. I have this grave secret I want to share, but I can't formulate the words.

Maybe I really am losing my mind.

She is fucking beautiful, but I find myself attracted to her because I want to…protect her. And I want to protect her because I feel…guilt. But I don't know what I did.

My new friend, who will be dubbed Old Timer, looks at me, appearing to realize I zoned out. I assume that happens often here. "You move it around," he explains like I am stupid for not knowing this inside info. "She wants to check your cheeks, you move it under your tongue. She asks to look under your tongue, you push it to the back of your throat. Get the idea?"

I nod, impressed with him being such a sly bastard.

Giving us our pills all at the same time, and in the same room, allows them to watch us easily. It also, however, gives the other patients like Old Timer here a front-row seat to the drugs other patients are taking.

"I give you my drugs, what do you give me?"

"Safety and power," he says, and I suddenly realize he is unsupervised. Usually, an orderly would unlock the door, but they sent Old Timer instead. "You can sleep easy knowing Noah and his friends will leave the pretty brunette alone."

Just the mention of that asshole has me clenching my fists.

"You work with me and I will make sure you and your friend are safe."

I have no idea what Old Timer gives Noah in return, and I don't want to know.

"Okay, I'm in. But only if this means Misha stays safe. If anything happens to her, I will make sure you and this place suffer in ways unimaginable."

Old Timer nods, but appears taken aback by my aggression, and he's not the only one. I have never been a violent person, but since waking from surgery, I feel like I'm barely holding on. I don't like it and decide to talk to Dr. Norton about it.

Something isn't right. I just don't know what that something is.

"Let's bounce."

The moment the words leave my mouth, I wonder why I would use them because I've never used them before. But they're out now and Old Timer gets the message.

I follow as he leads me from the room and when I step into the concreted hallway, I realize why it's so dark—we're underneath the main building.

"Are there tunnels under us?"

Old Timer looks over his shoulder, grinning. "You don't

miss much."

This changes everything.

I take it all in, passing rooms with locked doors. I wonder what's inside. It suddenly feels like there is a lot more to Parkfields than I thought.

"If you need some private time with your girl, you can come down here."

"It's not like that," I snap, feeling my temper spike again.

But it kind of is.

Luna awakens a fire in me, but in the same breath, I find myself feeling responsible for her. I want to throw her up against a wall and devour that gorgeous mouth for hours, but I also want to hug her and keep the monsters away.

In no way do I see her as someone who needs rescuing, but I feel protective over her. Last night, for instance, all I wanted was to comfort her and tell her it'll be all right.

We walk up some stairs, and when Old Timer opens the door, I see we're in the projection booth connected to the theater. I could run at any moment, but I don't want to and that's because I want to check on Luna.

I'm still surprised he's allowed to walk around unsupervised.

When we enter the bright, sterile corridor, I am actually thankful. All I want to do is shower and talk to Dr. Norton. Old Timer drops me off at my room, a silent nod the only hint of what we spoke of down below.

I guess I'll be seeing him soon.

There is no bathroom in my room. All the men have to shower in a communal block, just like in prison, which is what this place is. Monique rounds the corner, talking to a colleague who conceals a chuckle behind her hand.

Looks like Monique made good on her word and told anyone who would listen about what went down between us. I wish I had stopped it.

"I'll help you shower."

There's no point arguing because she is only following orders.

She says goodbye to her friend, who winks discreetly at me.

She leads the way and I have no other choice but to follow. "Once I'm done, I want to see Dr. Norton."

Monique looks over her shoulder, her lips forming a devious grin. "Okay. But you owe me."

And no guessing what she wants.

Thankfully, another patient was showering, so Monique couldn't divulge what form of payment she wanted. But I know she'll come calling again.

Once I was showered and dressed, Monique escorted me to my room and paged Dr. Norton. I've been waiting an hour.

"Are you sure you don't want to eat?"

Peering at the vomit-colored stew in front of me, I nod. "Very sure."

"Saving your appetite for tonight?"

"What's tonight?"

Monique collects my untouched food, making sure to lean in close. "Once a week, we have a movie night. The patients love it. They have popcorn, hot dogs, ice cream…everything you'd have at a regular cinema."

Sounds fucking awful, but I fake excitement because I have an idea.

I assume this movie night will take place in the theater, which means I will have easy access to the tunnels. I can't stop thinking about them. I want to explore them, and I want Luna to come with me.

"Maybe we can sit in the back row together," she says with a wink.

I like that she goes after what she wants, but I know if we weren't inside these walls, a girl like Monique wouldn't look twice at someone like me. I'm someone to pass the time with. If this were "real life," she would be going out with her friends, flirting with some jock who would call her babe, not insinuating to give me a blow job once the lights dim.

Thankfully, Dr. Norton arrives.

"Hello," she says, reaching for the clipboard off the end of my bed. She doesn't seem too impressed with Monique loitering, so she quickly makes herself scarce, but I know she'll be back.

She takes her time, reading over the information and if the deep frown is anything to go by, whatever is on my chart, can't be good.

"I'm surprised your body hasn't rejected your heart," she finally declares, flipping through the pages.

"No such luck, Doc," I quip with a smirk.

"Dutch—" she cautions in a low voice.

"I thought we aren't to use our real names?" I sarcastically scold.

But Dr. Norton isn't in the mood for games. "I don't understand. I thought this is what you wanted."

"No, I don't want this," I reply, tapping my temple. "The emptiness hasn't gone away. I can't hear anything."

"That's normal. I explained that's because of the medication."

"But for how long?"

She sighs, and I wish I could be more grateful for her, at least. "I honestly don't know. The studies vary from person to person. I—"

But I zone out because all I hear is Dr. Norton telling me, in a roundabout way, that I am fucked. Who I once was died the moment she took my heart, and gave me another.

"I want to know who the donor was," I blurt out, interrupting Dr. Norton.

"I can't share that information with you." She toys with the small key that hangs from a thin gold chain she wears from around her neck. I wonder what it unlocks.

"Why not? He's dead. He won't know any different."

Dr. Norton clears her throat, and again, I realize I am being really rude. "This is the reason why I need to know," I explain, not above begging. "Since the transplant, I feel…different. I don't feel like me anymore."

Dr. Norton stops writing something down. "What do you mean?"

I can see her interest is piqued, so I don't hold back. "I have visions that I've never once seen before. They feel like memories I should remember, but I don't. I am fucking angry most days, and yes, the fact I can't play music is part reason why. But I don't feel like me anymore. This…heart, it may be a match medically, but on every other level, it's a fucking foreign entity, eating me away."

I decide to leave out the inexplicable connection I have to Luna because I don't want to give Dr. Norton more of an excuse to separate us as I'm sure she knows why we were thrown into "the vault."

"Interesting," she says, which doesn't really help. "What are the visions of?"

I close my eyes and focus on the *lub-dub…lub-dub…*

In sync with it, I see headlights, I feel panic overwhelm me as I try to avoid them. I feel leather as I catch a football and hear the roars of the crowd. I feel the slap on my back as I bend low and snort a line of blow. I feel frustration as I try and find someone I have never met before.

I can't breathe as I try to be the perfect student…the perfect boyfriend…the perfect son.

Guilt tackles me harder than the guy in football gear as I deceive the one person who loves me more than anything in the world. I see the eyes of a woman I don't know. I smell roses. And then I see something which I've not seen before…I see me, but it's not me, as I am looking through the eyes of a stranger, staring up at a beautiful woman as she fucks me senseless.

Her face is blacked out, but she feels…familiar. And it's wrong…so very wrong.

Gasping for air, I almost launch off the bed as I rub over my chest, wincing in pain.

What did I…what did *he* do?

"It's okay, Dutch! Calm down. You're safe." Dr. Norton's composed voice is my anchor and I focus on it, afraid I will float away if I don't.

"What's happening to me?"

My heart rate soon settles, and the visions subside, allowing the present in. Once I can breathe again, I open my eyes.

I can see it—there's a reason for this, and Dr. Norton knows what it is.

"There have been some reports, which are very, very rare, but it's something called the theory of cellular memories."

When I look at her like she's just spoken to me in another language, she takes a seat near me.

"For decades, it's been reported that personality changes following heart transplantation have occurred. This includes a change in preference, alternations in emotion and temperament, modifications of identity, and…memories from the donor's life."

I stare at her, fucking speechless because what in the ever-loving fuck. This wasn't in the pamphlet when I signed on the dotted line.

"When referring to heart transplant patients, it's called heart memory transfer. Memories from the donor's life are said to be stored in the cells of the donated heart and are then "remembered" by the recipient following the transplant surgery. It's not common, which is why I didn't mention it. I didn't think it was possible."

"Well, it's very fucking possible, Doc," I correct, running a hand through my hair. "I'm living proof. Everything you just explained *is* me."

I knew this asshole heart wasn't mine. From the moment I woke up, I felt like I was living in someone else's skin.

"How do we fix it?"

"There is no cure for this, Dutch," Dr. Norton says slowly. "You must realize there is no real scientific proof. Studies have been conducted, yes, but with such a small number of transplant patients surviving, the data isn't accepted as medically sound."

"This is a bunch of bullshit!" I exclaim, slapping my palm over the healing wound on my chest. "Here is your proof! You know I'm different. You know music is my life, and for it to just vanish…something is wrong. Who was the donor, because from what I feel, he was one angry asshole who harbored a lot of secrets. I have the heart of a motherfucker in me."

Dr. Norton takes out a small notepad from her white jacket and writes something down. "Would you be willing to undergo some tests? They'll be with me. No one else. No one will know. This isn't my field of expertise, but I assume you'd prefer to see me and keep this delicate matter…private? I will consult with some friends and discuss their thoughts with you."

I don't even think twice about my response. "As I see it, what choice do I have?"

Dr. Norton nods.

I'm almost afraid to ask, but I need to know. "From the limited studies, was there a cure? What happened to the people?"

Dr. Norton's grim face says it all. "There is no cure, only more medication to assist with the visions and mood changes. And as for the people, it varied…"

"What. Happened?" I press, not interested in the PG version.

"Some lived a normal life. Some were committed as the visions were too much. Others fell in love with their donor's family or friends. While others…others preferred death over living with something that changed who they once were."

Oh my fucking god…how is this even real?

"This is why I cannot, why I will not ever divulge who your donor was. With what is happening, I am afraid of the repercussions if you were to ever find out who he was."

"What do you mean they fell in love?" I question because

that's just a horror story.

"I don't pretend to understand it, but the recipients have said they felt a connection to the donor's family."

I guess that makes sense, but what if they were blood family? Wouldn't that be kind of…weird? Not that any of this is "normal."

"Some reports have said that the recipient, in fact, marries their donor's spouse or siblings."

I don't even know how to process that. It's fucked up, but it's not like they were related. If this heart memory transfer thing is a real thing, I guess those feelings of love change due to the fact they aren't related by blood…well, not really.

"Take some time to think about it, and if you agree, we can start—" She pauses because what word is the appropriate one to use here?

This is so unheard of, if it wasn't happening to me, I would say it's nothing but fantasy. But I do feel better knowing I'm not going crazy. I just wish I could play music again.

Dr. Norton reads my thoughts. "Maybe as our sessions progress and it's safe to do so, I could organize a piano for you."

I should be happy, but I'm not and that's because this means my stay here is indefinite.

"Your playing was one of the most beautiful things I have ever heard."

Her innocent comment sparks my interest. "I didn't realize you saw me play."

"Are you kidding me? Everyone has. You're just too modest to see. You remind me so much of—" She lovingly reaches out, but soon stops herself and clears her throat.

For a moment, she went someplace else.

She stands abruptly, which just adds to the weirdness this day is turning into. "I will come see you tomorrow and if you agree, we can commence."

"I agree," I say, needing no time to think this over.

She nods, and just like that, things for the first time in days begin to make sense—well, kind of.

After today, being wheeled into the theater to watch *Gone with the Wind* seems fucking stupid, but here we are.

I did as Old Timer said and have an arsenal of drugs stowed away in my sock. This gown doesn't have any pockets, so I had to be resourceful as there was no way they were going in my butt. I couldn't get to Luna in time, however, and when she swallowed her stash in one big gulp, I knew I had to get her alone so we can speak.

So this is the reason I'm here because what better place to have a covert conversation than in a darkened room.

Monique wheels me to the back of the room like I knew she would while I scan the room for Luna. She isn't here yet.

Old Timer is handing out popcorn in red-and-white plastic containers. It seems no expense was spared to give us the genuine movie feel. The fact we can't take a piss unsupervised or that we are strapped to our chairs sadly cancels that out, however.

I can't believe we've come here to "get better." This place would drive anyone insane.

Old Timer makes eye contact with me and reads my facial charades perfectly. He continues giving entering patients their popcorn, subtly making his way toward me. I wonder what he has up his sleeve.

My question is answered when a piercing shrill fills the theater.

The excitement amongst the patients soon turns to panic because I've seen firsthand what chaos can do in this place, and so do the orderlies when they all run to the front of the room where a man is climbing a pillar, making monkey noises.

Monique talks into her walkie-talkie, asking for backup as she too runs toward the man.

Old Timer grins as he was no doubt behind this little diversion. The man is obviously in on Old Timer's plan. I wonder what he gets for his efforts. But whatever it is, I realize Old Timer is someone I want on my side.

"How'd you do?" he softly says, offering me a container of popcorn.

I shake my head, but when he nudges it toward me, insisting I take it, I realize this is yet another ingenious plan of his. My legs are strapped in, but my arms are free, so I accept the box and peer inside. There is nothing inside except for golden popcorn, but it's what I don't see that is the key.

"Once you're done, make sure you give the box back to me. We reuse them for next time," he informs me, which is code for "put your drugs in here so I can collect them later."

I assume one is to conceal their drugs in here as the pills will fit snugly once pressed into the popcorn.

"Where's Misha?" I ask because we don't have a deal if she isn't here.

Old Timer glances around the room, as if only just realizing she isn't here. He gestures to a young woman who is talking to her finger puppet of a cat with his chin. She ceases her conversation before leaving the theater.

I don't know what they did to be able to roam around unrestrained, but I want in. I guess Old Timer was right—I have to play by their rules to win, and I assume to do that, I have to pretend being here is helping me "heal."

Talking to Dr. Norton seems like a good place to start.

The girl and her finger puppet are back a minute later. The cat on her finger whispers something into Old Timer's ear. He looks at me and shakes his head. When I notice Noah isn't here either, panic overcomes me and I try to get the hell out of here, but Monique has put on the brakes.

Old Timer puts a hand on my shoulder and bends low to whisper into my ear, "You do that and they'll make sure you never see her again. Play it smart."

"Sitting here, dick in hand, while she is alone with that motherfucker, Noah, is not playing it smart," I counter through clenched teeth.

"She's all right. She's asleep, that's why she's not here. I take it you didn't speak to her?"

I shake my head. "How do I get away during the movie?"

When he hesitates, I subtly reach down and retrieve the pills from my socks and without detection, press them into the center of seven pieces of popcorn. I offer him the container. It took ten seconds.

He doesn't conceal his shock that I'm so efficient in hiding pills and I am too. It's like I've done it before. Images propel into me, similar to the ones I had earlier of someone other than me, snorting a line off the hood of a black car.

I don't know what the make of it is. But it looks fancy.

Old Timer accepts the container and passes it to the

redhead. I wonder who else is "working" with him. But from the way he looks at me with approval, I know I've just been hired.

"Just wait for my cue."

And that's all he leaves me with.

Seven

Luna

I hate the drugs they give me. But I also love them.

They make the pain go away.

I am a medicated zombie when I take them, but I've learned that they help with the guilt and memories which won't go away. The only times I feel remotely better is when I'm with Bowie.

They took me back to my room this morning and all I could do was look over my shoulder in hopes of seeing him. But the first time I saw him was in the sunroom where it seemed he wanted to tell me something.

Noah made that impossible, however. I can't believe he's still standing after being beaten to a near pulp by Bowie. I know the doctors have insisted he take some time off, but he won't, and that's what scares me.

I can't shake the feeling he is watching us closely, like a

predator would, waiting for the perfect time to strike, which is why I don't want to take the medication as it leaves me vulnerable.

But it also silences the screams inside my head.

I'm not sure how long I'm supposed to stay here for. I don't feel any better. I feel worse. Maybe if I were to do what Jade suggested and talk about my feelings, it might help. But I doubt it will.

The only thing which will help is seeing Misha again.

I can feel the tears spill from the corners of my eyes, but I can't wipe them away because my arms are strapped to my sides. I assume if I need to use the bathroom, the incontinent bed pad underneath me is where I'm to go.

This is utterly humiliating and I suddenly am so angry at Joy. How could she do this without my consent? I don't belong in here. But isn't that what everyone who's in here says?

I've never felt more hopeless than I do right now. Not just being bound to this single bed; I mean in every aspect in my life. I realize Misha was my reason for living and now, now I have nothing. Why would I bother to fight when I have nothing to fight for?

Or do I?

"Hey, baby. I've got you."

Misha?

That is what he used to say whenever I was having a bad day—*I've got you.*

But when I smell the ocean, I know it's someone who has wormed his way into my heart as well.

I try and say his name, but all that comes out is slurred gibberish. I wonder how he got in here without getting caught.

Whatever the reason, I'm happy he's here.

I float above myself, watching as Bowie quickly unfastens the leather restraints around my arms and legs. When I'm free, the slither of moonlight coming in from my window allows me to see he has something in his mouth—a syringe.

I don't panic when he removes the cap and lifts my gown to inject the needle into my leg. He rubs over it gently, peering at me to make sure I'm okay. I should be worried that I'm being fed more drugs, but I'm not because I know Bowie wouldn't hurt me, and he confirms this when he very carefully lifts me into his arms.

His touch is gentle and I rest my head in the crook of his neck.

He strokes my hair and kisses my temple. "We're going on an adventure."

That sounds like fun.

I watch as he walks us toward the wheelchair and he sits, still holding me tightly. I'm floppy and I will my muscles to obey, but they don't. But he won't let me fall as he secures me against his chest and wheels us away.

I trust him completely which may seem crazy considering I don't even know him that well, and we did meet in a psychiatric hospital. But my heart knows he won't hurt me.

The hallway is quiet and I wonder where everyone is, Noah included.

The wheels squeak along the polished linoleum and I hear Bowie clucking his tongue to the beat of the sound. Music is something which he clearly lives for. So it saddens me he doesn't play anymore. I wonder what happened for him to stop.

Did he also lose someone who was the rhythm of his heart?

With Bowie, I feel a sense of peace and I guess he feels it too. We are inexplicably drawn to one another and although I shouldn't because it won't lead to any good, I can't help but admire his good looks and how each gentle breath which escapes his beautiful lips has me wanting to seal my mouth over his.

A moan leaves me and when I am utterly embarrassed, Bowie seems pleased. "There you go," he whispers. "You'll be awake in no time."

I have no idea what he means until I realize what he injected into my leg must have an adverse reaction to the pills I took. This means I'll be coherent soon, which is a good and bad thing because I'm afraid of what I might say.

Bowie sweeping me away in the middle of night has everything inside of me tightening in all the right ways. It also reminds me it's been a very long time since I've had sex and that's because of choice, not lack of options.

I'm fussy with my shoes and they just go on my feet. So you can imagine what I'm like with a man. But Bowie is ticking all the right boxes, even if he is younger than me. I don't have an issue with it, and neither does he clearly as he gently rubs my exposed lower back as one of the ties on my gown has come undone.

It sends goose bumps from head to toe.

When we turn the corner, I feel a slow pull and am slowly being sucked back into my body. I no longer am watching Bowie, floating above. I am looking at him dead in the eyes and those blue eyes will be the death of me.

"You're back," he says with a relieved sigh. "Hello."

I open my mouth, but nothing comes out. I try again and

croak, "Hi."

He smiles which does nothing to help this growing obsession. "We're almost there."

All I can do is nod and even though my muscles are slowly regaining strength, I don't let Bowie go. I like being nestled against him this way. We pass the theater and stop in front of a small set of stairs which leads to the projection booth.

"This is our stop."

I arch a brow, but don't question it. I'm unsure if my unsteady legs will hold me up, but I carefully place my feet onto the cool floor and stand. Instantly, I wobble, but don't fall because Bowie quickly stands, wrapping his hands low on my waist.

"Okay?" he asks, questioning if it's all right to let me go.

I nod, but miss his touch the moment he does.

He ensures no one is coming as he climbs the stairs and opens the door. He waits by it, which is my cue to follow. And I do without question.

The moment I pass him by, his hand shoots out and he grips my upper arm. I peer down at our connection, certain where he touches me my skin is on fire. "Trust me?"

"No," I reply with a smile.

He laughs and the sound twists my stomach into knots. "Good, you probably shouldn't."

His warning only has me wanting to surrender all the more.

I enter the booth to see a patient sitting in front of the small window with a large movie projector behind him. *Gone with the Wind* plays on the screen. The theater is quite beautiful. It's fitted with red velvet seats and the walls are adorned with gold décor of various sculptures.

The large arch at the front of the theater sits above a small wooden stage. I imagine in its heyday, this place was the talk of the town. Now, it provides movie nights for people like me.

I don't know what to do, so I wait for Bowie to speak.

"How long do we have?"

"Fif-fifty on-one minutes," the man says with a stutter. I like him as he has kind eyes.

Bowie nods, accepting the watch from him. "If we're not back in time, you know what to do."

The man nods, and I don't question it as Bowie opens a door, indicating this is our exit. The darkness welcomes us.

Bowie reads my apprehension and extends his hand. I can turn around at any time. He is giving me a choice, one which I accept as I place my hand into his. The moment I do, a shiver robs me of breath. It's not a bad feeling.

But it's not a good one either.

I ignore it and follow Bowie as he leads us into the unknown. I watch my footing but the moment my bare feet touch the ground, I realize where we are.

"Why are we down here?" I ask, tugging on his hand and digging in my heels. I'm unsure why he's leading us back to the place we wanted to escape.

"Because this time, we're here of our own accord. Let's find out what secrets this place holds." He squeezes my hand gently.

This may be a silver lining as such. Even though we're both cooped up here against our own will, this may provide us with an adventure we need to forget where we are, and why we're here.

With that thought in mind, I let go of my reservations and hold on to Bowie's hand as he leads me down the dark corridor. It's so quiet down here. I can almost forget a world exists outside

Bowie and me.

We are in a tunnel and I wonder what a hospital would need one for. I observe the many rooms we pass by and wish there were windows on the doors so I could look in. I know Bowie doesn't want to waste time as we don't have much of it.

I'm guessing he wants to explore as much of the blueprint as we can tonight, so we know its layout for when we come back as I assume we will be back.

He never lets go of my hand and I like that he doesn't. We walk in silence, both taking it all in. We turn a corner and both gasp when we see the tunnel branches off into two directions.

"Which way?"

Nothing distinguishes either tunnel, so I shrug. "Oh no, I'm not taking on that responsibility. If we die, it can be on both our heads."

His gravelly laugh bounces off the concrete walls. "Fair enough. I would say flip a coin, but—" And he pats himself down with a smirk. "No pockets."

"Eeny, meeny, miny, moe?" I offer as a solution.

Bowie turns over his shoulder and smiles. "Looks like it then."

I expect him to do the honors, but he catches me completely off guard as he stands behind me. I almost forget to breathe when he runs his fingers down my arms and latches on to my wrists. He is tall, I'd say six-four.

I'm not short, but I still feel shadowed in his presence and I know that has everything to do with the way he carries himself.

His breath is warm against my neck and I shift against him subtly so we're pressed back to chest. Nothing has ever felt so right.

He raises my arm and coaxes me to point my finger as he commences, "Eeny, meeny, miny, moe…"

The entire time, I hold my breath, my heart sounding so loudly, I'm certain Bowie can hear it.

"Moe," he concludes, my finger landing on the tunnel on the left.

I've forgotten everything, however, except for the way Bowie feels pressed up against me. He doesn't let me go. He instead traces a finger along the underside of my wrist. The touch is purely innocent, but it evokes a hunger in me.

It takes all my willpower not to turn around and give in to my needs of pressing my mouth to his as I wish to see if he tastes as good as he smells.

He lets me go and I instantly miss his hands on me.

He walks toward the tunnel without fear, while I catch my breath. I follow, still reeling from the way my body responds to him touching me. He seems unaffected, however, so maybe it's just me.

The ground is wet and I peer above to see small droplets of water clinging onto the cracks in the ceiling. I wonder just where we're headed.

"What are these used for?" I ask, my voice echoing around us.

"I don't really know," he confesses, walking with caution as this tunnel is long and doesn't seem to end. "If I were to guess, I would think to transport patients—dead or alive, in secret."

I blanch, but it makes sense.

"It's also a really good place to hide things."

I have no idea what he means until he points to the walls.

I squint and am almost doubtful I see them, but when I

reach out and feel the indents made into the walls, my stomach roils in disgust.

They're fingernail marks, as if someone was clawing at the walls to stop from being led down this nefarious path.

"I don't like what's behind door number one," I say in a mere whisper as it suddenly feels very wrong being down here.

We continue walking until the tunnel opens up and we're faced with two pathways. When I see the claw marks continue to the right, I gesture with my head to the left.

Bowie nods as I need time to prepare for whatever faces us on the right.

We take the tunnel to the left and I notice it's not as cold this way. It's probably my imagination playing tricks on me. I've never done anything like this before. Having Misha when I was so young meant I couldn't do all the stuff teenagers my age did.

When my peers were out causing trouble, I was scrambling for money to feed my son. I don't regret it, but doing something like this does feel a little fun.

And when I see a ladder up ahead, the fun it seems, has just begun.

Misha stops by it and peers up at the manhole. He waits for me to give him instruction.

I nod because there is no way we're turning back now.

"Wait down here."

Scoffing, I gesture he's to climb the ladder as I will be following close behind. This isn't negotiable.

He takes the steps carefully as they are pretty narrow and they lead up quite high. I follow behind, the cool steel rungs stinging my bare feet, but I persevere. He reaches the manhole and this is the moment of truth.

There aren't any handles, so he places his hands on the steel and attempts to shift it. It doesn't budge. But he doesn't give up.

He tries moving it from different angles, putting everything behind it. I hold my breath. This can't have been for nothing.

Just when I'm about to tell him it's useless, I hear it—the shifting of dirt.

"Oh my god," I gasp, straining my head back to see if he in fact did it.

He did.

When he's able to slide it across just enough for him to slip his fingers through, Bowie grips the edge of the manhole and using his body weight, he moves it across until we are staring up into a star-filled sky. I don't believe my eyes.

Sliver by sliver, the world is unveiled before me and it's like I'm seeing it for the first time.

Bowie bolsters himself through the hole with ease and when he's out, he offers me his hand. I accept and when I join where he stands, I take a moment to appreciate our surroundings.

We're outside—and I mean that in every literal sense there is.

Turning around, I see we are standing outside the east wing of Parkfields. And when I say outside, I mean we are standing on the other side of the fence. No longer are we trapped inside looking in; we are outside looking in.

"You've got to be shitting me." I can't believe we are out.

Bowie's cheeks bellow and a puff of smoke escapes him. "That was easy."

A laugh spills from me because it really wasn't. But here we are.

I feel like a bird being freed from her cage—this is my

freedom. But am I ready to spread my wings and fly free?

I take a moment to peer into the skies and just be present with the universe. I've not done that in a long time because I haven't wanted to be a part of this world. I still don't want to be, but I want that choice to be mine.

"Why are you in here?"

Bowie and I are well past formalities. If we're to do this, then it's time we bare our souls. But this is the first time I'm telling another person what happened, what *really* happened.

There aren't enough breaths I can take, or the appropriate words to use, to explain something which to me still makes no sense. So, I decide to strip it all back and just be honest.

"My son…he died, and well, I died too. I didn't want to be here without him, so I…I took a bunch of pills."

Silence.

"You're thinking what a coward, right?" I finally meet his eyes, expecting to see judgment. But that's not what I see.

I see understanding, like Bowie has lived the same life I have.

"Not at all." He steps forward, brushing a strand of hair from my cheek with the back of his knuckles. "I was thinking of the immense pain you must have felt losing your son. I know that you loved him very much, your actions prove it."

He doesn't remove his hand from my cheek. Instead, he sweeps a finger across the apple of my cheek. I can't suppress my gentle whimper.

"You're not going to say things are going to get better? That with time, I'll heal?"

He shakes his head, the full moon intensifying those blue eyes. "No, because they won't," he declares with honesty. "Time allows us to accept our fate, but do we ever heal from something which changes us forever?"

I wait for him to deliver me with his wisdom because I need to hear it from someone else. I need to hear that I'm not the only one who lives with this burdening pain where it's impossible to breathe.

"No, we don't," he concludes, his fingers sliding down my cheek, across to my parted mouth. "We just learn to deal."

And that's it.

No psychological nonsense. No finding your inner strength to go on. Bowie has just perfectly summarized a pain so deep, it has not only cut you in half, it's broken you into a million irreparable pieces. He has said the words which any therapist has failed to say.

We just learn to deal.

"Wh-what about you?" I say, only realizing his finger is tracing the outline of my upper lip.

"What about me what?" he replies, fixated on my mouth.

"Why are you in here?"

I expect him to deflect, but he doesn't. He doesn't take his eyes or finger off me as he professes, "I lost myself, Misha…and I don't know how to get it back."

Tears spring to the surface for so many reasons, but at the forefront is the fact he used my son's name and it felt like I was hearing it spill from Misha himself.

"I tried to cut out my heart, but it's not as easy as it sounds."

My own begins to race because I can't help but think of Misha's heart which gives another life. I hate that person. I know it's selfish, but I wish that person didn't need his heart because it's Misha's. It doesn't belong to another.

I assume Bowie is talking in the metaphorical sense because could it be his heart is broken too?

"You can't play music because you lost a part of yourself?"

"Try *all* of myself," he corrects, swapping his finger for his thumb which takes off from the tortuous exploration of my mouth as I want his tongue, not his thumb.

"I can't play music because I can't hear anything in here"—he taps against his temple, before reaching for my hand and pressing it over his heart—"or in here."

His heart beats fiercely and the echo is like coming home. I am in sync with it, and I never want the sound to end. I understand why Bowie wanted to end his life because music is his life and without it, he'd rather not live.

"How does the music return?" I whisper, my knees heavy as he slips the tip of his thumb past my parted lips.

"I don't know, but with you...I hear it," he confesses, robbing me of air and breath. "It gets louder and louder each time. I don't understand it. But I don't want to. The best things don't ever make sense."

I don't know what's happening. Everything simply fades and it's just Bowie and me...and the sound of his heart.

"Then come with me," I say, unsure what exactly I'm offering. I just know I don't want to leave here without him.

But I see it even before he speaks the words. "I can't. If I go back out there, I'll never find out what's wrong with me. And if I can't play music, I don't want to exist."

And here is the conundrum—I am faced with literal freedom, but do I want it? It seems so...pointless. What am I going home to? An empty house filled with bittersweet memories. But in here, maybe I can find myself again...just like

Bowie.

"No, don't you do that," he commands, reading my thoughts as he cups both my cheeks in his large palms. "You want this, you take it."

But that's the thing—I don't know what I want.

A beeping alarm shatters the beautiful moment between us and when Bowie looks down at his watch, I realize we're running out of time. Time, it really is the one thing in life we cannot change, only learn from. And I've learned that life is short, too short for regrets.

So with that thought in mind, I reach for Bowie's hands and wrap them around my waist. I step into his embrace and do what I've wanted to do since the first moment I saw him—I press my ear to his chest and listen to his heart beat.

I feel warm. And happy.

"I want to stay."

There is no other place I want to be than right here, in Bowie's arms, listening to the cadence of his heart.

Eight

Dutch

Here I am, lying on a black leather couch, about to divulge my deepest, darkest secrets to Dr. Norton.

On any other day, I would rather cut out my own tongue and eat it, than talk about what is wrong with me. But if I don't do this, I'm afraid I'll never be able to play piano again.

But for the first time in a long time, I have hope that this is temporary because last night with Luna inspired me in ways I don't understand. She had the chance to run, but she didn't. She chose to stay. She didn't specify what the reason was, but I like to think I have some part in it.

Touching her feels so natural. She's fucking beautiful, but that's not what it is. I feel like a tether connects us together and at times, it's us versus the world. I've never felt such a deep connection with another human being before.

It's no wonder I want to play whenever she's around. I've

only ever felt this way with music.

"So, I've spoken to colleagues and they've suggested we start with when you first woke from your surgery," Dr. Norton says from her high-back chair, legs crossed as she opens a spiral notepad.

She's not wearing her usual doctor getup today, but instead, has on a tight black dress and heels. I realize I don't know much about her. She looks to be in her thirties and I'm sure is not short of admirers. Not only is she smart, she's beautiful as well.

I don't want to do this, but I close my eyes and try to remember.

"The first thing I remember is the sound of…it."

"Of your heart?"

"It's not my heart. It never felt that way. It still doesn't. It's *his*."

"That's just your mind playing tricks, Dutch. It's completely normal for one to feel that way. It's similar to an amputee who can still feel the limb. It's called phantom limb sensation."

"But in my circumstance, my limb isn't missing, it's been replaced with this diabolical imposter."

I can hear her pen frantically scribbling across the paper. I wonder what she's writing.

"What did you do with it?"

A sudden pause in her scribing.

"With what?"

"My heart."

"It was disposed of with all of the other medical waste."

Shaking my head, I can't kick the sudden sadness at the thought. "It wasn't medical waste. It was my heart."

This is totally irrational.

"It may have malfunctioned, but at least it allowed me to compose. It didn't block me from feeling…anything. How is this possible?"

I know this sounds like the ramblings of a crazy person. Maybe I am.

"You spoke of memories? Visions? Can you share those?"

I dig into my psyche, but I know if I push too hard, I don't think I'll ever return. "This dude was one fucked-up asshole," I say, suddenly feeling breathless, like I am running a football field. "He played football, right?"

Dr. Norton doesn't need to answer. Her silence speaks volumes.

"He also liked to party. No wonder I can't play music. With the amount of blow this guy did, I'm surprised it was a car that killed him and not the drugs."

"How did you know he was involved in a car accident?" Dr. Norton asks calmly.

"You told me."

"No, I didn't," she corrects. "I've been very mindful of the information I've shared with you. And that is something I am certain I did not reveal."

"So he died in a car crash then?"

Again, I don't need the doctor's confirmation because I know that he did. I can see it.

"I am behind the wheel," I say, the vision coming to me in a broken sequence. "I'm going out to get something for someone I love very much."

His heart begins to beat faster.

"Music is playing over the speakers." A smile instantly spreads across my face. "'Heroes' by David Bowie. I'm keeping to the speed limit. It's raining."

Swish.

Swish.

Swish.

The wipers lull me into an almost trance.

"What happens next?"

My eyelids flicker as I wade through the fog. I see bright lights. I feel panic.

"There's a car on the other side of the road. No…"

"What's wrong, Dutch?"

A pain strikes my temple and I gasp for air. The headlights are blinding and I shield my eyes.

"I don't, I don't understand," I say as the memory appears as if…

"You don't understand what?"

My head smashes into the steering wheel. The car was on its side of the road…and then it wasn't. It was as if…

"It wasn't an accident," I reveal breathlessly, seeing and tasting his blood.

My head begins to pulse in and out on its own as my body begins to die.

"The person in that car wanted him dead. They knew him…"

And then, everything fades to black.

I spring upright, my eyes popping open as I take in where I am. My breathing is erratic and I am drenched in sweat. Dr. Norton looks as if she's seen a ghost or witnessed an exorcism. I don't know what to think of any of this.

"Am I going crazy?" I ask, hating to use that phrase, but there are no other words for it. "I mean, Beethoven contemplated suicide after losing his hearing when he was twenty-eight. Is this what is happening to me? But instead of my hearing, I lost my heart."

"But Beethoven composed some of music's greatest masterpieces while completely deaf," Dr. Norton counters, which is true.

"I don't want to be completely deaf, though, because for me, deaf equates to dead. At least Beethoven could compose. I can't hear a single thing, other than—" But I catch myself out before saying anything about Luna.

I don't know why I don't want Dr. Norton knowing about her. My gut is just telling me to keep her a secret.

"But we really shouldn't be comparing myself to Beethoven," I say, quickly changing the topic of conversation. "I can only wish to be as talented as him."

"You're very special. That was why I wanted to give you the transplant," Dr. Norton reveals, a strain around her green eyes. "I wanted to help save you because not everyone gets the chance."

Suddenly, I get the sense Dr. Norton is speaking from the heart.

"I feel terrible you're going through these difficulties, but I don't regret the decision I made. It saved your life, and your life is worth saving."

I don't know what to say as I suddenly feel so undeserving. She is right. I'm in the minority and here I am, bitching and moaning about getting a second chance at life. I don't want to make Dr. Norton feel like shit.

She is going above and beyond for me when she doesn't have to. She's doing this as a favor to me.

"I'm sorry, this isn't your fault at all," I reveal, hoping she forgives me. "I am so thankful for you, for everything you've done. I just am…frustrated. I don't understand what's going on and the explanation you've given me sounds like something out of a B-grade horror movie."

She runs a hand over her immaculate blonde hair. I'm clearly making her feel worse.

"I just want to play music again," I confess, hoping I can express myself better this time.

"We all want that. Maybe if you start doing everyday, normal things it might help?" she suggests, and at this stage, I'm willing to try anything.

"I'll ask your mom to bring in some of your things. Clothes. Personal items, those sorts of things."

That sounds fucking dreadful because that means Dr. Norton thinks my stay here will be long term.

"Speaking of." She stands and opens her desk drawer, producing a small bag. "Here."

I peer inside and see my jewelry.

Instantly, my mood lifts because I've just been given back a part of myself. Seems trivial; something I took for granted gives me much joy. I slip on my rings and look at my hands. They look the same, but there's one big difference—they can't play.

Pushing aside my anger, I put on my chains, feeling at ease when the crucifix sits around my neck.

"I had an idea, but I'm not sure if it's too soon."

"Nothing is too soon. Every minute that passes feels like ten."

Whatever she's thinking, I'm ready to listen to because it can't be any worse than her telling me the heart within my chest is making me one with its original owner.

She nods, and I watch with interest as Dr. Norton walks over to the record player in the corner of the room. I like that she doesn't have some bullshit computerized gadget. "If this gets too much, you must tell me."

Now my interest is really piqued.

I shuffle forward and place my elbows onto my thighs, interlacing my hands and wait. She moves with intent and I suddenly second-guess my willingness to obey.

"I've always loved music," she begins, revealing something personal to no doubt distract me from what's to come. "The way it's able to transport you to another world. When you really connect with a piece of music, it allows you to escape and it also allows you to remember…"

I lift my downturned chin slowly because she has chosen her words wisely, and when Mozart's Sonata No. 11 crackles over the speakers, I realize she is trying to do that right now.

She wants me to remember.

Instantly, I feel the musical notes wrap their arms around me into a tight embrace. My eyes slip shut and I lose myself to the place I go to whenever I hear music.

Usually, this is the place I go to when I play, but today, that place is dark and won't let me. I bang invisible palms against the locked door in my mind, demanding entry. But it won't budge.

"Don't fight, Dutch. It'll come in time." Dr. Norton's smooth voice calms me somewhat and I try to do what she says.

I appreciate the music because although I'm not the composer, it still fills me with a new lease on life.

"Remember what it felt like the first time you heard it. Tell me about it."

My body moves on its own as I'm no longer in control. Music is—it always is. I surrender everything I am and allow myself to venture back to the time when I was flicking through my dad's records and found Mozart.

"Most kids would have not looked twice at the old dude on the cover," I say, flashes of the front of the record flickering before me. "But it called to me in ways I still don't understand. My dad put it on and the moment I heard…I heard nothing but the music. I listened to it over and over again, my mind trying to compose the notes in my head."

My fingers move on the invisible keys on my legs, attempting to play along. But they are clumsy and out of time.

"Just how I'm trying to do right now. But all I hear is the music playing over the speakers, and not hearing and feeling it inside my head." I can't mask my frustration, and on instinct, I rub over the scar on my chest through the gown.

I haven't looked at it since I stabbed a pen through the middle of it. It's tender and feels raised. I can imagine it looks as grotesque as it feels.

"Do you think your heart is the reason you can't play?"

"Yes," I counter quickly.

Hasn't she been listening?

"Since the surgery, I can't hear anything. Music used to be a part of me. Now, I'm an outsider, looking in."

"I think it's all in your head, Dutch," she reveals, surprising me because this is new. "I think there's something else which troubles you. Your heart doesn't control your creativity, you do. Something is obstructing that, and until we can get to what that something is, I believe you'll be stuck with these destructive thoughts."

103

My fingers run up and down, up and down along the scar. Each stroke incites the anger within.

"That makes no sense. No, I disagree," I reply, refusing to believe her.

"I'm not here to judge you. I know you're upset."

"Yes, you could say that," I snap, the music suddenly speeding up. "You'd be upset too if something you lived for was taken away."

"I understand that in more ways than you can imagine," she confesses with heart, and I feel like an asshole for snapping. "How do you feel right now?"

"Like I want to cut this bastard out of my chest."

"Why? You know logically, that makes no sense. Your heart has nothing to do with what's going on."

"Then what is?" The music continues to get faster and faster, as does his heart.

"I think you use music to protect yourself," she says softly. "To not let anyone in. I think you're scared of connecting with another human being in fear of rejection. You've also been different your whole life, and that's not a bad thing. It's extraordinary. But I think you should have been diagnosed with your condition a long time ago. And my colleagues, who have read over your file, agree."

"Excuse me?" I slowly open my eyes, taking her in. "What condition?"

"I think you're suffering from a form of schizophrenia and this is all in your head. I've read your files many times, and I know you've been medicated for depression, but you stopped taking your medication before the full effects were able to be seen."

"No, I stopped taking them because they made everything fuzzy. I couldn't compose when I was on them. I didn't need them because there is nothing wrong with me!"

However, I suddenly feel like there is.

"Why are you so angry?"

"I'm angry because you're accusing me of being crazy!"

"No, I'm not. And I hate that word," Dr. Norton calmly says. "I think it'll help you immensely to see another doctor. Someone who specializes in this area. I can recommend someone. A friend—"

"A shrink, you mean?" I can't control my anger because I suddenly feel like she tricked me. She welcomed me into this warm, safe bubble, only to burst it with claims of me needing psychiatric help.

"Yes."

I give her credit for not sugarcoating anything. But I refuse to accept her diagnosis.

"No."

Her lips pull into a thin line.

I know she's only trying to help, but I don't want it because her "help" is not helping me—at all.

"What's obstructing me then, Doc?" I ask, coming to a slow stand.

Dr. Norton leans back in her seat and her cheeks turn a lovely pink. And when she nervously licks her lips, I realize therapy has just turned into something else.

"I think there are a number of things, which is why I want to help."

"Why have you shown such an interest in me, Dr. Norton?"

"I take an interest in all my patients," she replies, but she's lying.

"But why me? I know there would have been other candidates, but you chose me?"

She straightens her back and I really look at her for the first time. She's slender, but her body is shapely, like she works out. Her blonde hair is immaculately styled. Her eyes are green. Her lips plump. She certainly doesn't look like the stereotypical doctor.

"You and the donor were a m-match." She's nervous, clutching at the key around her neck like it's her lifeline.

"Yeah, you already said that." I stroll toward her, and I suddenly feel like a predator stalking its prey.

I know I'm being incredibly arrogant, but she has pissed me off. And I also can't help it. I want to say I would never react this way before the transplant, but now, I'm not so sure.

At Juilliard, everyone thought I was arrogant, while I just thought I was uninterested in most things. But were they right? I begin to doubt everything, and all because Dr. Norton thinks I'm using my transplant as an excuse to hide the truth.

Which is…? I don't know.

"But why was I worth saving?"

"Every life is worth saving," she corrects, but the closer I get to her, the more nervous she becomes. "It's my job."

"I can't help but think you're taking your job very seriously when it comes to me."

Her chest begins to rise and fall quickly, drawing attention to her ample breasts.

"So, if you were to give me your professional opinion, what do you think is wrong with me?"

She holds her ground, and I like that.

"I think you used your heart as an excuse as to why you were different. To why you never connected with anyone. To why you saw, felt, and experienced the world unlike anyone else.

"But now that you've got a functioning heart, you're blaming it for being unable to write, when in reality, you're afraid to try and live a normal, long life. And this is very common for people who are given a second chance at life.

"The notion was perceived in your mind since you were little that you were different and now that you're not, your mind is playing tricks on you. It has you believing that you're no longer special or different, so how can you write something which is just that?

"But this heart allows you that, and so much more. The blockage is no longer in your heart. It's now in your head and I want to help you. I want to help you finish that masterpiece you've been working on."

Well, fuck me.

I don't want to accept what she's saying, but it makes more sense than a donor heart being the reason for this creative clam-up.

She watches me closely, allowing me to process what she just shared. But I don't want to. If what she's saying is true, am I really just unhinged then?

She stands cautiously like she would if approaching a rabid animal. I suppose I am.

The space between us suddenly fills with something electric. I don't know what it is.

"I only want to help. I want to show you that it's all in your mind."

Before I know what she's doing, she reaches around my shoulders and commences untying the string from my gown. I would ask, but curiosity, as well as shock, has rendered me speechless. I can only watch as she finishes unfastening my gown, before sliding it off my shoulders.

Thankfully, I'm wearing boxers because standing in her office naked is fucking weird. Yes, she's my doctor, but something about this feels like we've crossed a line. We're definitely not in Kansas anymore, Toto, when she places her hand against my chest.

But not before toying with the crucifix around my neck.

She notices me purposely avoiding looking down at the scar. "Look at it. I want you to see what this is."

When I turn my cheek, she grips my chin and coaxes me to look.

For a moment, I simply stare at it, not knowing what to think. I just feel numb.

It's not as hideous as I thought it would be. In my head, I envisioned a red, raw mess. But it looks like any other scar would. I'm slightly disappointed.

"See?" Dr. Norton says, reading my thoughts. "It's just flesh."

To accentuate her point, she runs her finger along the jagged scar.

"There is nothing supernatural about this. Or what's inside."

Her touch doesn't feel unpleasant, but it also feels out of place. Unlike Luna, who was able to set me on fire.

Dr. Norton's fingers begin to dance over my chest and as her lips part, I know we are venturing into dangerous territory. "I want what you want—I want to hear you play again."

"When did you see me play?" I ask as I had no idea she ever

saw me play.

"It was the June Meriweather forum recital at Juilliard. The hospital was a sponsor."

That makes sense, but what doesn't is why she never told me she came.

"You were unlike anyone I've ever heard before," she says in a faraway voice, her fingers continuing to explore my skin. "La Campanella is one of my favorites."

I arch a brow, confused. "I didn't play Liszt at that recital. It was Bach. Are you sure it was me?"

My question snaps her from wherever she just went.

She shakes her head and removes her hand from my chest so abruptly she almost falls on her ass. "Oh, sorry. I got the names mixed up. Sometimes, I like to think I'm a classical music expert."

Her fingers tremble when she brushes a piece of hair behind her ear. A surgeon's hand should never tremble and the perfect scar down my chest is proof of that.

Something is wrong…but I don't know what that is.

Her doctor persona slips back into place as she bends low to gather my gown. She offers it to me with her face turned, and suddenly, this feels awfully sordid.

I'm in no hurry to dress, but Dr. Norton seems to be desperate to flee as she stuffs her leather briefcase with her belongings. "Give some thought about what we spoke about today. There's no harm in talking to another doctor."

"Sick of me already?"

It's a joke, but when her bottom lip trembles, I realize my sense of humor is only funny to some.

"What about the stuff you said about heart memory

transfer? We didn't discuss that. The donor—"

"I really have to go. Can this wait for our next appointment?" The needle screeches across the record as she practically rips it off the player.

I recoil on instinct because I treat my records like they're the most precious thing in the world because to me, they are.

"Sure," I reply, wondering what's going on.

I don't even have the gown tied up properly before she's shoving me out the door and rushing down the hallway, leaving me unsupervised—the first time she's ever done that since I've been admitted.

I wonder if I should chase after her and make sure she's all right. Something obviously spooked her. I think the correct phrase there would be *I* spooked her.

The way she looked at me and touched me, it was like I was someone else.

Jesus fucking Christ.

This heart has done nothing but cause me problems. Now my doctor can't even look at me without freaking out.

The corridor is quiet and any other dutiful patient would return to their room, ready to be spoon-fed their lunch. But not me.

I could make a break for it seeing as today was a total waste of time. I thought seeing Dr. Norton would help, but all she did was confirm that I'm as batshit crazy as I feel. But if I do that, that means Luna will be stuck here alone.

I don't want to do that to her, especially after last night when she chose this prison over freedom. And the truth of the matter is that I don't want to leave here without her.

This is getting weirder by the second.

110

I decide to go find her because the thought of seeing her calms me down.

Trying my best to remain as inconspicuous as possible, I blend in with the settings and any nurses I pass by, I simply smile and continue walking as if I'm supposed to be here. I turn the corner but quickly backtrack and use it as a barricade as I peer around the wall.

It shouldn't surprise me, but it still fucking pisses me off when I see Old Timer talking to Noah. They're clearly up to no good.

Noah peers around, ensuring they're alone, and extends his palm out where Old Timer places a bag of pills into it.

Explains where our pills are going. I hate that I had a part in helping this asshole out.

Noah quickly pockets the bag and in return, gives Old Timer a carton of cigarettes and a few bars of chocolate. I wait for more, but there is none.

We're risking our asses so Old Timer can smoke himself to death? This is a bunch of bullshit. The exchange is over as quickly as it occurred and the two men go their separate ways.

I have two choices—follow Old Timer and smack some sense into him. Or I can see what Noah is up to when he skulks off because I have a feeling he's not going back to work. I decide to go with the latter because Old Timer can wait.

Noah is clearly offering to turn a blind eye and grant Old Timer special privileges, as well as his bogus payment of smokes and chocolate. But for Noah to be in a position to do so, he clearly has some pull around here.

And that makes him dangerous. It especially makes him dangerous because he seems to have taken an interest in Luna.

He hasn't harmed her yet because of Old Timer; I'm sure of it. We are in his "circle," but that doesn't mean I trust either of them. The sudden realization that we should have got the fuck out of here hits hard and protecting Luna just becomes all the more serious.

I follow Noah, who is in a hurry to get to wherever the hell he's going to notice he's being followed. And when he heads toward the projection booth, I know this isn't going to end well. He enters casually.

I wait thirty seconds before following.

I hold my breath, hoping he isn't inside and gone down into the tunnels. I open the door and let out a breath when I see he's gone. But when I realize *where* he's gone, I realize that breath was taken in vain because whatever he's doing down in those tunnels is going to be bad news.

I try my best to silence my footsteps, but everything down here is amplified.

I'm thankful I know the layout of the place somewhat, but with the tunnels branching off into different directions, I have to hurry because I don't want to lose Noah. I go with my gut because after the scratch marks I saw carved into the walls, I dare say that's where Noah is headed.

I've lost sight of him, so I continue walking in hopes I'm right.

I venture down the tunnel Luna and I bypassed last night. I run my fingers along the walls as I walk down it. The scratch marks continue and get deeper the farther I go. I get the sense that whatever goes on down here is done in secret, and when I hear a muffled cry, I don't know if I should be thanking or cursing my gut instinct.

I persevere, not sure what I'm about to walk into. I prepare myself for anything. His heart begins to beat faster—it too can sense something awful on the horizon.

I focus on the sounds, just how I always do, but instead of music, I hear cries, followed by someone being slapped. Over and over again.

I forget secrecy and run toward the sound but as I get closer, I realize I prepared myself for anything…but this.

I was right.

Noah is down here, but what he's doing is beyond horrifying.

The woman with the cat finger puppet is down here, on her hands and knees. I know it's her because that's the first thing I see; that fucking cat on her finger as her hands are splayed out in front of her as one of the orderlies is fucking her from behind.

There are three of them, including Noah, who holds a video camera, filming the entire thing.

"Meow for the camera," he mocks, getting low and shoving the lens into the woman's face.

The men laugh while she does as Noah says.

This is fucking sick.

I don't have a weapon. I'm outnumbered. But there's no way in hell I'm letting this happen. His heart suddenly animates me with the strength of a superhero and I reach for the belt on the floor and whip the orderly who is egging his friend on to 'fuck her harder,' on the back of the neck.

He drops to the ground, his screams echoing through the tunnel as the gold buckle tore away a piece of flesh at the side of his throat.

The animal pauses mid-thrust, which is all I need to shove

him on the front of the shoulder and when he recoils backward, I draw the belt down onto his cock. He slumps backward, gasping for air because I'm pretty sure he won't be defiling anyone ever again.

Noah drops the camera, it shatters with a thud as he dives for me. But I'm faster as I strike out and punch him in the mouth.

His nose is still taped after Luna nearly bit it off, so when I punch that next, I know he's going to go down.

He drops like a sack of shit, and I pin him down with one arm pressed to his shoulder, while with the other, I begin beating his face into a bloody pulp, but this time, I won't stop until he ceases breathing.

Cat woman is howling, a sound of fear and excitement. I then wonder if she was a willing participant. I hope not. A rage so fierce overwhelms me and I'm fueled by nothing but this need to kill.

His heart trounces in excitement, egging me on to hit him harder, to make him pay for the vile things he's done.

Blood somersaults into the air, backflipping and tumbling with grace as I deliver each punishing blow. A gargle spills from Noah and although I can barely make out what he said, his promise turns my stomach.

"She's going to pay for this."

I know he's talking about Luna which means there is only one thing I can do—reaching overhead for a fallen brick on the ground. I raise it above my head, ready to silence him for good, but sadly, I'm tackled to the ground.

"Drop it!" I don't recognize the voice, but from the strength of him, I dare say these assholes have called for backup.

I try and fight, but now I know I really am outnumbered when I hear the fucker on top of me bark orders into a walkie-talkie. "I need men and restraints. Now!"

"You bastard!" I scream, trying to buck him off me. "You're defending these rapist assholes!"

"No one is raping anyone," he replies, which throws me for a loop. He pries the brick from my hand, tossing it aside.

"Are you fucking blind? I'm pretty sure the girl down here would object to your claims. Tell him, kitten." I lift my chin from the floor, but when I see she's not here, I do a double take.

"What girl?" he asks, his words coming out in breathless pants as he tries to keep me subdued.

"The girl with the finger puppet! She's there." I look at the spot she was at, certain she's still here, but she's not.

"It's going to be all right. We're going to get your medicine, and then you're going to have a nice nap."

"Stop talking to me like I'm crazy!" I holler, spittle running down my chin.

"It's going to be all right," he repeats, which just makes me feel even crazier.

With his knee pressed between my shoulder blades, I can't move, but my eyes scan the tunnel, and I wonder how they got rid of the girl so quickly. I look for the smashed video camera, but notice that is also missing.

What's going on?

I don't have time to answer my own question because before I know what's happening, two hands become six and I'm rolled onto a stretcher. I don't have time to fight because one set of hands are strapping my feet. While another pair is tightening the leather belt around my chest.

And the last pair is stabbing something into the vein in my arm.

"Motherfuck—" But I don't get to finish my sentence because everything soon quietens, and down the rabbit hole I go.

Thy drugs are quick.

Nine

Luna

I'm worried.

It's been two days since I've seen Bowie.

When I asked the orderlies about him, all I've been greeted with is a big fat nothing. Something isn't right. My heart aches, and I don't know why.

This place has a way of making an hour feel like ten. I need to get out of here because the longer I'm in here, the worse my mental health becomes. There are whispers among the patients that something happened to Noah, which is why he's not been at work.

I'm not complaining about the fact, but I know that the reason has got something to do with Bowie.

"You've got a visitor."

I peer up from my chair by the window and see the smiling face of a young nurse. She must be new. Give her a month, and

I doubt she'll be smiling.

She wheels the chair over to me, indicating walking isn't an option. I don't bother arguing because I want to see who's come to see me. I sit in the chair and don't flinch when she straps me in.

Bless her when she attempts to make conversation, like this is a normal occurrence. "They said we're supposed to get some sun this weekend. Should be nice."

You know what would be nicer? Getting the fuck out of here. But I play along.

"Sounds lovely. You'll have to enjoy it for me." *Seeing as I'll be strapped to my bed,* I silently add.

She doesn't bother with any further conversation after that.

She unlocks the door to the visitors' lounge, and when I see Joy, a bag of mixed emotions weighs me down. I want to be happy to see her, but she's the reason I'm in here.

When she sees me, she stands, nervously straightening out her sundress. Correction, *my* dress. I don't know why it pisses me off because it wasn't uncommon for her to ask to borrow my clothes. But that's the thing, she *asked*.

Now, it just feels like an invasion of privacy.

She reads my expression for what it is and sits quickly.

The nurse wheels me over to her but doesn't unstrap me. She smiles and gives us some privacy, which is horseshit as there's no such thing in this place. Joy toys with the gold crucifix around her throat. If she's waiting for me to speak first, it's probably best she goes back home.

"How are you?" she asks after a full minute of silence.

"How do you think I am? Seeing as you think you know what's best for me." I can't keep the cattiness from my voice because I'm angry.

"I did what I thought was best," she says, eyes filled with tears.

"Well, you thought wrong. How could you throw me in here? I'm not fucking crazy!"

Joy peers around the room, embarrassed as my raised voice has drawn the attention of other visitors. My fellow patients, however, have heard worse.

"Luna," she says in a patronizing tone. "I love you. I only want you to get better."

A maniacal laugh bursts from me, and tears leak from my eyes. "Better? There is no better. Misha is dead! And unless you can bring him back to life, then this is the best you're going to get."

"The doctors said they could help."

"Well, they fucking lied to you!"

"Could it be because you aren't really giving it a go?"

"Giving what a go? Giving being force-fed while tied to my bed a go? Or maybe getting a male orderly to help me go to the bathroom a go? How about given drugs to turn me into a medicated zombie?

"Is that what you're telling me to give a go? Because no offense, Joy, but you can go fuck yourself."

She gasps, eyes wide because I've never spoken to her that way before. But I'm angry. I also feel betrayed.

"And why are you wearing my dress? Just because I'm not home doesn't mean you can come and go as you please."

"Your dress? It's not...I'm s-sorry." She stumbles over her words, and I feel awful, but I can't stop.

"Well, stop being sorry and get me out of here. Apparently,

119

you're the only person who can do that. Because I'm crazy and all," I whisper sarcastically.

"I can't do that. Not until you're better."

I blink once, wondering if the entire world is on crack. "Have you been listening to me?"

"Yes, and that's why being in here is best for you."

"Who died and made you Mother Teresa?" It's out before I can stop myself, but instead of crying, I laugh—because if I don't laugh, I'll fucking cry and won't stop.

"What's happened to you?" Joy covers her mouth, horrified by my etiquette. Or lack of.

"Nurse!" I call out, so done with this conversation.

"Luna! Please!" Joy pleads, and when she attempts to touch my shoulder, I lunge and bite her hand. "Oh my god!"

She recoils, cradling it to her chest as two orderlies run over to wheel me away.

"Oh, and by the way," I call over my shoulder. "Stay out of my fucking house!"

The last image I have is of Joy covering her mouth, horrified at the monster she once called her best friend.

The moment I'm wheeled back into the sterile corridor, I actually feel better. Ironic, I know. But being out there, in the real world, it forces me to deal with reality; the reality that Misha is dead.

A longing hits hard, and I instantly want to see Bowie. But how do I manage that? I don't even know where he is.

Once I'm back in my room, I don't fight when they lift me out of my chair and strap me into bed. Now that I've calmed, they don't give me any sedation—for now, at least. When alone, I stare at the walls and wonder what comes next.

I have no family left. Joy no doubt wants nothing to do with me after I almost bit her like a rabid dog. But how could she do this to me? I don't know how I'm going to get out because if Joy is my only hope, then looks like I'll be staying here for good.

I wake with a start, aware someone is watching me.

"Shh, it's okay," says a man as he raises his hands in surrender. "I'm a friend."

"What do you want?"

I don't want any part in his comradeship until he reveals, "I know where he is."

I don't play coy. "Take me to him."

The man nods and unties me.

I don't waste a second and leap from the bed but reach out and steady myself against the wall. "Why are you helping me?"

The man smiles, revealing a mouth full of missing teeth. "I like the kid."

But I don't buy it.

A hoarse chuckle leaves the man when he reads my thoughts. "I can see why he likes you."

Bowie likes me?

The thought thaws the pain from around my heart.

"Let's just say we have come to an understanding. He helps me. I help him. And he's the best help I've had in a while. He calls me Old Timer, by the way."

I don't ask questions because I don't think I want to know what Bowie's "help" entails. If he trusts Old Timer, then so do I.

We quietly make our way from my room, and I'm surprised how quiet it is. I suspect Old Timer chose this time to come and find me because of this fact. I follow him cautiously because I still need to be on guard.

He retrieves a pair of keys from his pocket, muting the jingling by cupping them into his palm. We turn corner after corner, and before long, the lights grow dimmer and the atmosphere colder—in every sense of the word.

It's evident from the derelict state of things that this part of the building isn't used. The hallway is lined with broken hospital beds and wheelchairs missing wheels. It seems to be more of a storage area than functioning ward.

Red, white, and blue streamers limply hang from the ceiling—a Fourth of July memory captured in time. A red telephone booth with a black phone is randomly pressed up against one wall and across from it, a faded poster of Marilyn Monroe.

Goose bumps scatter across the back of my neck. This place gives me the creeps.

There are thick white pillars in front of windows which have steel bars fastened over them. Wall sconces replace low-hanging light bulbs which barely provide any light, but I can see the doors at the end of the corridor.

Above the doorway are the words, *Acta, non verba*, which is Latin for 'deeds, not words.' In plain English, actions speak louder than words.

I wonder what actions are carried out behind these doors.

Old Timer pushes open the heavy door with the old brass key. The first thing that hits me is the smell—the stench of decay. If Bowie is in here, I'm scared to see the state he is in.

He looks over his shoulder, silently asking if I want to continue.

I nod.

He leads the way, clearly knowing his way through this dark, dank corridor. It's deadly quiet—the only sound I hear is a drip…drip…drip from a leaking pipe somewhere. The buzzing fluorescents flicker on and off, the strobe effect hurting my eyes.

But I persevere because I cannot leave knowing Bowie is down here.

My bare feet are frozen and I wonder if Bowie has a blanket. But when I peer inside a derelict room, I realize that's the least of his concerns. The room is caked with utter filth. The once-green walls are sullied with brown smears. The ceiling yellowed over time.

This place is hell.

My heart begins to race and I know that's because Bowie is close. Old Timer stops in front of a brown door, pursing his dry lips. He is giving me one final chance to back out.

I shake my head.

With a sigh, he opens the door and when I peer inside, I understand why he hesitated. This was not what I was expecting because this isn't a bedroom but rather, a bathroom.

A single white tub sits in the middle of the room, and unlike the other rooms, this one is immaculate. It's so damn white, it actually hurts my eyes. But the white is overruled by black writing, scribbled all over the walls.

It appears like someone was punished and forced to write a single line a hundred times.

That line reads: *Cleanliness is next to godliness.*

It's written all over the walls, the ceiling; it's everywhere.

But when I see Bowie, I forget everything but him.

Running over to him, I gasp when I see the state he's in. He's

123

wrapped in a wet bedsheet, the only thing visible is his head above the water, and when I dip my hand into the water, I yank it out because it's ice cold.

He looks like he's been mummified. His lips are blue, but he doesn't move. Is he dead?

"Bowie!" I cry, dropping to my knees and gripping his face into my palms, coaxing him to look at me. But his eyes are vacant. There's no life behind them.

"Get him out of here!" I tug at the leather straps securing him down, but they won't budge because they're locked with a gold padlock.

"It's called hydrotherapy," Old Timer explains calmly. "It's a continuous bath. The cold water is used to treat manic depression and agitated behavior."

"I don't give a fuck what it's called!" I scream, cupping Bowie's beautiful face in my palms. "Help me!"

But he doesn't.

"Oh, god, what have they done to you?"

Bowie's stare is dead, and with hesitant fingers, I check his carotid pulse. It's faint, but it's there.

I peer around the room, desperate to find a tool to unfasten the locks, but there's nothing.

"Why did you bring me down here if you're not going to help me?" I shout at Old Timer, tears of anger streaming down my cheeks.

"Because you need to see what happens when you don't listen. You won't win," he explains, leaning against the wall. "To survive in here, you have to play by their rules."

"You mean be a fucking snake," I snap, realizing Old Timer is in bed with the enemy because that's the only explanation for why he's walking around unsupervised.

"You'll both see I'm a friend you need. Bowie knows what I want."

Right now, I want his head for being another power-hungry asshole. But I focus on Bowie, gently caressing his cheek.

"It's going to be okay," I whisper, staring into his eyes and brushing the wet hair from his angelic face. "We're going to get out of here. I promise you. No one is going to hurt you again."

My finger is suddenly wet and the moonlight streaming in from the window highlights a single tear slipping down Bowie's cheek.

He may not be able to talk, but he can hear me. Being held this way, he is literally a prisoner in his own body. This is the worst form of torture.

Suddenly, I hear the click…click…click of heels echoing down the corridor. The sound sends chills down my spine.

I don't know what to do. I fruitlessly tug at the straps, but they won't budge. "Tell me what to do!" I plead, peering into Bowie's beautiful eyes.

"We've got to go. Now!" Old Timer whisper yells. "She can't find us down here."

His terrified tone reveals whoever *she* is, is the person responsible for doing this to Bowie.

"Should I stay and fight?" I ask Bowie, my hands still pressed firmly against his cheeks.

There's no movement. He simply stares straight through me.

"Or, will that make things worse for you? Do I hide and watch, and when the time is right, strike?"

That sounds like the coward's way out, but I have no

weapons and no way to get us out of here safely.

"We've got to go!" Old Timer repeats, but he can wait.

"You want me to go?" I ask Bowie, clutching his cheeks, and when he blinks once, a sob gets caught in my throat.

Even stuck in a medicated nightmare, he's trying to save me. And this is the only way I can save him.

Kissing him lightly on his icy lips, I ignore the agony in my heart and follow Old Timer out the door. But when he attempts to leave, I grab his arm and shake my head.

"No fucking way," I state, as this isn't negotiable. "I'm not leaving until I see who did this to him."

"Why?" Old Timer questions, his fear cementing my need to stay.

"Because I want to know who needs to pay for what they did to him. If you're too chickenshit, go. But I'm staying."

I quickly hide in the room across from the bathroom and keep to the shadows to remain unseen. I'm surprised when Old Timer follows. The footsteps get louder and louder, and I prepare myself for anything.

But who I see leaves me confused.

A beautiful blonde woman appears, wheeling a chair, her spotless white doctor's coat hinting who she is. But I've never seen her before.

She enters the bathroom and stops beside the bathtub. She exhales when she peers down at Bowie. I don't know what it is about her, but I instantly don't like her. Even though she wears a doctor's uniform, I don't think she's here to help.

"I'm sorry, but you gave me no choice," she scolds, arms folded. "I can't show special preference because of who you are."

What does that mean? Just *who* is he, then?

"You can't behave that way," she continues, talking to him like a child. "I'm trying to help you. I'm trying to make you better so you can play music again. I know that if you can do that again, everything will be all right.

"*We'll* be all right again. I love you, Jonathan. Please come back to me." She produces a key from her pocket.

My stomach drops, and I want to be sick. But I watch as she kneels by the bathtub and presses her lips to Bowie's…or rather, Jonathan's.

She kisses him passionately even though he is non-responsive. But she doesn't seem to mind if the moans coming from her are anything to go by. She unlocks his restraints, and when I hear the water sloshing, I charge forward, ready to rip off her hand.

Old Timer, however, snares the back of my gown. "No," he mouths, eyes wide.

But I can't just sit here while this doctor gives a comatose Bowie a hand job. It's so unethical and, not to mention, a total violation. This is wrong—on all accounts.

But then I remember her calling him Jonathan and how if he was responsive, the hand job would probably be welcomed. I suddenly feel so stupid. What was I expecting? To ride off into the sunset happily and cured of the voices?

That only happens in cheesy movies and clichéd romance novels.

This is real life and I really need to accept that Bowie is romantically involved with this doctor who looks like an angel.

The sloshing ceases and I release the pent-up breath I was holding.

"It's okay," she says, wiping her wet hand on her jacket.

"Next time when you're feeling better."

She unfastens all the restraints and uses some machine to help lift a sopping-wet Bowie from the bathtub. He's suspended in midair, like some lifeless doll. She lowers him into a wheelchair and removes her jacket to cover him.

She hums under her breath as she escorts him from the room while I question what the hell I just saw.

Ten

Luna

One Week Later

I sit, staring vacantly at a robin perched in a tree. It looks so happy. So carefree. And why wouldn't it be? It gets to fly freely, deciding its own fate.

How envious I am of that bastard. I want what he has, something that I once took for granted. Now, I can't even go to the bathroom alone.

The bars across the window in front of me is just another reminder of where I am—in prison. Or, a better description… I'm in hell.

I haven't seen Bowie since that night in the bathroom. Nor have I seen the lady, who I'm assuming is his doctor.

This entire situation makes me sick. I need to get out of here, and I regret not doing so when I had the chance. But until I know what happened to Bowie, I can't leave. If he's still here, then I'll do everything in my power to find him.

I don't understand the pull I feel for him. And now that he's gone, it's even stronger. The longing keeps me awake, and I now welcome the drugs they give me to help me sleep. It's the only time I'm at peace, when I knock myself out cold.

The dreams have subsided, as has Misha. I don't hear him anymore. I don't like it. If hearing him makes me crazy, then I'll happily accept that diagnosis because I prefer that than feeling this…emptiness.

His memory is fading day by day…minute by minute.

I squeeze my eyes shut and force myself to remember him; remember his beautiful face, his contagious laugh, and his kind heart…the heart which now beats in a stranger's chest, helping him live a life Misha will never live.

I fucking hate that person with every fiber of my being.

A hysterical laugh slashes through the air, but it's a common occurrence here. A laugh which usually signifies something joyful, is anything but at Parkfields.

Opening my eyes, I see Starlight being restrained by two orderlies. She's a sore loser which is why no one wants to play any board games with her. The last person who did was force-fed the top hat playing piece from Monopoly.

She kicks and screams, and when a nurse in white comes rushing into the rec room, syringe in hand, I know Starlight won't be doing much of anything soon. She's jabbed in the arm, and after a few seconds, she's quiet.

This place isn't helping anyone. Instead of offering support and care, they simply turn their patients into medicated zombies, which is their "cure."

It's my goal to expose this place for what it really is. But first, I need to get the fuck out of here.

The gates open, and I know Jabba and the Hulk are waiting by it, looking for their chance to escape. I give them credit for their perseverance. Not bothering to pay anything attention but the robin outside the window, I don't realize someone is wheeled by me until I hear the wheels being locked into place.

I return to the now, and two things happen—my heart begins to race, and I hear him. I hear Misha.

"Miss me?"

Snapping my head to the right, I'm thankful to be strapped in my chair because who I see beside me leaves me a mess. I don't speak. I wait for the orderly who has a bandage around his throat to leave. But the way he looks at me, I know he's somehow involved in what happened to Bowie.

I haven't seen Noah, but I know he'll be back. In the meantime, his goons are keeping an eye on me, reminding me that it's not over.

Once he's gone, I take a moment to look at Bowie, or rather, Jonathan. I prefer Bowie, however, and refuse to acknowledge him by any other name.

He's in a starchy hospital gown, and his long hair looks freshly washed. I blanch, however, wondering if that's because he has been subjected to that torture in the bathtub once again. I know that bastard orderly placed Bowie next to me for a reason.

A warning, perhaps?

His head is drooped forward, and saliva hangs off his chin. The crucifix around his throat is like a pendulum. My vibrant boy is no more.

"What have they done to you?" I whisper, tears in my eyes.

"Bowie, can you hear me?"

I hope, like in the bathtub, he'll give me a sign that he's here. That although he may be caught in a drugged stupor, he's still present.

But I get nothing.

Bowie sits beside me, but what animates him is gone. His bitch of a doctor made sure of it.

"I'm not giving up on you. I know you're in there. You just have to try. This isn't for nothing," I continue, swallowing past my tears. "I won't let them get you too."

Bowie is the first person I've felt any connection to, besides Misha, of course. And I don't give up on the people I...love?

I don't love Bowie. Well, I don't think I do. But I can't deny the attraction I feel is not just physical. It's beyond that. Far deeper than I can explain.

The TV is on, and I pretend to watch it as I strategize ways to get the hell out of here, and when Old Timer comes into view, sweeping the floor, I know he's my only hope.

He notices me watching him and casually sweeps his way over to me. When close enough, he looks at Bowie, his anguish clear.

"I need your help," I whisper, ensuring no one is listening.

He nods but goes about doing his job, not to stir any suspicion.

"Can you get us out of here?"

He nods once again.

"Tonight?"

He shakes his head.

"When?"

"When the time is right."

"The time is now!" I whisper a little too loudly as my anger explodes.

Old Timer sweeps around us, his back facing the nurses' station. "How are you going to get him out of here? Carry him?"

He's right. I need Bowie semi-mobile for this to work.

"When will they stop drugging him like this?"

"When he learns to behave," he counters quickly, his astute eyes scanning the room. "I've seen it before. They're making an example out of him. He's a warning to other patients. You can't win against them. The only way to get what you want is to play by their rules."

"I want them all dead," I spit, surprising myself because I actually mean it.

"I know, we all do."

His comment surprises me. "Why are you in here? You seem…fine?"

I don't know what the politically correct term is. Normal is so cookie-cutter because what's normal anyway?

He appears taken off guard that someone actually asked about him. I guess in this place, everyone has their own cross to bear, let alone dealing with someone else's shit.

"Where am I to go?" he poses, and his sweeping ceases. "Out there? I've got nothing waiting for me out there. This is the only home I know."

A sadness so great overcomes me. Old Timer prefers these confines because freedom appears to be a lot scarier than being in here.

"Tell me how to help him."

"The alarm—" But he never finishes his sentence because the room suddenly grows cold, and I mean that in every sense

133

of the word.

The patients, it seems, go into hiding when the familiar heels clicking on the polished floors sound loudly. It has the opposite effect on me.

I rivet my attention to the steel gated door and when it opens, the antichrist in heels enters. She is even more stunning in the daylight. Too bad she's an evil bitch who tortures those she's meant to be helping.

Old Timer discreetly sweeps away, but the doctor knows we were up to no good, and when she sees Bowie beside me, her red-painted lips pull into a tight line. She ignores everyone and heads straight for us.

I try my best to remain impassive, but the closer she gets, all I can see is her giving a comatose Bowie a hand job. The moment she stands in front of me, blocking my view of the window, it's apparent the hatred runs both ways.

"Hello," she says, attempting a smile. It's more of a sneer. "I'm Dr. Norton."

She's not exactly what I expect a doctor to look like. She's blonde, beautiful, and tall. But there is no warmth behind her green eyes. But that changes when she looks at Bowie. It seems like everything ceases to exist but him.

It sounds romantic, but put aside the fact that we clearly like the same man, but there is something…wrong with the way she looks at him. It's not that of a lover but rather of someone who is infatuated to an unhealthy degree.

When she realizes I'm watching her closely, her doctor mask slips back into place. "I hear you and…Bowie have become good friends?"

I have to play it cool.

"Can one really make friends in here?" I pose, knowing the less I reveal, the better.

Dr. Norton nods, and I know she's scrutinizing everything I say. "That's true. I've read over your file. You're a very smart woman. You don't belong in here."

I hold my breath because although these are the words I've wanted to hear since awakening in this nightmare, I know what she's doing.

"Therefore, I'm going to override any medical diagnoses and sign your discharge papers. You'll be free to leave in the morning."

A lump forms in my throat, but I smile. "Thank you so much, Doctor."

She nods, but there is no kindness behind her actions. She's doing this to keep me away from Bowie. She realizes I'm a threat to whatever she has planned for him, which means…I can't go. I won't leave him here to rot.

"You're most welcome. You suffered in ways unimaginable. It's natural for the response you've had. But does that warrant a stay in here? No."

I want to ask what Bowie did then for him to be subjected to the torture he's endured, but I don't.

"I'll organize a doctor to see you once you're home and settled, but the best medicine for you is to be at home and attempt to heal."

She's overlooked the small fact that when I was there last, I tried to kill myself, so I don't think being home is the best place to "heal." But this isn't about me.

This is about Bowie.

She walks around and grips the handles of his wheelchair.

"It's time for his medicine," she says while I bite the inside of my cheek to stop from screaming out in protest.

How much more medicine can he take?

Dr. Norton reads my expression and smiles, but there is nothing comforting in the gesture. "Don't worry, his heart is… strong."

If that's supposed to be a joke, I don't get it.

"By the way," she says over her shoulder as she wheels Bowie away. "That elderly gentleman you were talking to… don't believe a word he says."

"Why?"

"Because he's in here for being a compulsive liar."

And with that, she walks away, humming happily, while I question everything I thought I knew.

Two thousand and twenty.

Two thousand and twenty-one.

That's how many small dots I've counted on the ceiling. The pattern I'm certain is to drive one crazy, or crazier, depending on who you speak to.

Usually, I would be sound asleep, but I guess because I'm being discharged tomorrow, Dr. Norton didn't see the point in drugging me. As far as she's concerned, I'm a problem she no longer has to worry about.

Anyone would be thankful their wish has been granted, but I just can't leave. I know if I do, I'll never see Bowie again.

I need to help him. I just don't know how.

"I heard it's your last night in here. Noah won't be happy."

Turning my head toward the doorway, I see the man who

wheeled Bowie into the rec room. If he knows Noah, then he's not a friend.

I remain quiet because I wonder if this is a sign. Is this bastard my meal ticket to stay?

He peers down the hallway before entering my room and closing the door behind him. It's dark, the only light is coming in from the window from the moon.

"Such a shame," he continues, walking toward the bed. "We were going to have fun with you, but thanks to your *friend*, Noah is still pretty messed up."

He means Bowie. Bowie is the reason Noah hasn't been here. I wonder what he did.

"But that doesn't mean I can't have my fun with you. I mean, it would be a shame not to. I've jerked off to your pictures so many times. But you're so much better in person."

I don't panic because I've been around men like this before. They think they're God's gift to women. If he wasn't such a bastard, I would say he's attractive, but it's because of his looks that he believes he can get whatever he wants.

And the fact I've shown no interest in any of them is the reason they want me—they see me as a challenge, one they want to conquer. But they've underestimated the wrath which runs through me.

"If you scream," he warns. "I'll gag you. But I don't want to do that because I prefer that beautiful mouth to be gagging on something else."

He commences stroking over the front of his white trousers. Bile rises, but I remain calm.

"I'm going to loosen your restraints, but if you try anything, I will knock you out. Got it?"

I nod.

"Good girl. I don't need you awake for what I want anyway," he adds, which just confirms this bastard deserves everything I'm about to inflict on him.

He sits on the bed and gently brushes the hair off my brow. I remain passive. He unfastens the leather strap from around my chest. I exhale deeply because I can breathe a little better. He then unfastens one of the leather cuffs from around my wrist but leaves the other bound.

I don't move.

He takes a moment to look at me. "You really are beautiful. Too bad you're a crazy bitch. But you know what they say about crazy people—"

He leans down and smells the side of my neck. "They are crazy in bed."

I try not to cringe because who speaks so disgustingly? He laps at my throat with his revolting tongue. I'm going to take great pleasure in hearing this pig squeal.

As he is molesting me with his mouth, I discreetly use my free hand to search for a weapon. I don't have a plan, so I need to think on my feet. All I can feel is the tray which has nothing on it.

"You're so sexy. No wonder Noah wants you. I can't wait to tell him." He runs his slippery hand over my body before sliding them under the hem of my hospital gown.

My legs are still strapped in, so he can't gain access to where he wants with ease. He grunts in frustration. I've always been blessed in the chest, so I use it to my advantage and arch my back. It works like a charm as his attention diverts to my breasts.

He licks his lips like a salivating dog.

"Kiss me," I whisper, batting my eyelashes. "If you're going to fuck me, the least you can do is kiss me."

Being crude is what this vile snake wants.

"Oh, baby, I'm going to kiss you all over." He plants his mouth over mine, shoving his tongue in deep.

It takes all my willpower not to bite it off because I have another idea. Men like this only think with the head between their legs which is why I grip his brown hair and yank his head away. Before he has a chance to reply, I slam his temple into the tray table.

He's utterly stunned, which is why I do it again and again until he goes limp. I don't wait a second and unfasten the restraint around my wrist before unfastening the one around my legs and feet. Once free, I shove the asshole to the floor and jump out of bed.

I decide to try to find Bowie, and if I can't, then make enough noise to alert the staff that I'm free. Opening the door, I look from left to right, and when I see the coast is clear, I tiptoe down the corridor. It's so quiet which means the patients were given a double dose of their sleeping medication.

The staff are no doubt up to no good, and when I hear music down the hall, it confirms my suspicions. I look through the small windows of each room, hoping to see Bowie, but I don't. What I do see saddens me beyond words.

Each patient is sedated to the point of nigh on being in a coma. This place doesn't help anyone. Turning the corner, a soft whimper catches my attention. I need to keep walking, but when the cries become unintelligible words, curiosity gets the better of me.

I creep toward the voice which is female.

I still can't make out what she's mumbling, but it's evident she's in pain. The rooms along here are offices or therapy rooms, which is why my curiosity is piqued. The voice gets louder and now I can make out a few words.

"I'm going to make you better. It's going to go back to how things were."

A shiver racks me from head to toe because I recognize that voice—it's Dr. Norton. I know I should turn away, but I can't.

With my heart in my throat, I slowly peer through the crack in her open door and what I see confuses and chills me to the bone all in one breath. Dr. Norton is talking with a man who is lying on her leather couch.

His sandy blond hair is shaggy, and he wears a hospital gown. I know it's not Bowie because his hair is longer and this man's is a lot thinner. I can't see his face because he's facing the other way. The overpowering fragrance of lavender hits my nostrils, and the overkill has me believing it's used to mask another smell.

I just don't know what.

Dr. Norton smiles, peering down at the man on her couch, and it's evident she has an attachment to him as well. She clearly takes her role very seriously.

She walks over to the record player, and when Beethoven sounds, I press my nose closer into the doorway to ensure it's not Bowie.

It's not.

As the music sounds, the doctor sips a brown liquid from a crystal glass and sways gently. She seems relaxed, but I'm not. I feel like I'm about to witness something monumental. And when Dr. Norton finishes her drink and places the glass on the edge of her desk, I realize now is the time to turn around and leave.

But I can't. I need her to confirm this hunch I have in the pit of my stomach that she isn't a good person. And when she turns up the volume on the record player and wets her lips, I know I'm right. She walks over to the couch where the man lies, completely still. I wonder if this is her thing—taking advantage of those who are impaired.

"It's going to be all right," she says in an almost hypnotic state as she mounts the man. She lifts his hospital gown, and it's very apparent what she's doing when a sated moan leaves her.

She begins rocking, her eyes slipping to half-mast as she tosses her head back. The man doesn't make a sound, however. He doesn't even move.

It sickens me she would abuse her power this way. I hate to think how many patients she is doing this to.

Her movements become faster, which is my cue to leave because I've seen enough. I need to keep her away from Bowie. But what I'm confused about is that she spoke to him so lovingly, but now her actions with another man are far from loyal.

This place is poison. The more I uncover, the worse things are.

I quietly step back because although I wanted to cause a scene, I know barging in on Dr. Norton riding a patient into next week won't be wise because Bowie will suffer the consequences. But I now know she is no friend.

I decide to continue my search for Bowie, but when a light shines brightly in my face, it seems my hunt is up. "What are you doing out of your room?"

I need to think fast.

"Hey, big guy," I coo, giving him big doe eyes. "I was looking for Noah and his friends."

I can't see who is pointing the light into my eyes, but the fact it's a man makes it a good probability that he's a pervert and probably in cahoots with Noah.

"Noah isn't here," he replies. "But I can be your friend."

I'm no longer blinded as he switches off the flashlight. It's an orderly I've never seen before. I walk toward him and smile. "I'd like that."

If I'm going to make a scene, I plan on taking down as many assholes with me. He grips my elbow and leads me away, giving me time to execute my plan.

"I don't suppose we can get my friend to join us?"

"Who's your friend?" he asks, appearing pleased with the possibility of more victims to exploit.

"Bowie," I casually reply.

When a chuckle escapes him, my hopes get shot to hell. "Good luck with that. Dr. Norton won't let him out of her sight."

But that's not entirely true. I mean, she is currently having sex with another man.

"Where is he?"

Silence.

Our footsteps echo an uneasy rhythm which only amplifies the farther we walk. We turn the corner and head toward the "treatment" rooms. A sense of dread fills my stomach, and I realize I've made a very big mistake.

"HEL—" My cries for help are muted, however, when the orderly presses me against his chest and fixes his hand over my mouth.

I try to bite his fingers, but he only fastens his hold and

drags me into a sterile white room. I try and fight, but he's strong and lifts me off the ground with ease. He tosses me onto a silver gurney and when I try to launch off it, he punches me in the face.

The world spins for a few seconds as I attempt to gather my bearings, but when I feel my arms being restrained, I know it's useless.

"You sick bastard!" I scream, kicking my legs as he secures my ankles with leather straps. "I'm going to kill you all!"

Spit dribbles down my chin because right now, I'm rabid. I thrash about as best I can, but being tied down prohibits me from moving. When I hear the sound of heels clicking against the floor, it seems my wish has been granted as this little stunt will ensure I'm not going anywhere tomorrow.

Dr. Norton enters, and she looks almost disappointed. "You just can't seem to stay out of trouble, can you?" she says, shaking her head.

All I can smell is fucking lavender.

"Just how you can't help taking your role as doctor a little too seriously," I spit back, ensuring I make clear I know what she's been up to.

She is taken aback that I'm privy to her secrets.

I watch as she walks toward a machine in the corner of the room and wheels it over. "You were out of here in the morning. Why?"

"She asked about the patient, Bowie," the orderly reveals.

Dr. Norton sighs heavily. "If you want to help him, then stay away from him."

"The same could be said about you."

She snickers, her anger shining through. "Have it your way

then, because after I'm done with you, you won't remember a thing. Harrison."

She nods at the orderly who shoves a rubber mouth guard into my mouth. I try to spit it out, but he holds the end of it as he pins me down. My heart beats frantically because, for the first time since arriving, fear has replaced my anger.

I scream around the guard, thrashing from side to side as Dr. Norton places two paddles against my temples. The sting of the metal is cool. I lift my chin to watch what she's doing when I hear her turning on switches.

I shake my head, begging she doesn't do whatever it is she intends to. But she simply smiles before I hear a buzz and feel my entire being get shocked into submission. I lose control of my body.

I can't think.

I can't breathe.

All that I can feel is unbearable pain.

The machine suddenly stops buzzing, and the pain subsides, but the echoes of the shock Dr. Norton just delivered whirl around in my brain. It's like a rainbow of colors competing to win an imaginary race.

I can't keep up.

And when I hear the machine fire up once again, I brace for death. But this is far worse when she pushes the button and an electrical current shoots through me so fiercely my body becomes numb before I begin to seize.

I don't remember anything after that.

Eleven

Dutch

I don't remember anything. I barely remember my name. But there is one name I can't forget…

Luna.

My memories are vague and trying to remember them is like wading through mud. I don't know what's real and what my mind is attempting to cope with whatever the hell has happened over the course of hours. Days? Weeks?

I don't even know what month it is.

I fight against this fucking fatigue and open my eyes. I have no idea where I am. It looks like an infirmary from the number of beds in the large room. But I'm the only person in here.

No surprise, I'm restrained to the bed.

"You're awake." I recognize the voice as Dr. Norton. "How are you feeling?"

"Like I've been slipped a Mickey," I reply honestly. "And this comedown sucks ass."

Dr. Norton sits beside me in the orange plastic seat and opens a notepad. "What's the last thing you remember?"

That's a good question because my brain is completely fried. I push aside the fog and cling onto the only solid memory I have—it's when Luna pressed her ear to my chest and listened to this foreign bastard giving me life.

It was the only time I felt at peace and that this heart was mine.

"Are you still experiencing memories which you cannot recall?" Dr. Norton asks as if reading my mind.

"Honestly, Doc, at the moment, I'm not experiencing anything other than wanting to dig my brain out with an ice cream scoop."

"What about your heart?"

"What about it?"

"Are you still feeling…ill at ease with it?"

I burst into laughter. "That's a real nice way of putting it. But I guess the urge to cut the motherfucker from my chest has subsided a little."

She writes something in her little book. "That's good. That's progress."

"What the fuck happened?"

Dr. Norton clears her throat.

"Don't give me some medical mumbo jumbo bullshit. I want the truth."

She adjusts her glasses, but I think it's merely nerves. "We were forced to sedate you because you made some very serious claims about certain staff members."

I did?

I squeeze through the tiny tunnel of light in my mind and grasp on to any solid memory I can. It's of me beating the shit out of three lowlife scumbags.

"Motherfucker," I curse under my breath when I remember what happened in that tunnel. "Those claims are fact. Those assholes were abusing their power, and the only regret I have is that I didn't kill those assholes when I got the chance."

Dr. Norton gasps, and her cheeks turn a lovely shade of pink.

Taking a closer look at her, I realize she isn't horrified by my words—no, she's turned on.

"Why are you here, Alanna?" I ask, using her name for the first time. I've done so with intent because it's evident her interest in me isn't purely professional.

"You're my patient—"

"Enough with the bullshit," I interrupt firmly. "I'm in a fucking asylum. Pretty sure this is out of your jurisdiction. What gives?"

She takes a moment to compose herself. "You intrigue me," she confesses, finally giving me the truth. "What you've described is happening to you…it can change medical history."

And now I understand why the sudden interest.

"You see me as your lab rat? You're the one who did the operation, so you think you should be the one who studies me and reports back to your medical board for a pat on the back and promotion? While I sit in here to rot? Is that it?"

"Dutch, no. Of course not!"

But we both know that's a lie. I am just someone she can make history with. She doesn't care at all. She's just using me as a science project. I can only imagine what this would do for

147

her career.

"Don't insult me," I snap, leveling her sternly. "I'll do whatever you want, but on one condition. You get me and Misha out of here."

The slight flaring of her nostrils reveals she's not pleased with this arrangement. But we don't have a deal otherwise.

"What is it about her?" she asks, studying me closely.

"I don't know," I confess honestly. "I just know that when she's close to me, everything feels…better."

"Your heart too?"

"Yes. It's the only time it feels like it's my heart as well."

She writes something down in her notepad. "Would you be willing to try something?"

"If it gets me the hell out of here, then yes."

She closes her notepad and places the pen in her high bun as if not to forget it. I watch as she stands and wheels over a wheelchair. "If I untie you, you promise to do what you're told?"

"I'll try my best."

That's hardly comforting, but Alanna unfastens my restraints as whatever she has planned is clearly important to her. She pulls back the gray blanket, and I wonder if my legs will work. It takes a moment for my brain and body to connect, but eventually, my legs do what they're told as I swing them over the edge of the bed and place them on the cold floor.

I take in two deep breaths before lifting myself off the thin mattress and carefully sit in the wheelchair.

Alanna arranges a blanket over my legs, and I hate that I feel nothing but like an invalid. If I had the choice again, I would have never answered her call. But here I am, being wheeled from this asylum infirmary, at the mercy of my doctor.

The hallowed echoes inside my head confirm that the music hasn't returned. I am still musically crippled. A part of me is missing, and I don't know how to get it back.

The corridor is quiet; the occasional moan or cry for help is heard. Alanna wheels me into a room I've never seen before. I would have remembered if I had because of the grand fucking piano sitting dead center.

The moment I see it, his heart stirs in interest. It's the first time I remember this happening.

Alanna is quiet as she wheels me over to the piano and positions me so I can play in the chair. But I shake my head. "I won't play confined."

I don't wait for her response as I kick off the blanket and stand. It's probably my very fragile mind playing tricks on me, but I suddenly feel stronger. I inhale deeply and close my eyes. Underneath the sterility, I smell polish and wood.

This would usually be the time I leave this world and make my own in a universe built solely for me. But the white noise suffocates me.

"Take your time," Alanna softly encourages.

I'm not a fucking wimp, so I open my eyes and take in the beautiful creation in front of me. I'm not a piano snob. As long as she sounds good, I'll play, but this piano is expensive. And that surprises me.

Parkfields doesn't exactly spend lavishly on the essentials such as food or soap, so to have this here is a mystery. And that has me wanting to play all the more.

I run my fingertip over the closed fallboard. My dick instantly gets hard. I pull back the stool and take a seat. I don't do anything. I just sit. The sense of peace which overwhelms me angers the voices inside my head because they need chaos to survive.

But as I lift the fallboard, revealing the keyboard, everything fades into nothingness. The black and white keys speak to me in morse code. I place my fingers on them and exhale slowly. This would be the time music floods my brain and I play without thought.

But as expected, I hear nothing…but the deafening sound of his heart dragging his ass in my chest cavity.

"What do you feel?" Alanna asks, and I almost forgot she was here.

"I feel…nothing."

I close my eyes and wade through the darkness to reach the other side. Sweat collects along my brow as I desperately try to remember…anything.

"How do you know that?" Mom asks me—a six-year-old me who simply shrugs as I run my fingers over the toy piano she bought at a yard sale and start playing 'Amazing Grace.'

"Your son is a prodigy."

"Your son is a freak."

The voices get louder and louder, kicking against my temple. But I welcome the pain as I almost double over. The pain is what helps me play.

"I need you to do this for me. For us."

Who said that?

It's a voice I don't recognize.

The pain is replaced with intense sadness, and I don't know why. I don't even know whose memory it is.

"If you love me, you'll do this."

"I'm short. Can I pay you next week?"

I taste blood.

I can't breathe.

I see a sign: *Woodland Waterfalls.*

His heart begins to beat faster, but it's not a feeling of unease. It's a feeling of belonging.

And just like that…I hear it.

Music.

It ricochets in my mind and is suddenly an extension of my fingers—just how it once was. I come back to what I know—Moonlight Sonata.

I play with my eyes closed because you don't see music; you feel it. And that's the reason I couldn't play. Because I wasn't feeling…anything.

I lose myself to the music, and although it's far from my best, it feels incredible to be able to play again. The fire within burns brighter, hotter, so hot, I'm certain I'll be set alight.

"Open your eyes…"

It's the first time I've heard his voice, but I know who it is—it's the owner of my heart. So, without choice, I do as he says and what I see has me slamming my hands onto the keys, a reflection of the heaviness in my chest.

In front of me is a large window which looks into the adjoining room and who's inside has me realizing *she's* the reason I was able to play.

I launch up, but Alanna places her hand on my shoulder. "She's all right. I've just prescribed her something to help her sleep. Keep playing."

My eyes are fixed on Luna, who is strapped to a wheelchair. A belt is secured around her forehead and tied to the headrest to stop her from slouching forward. I don't want to play. I want to go to her.

But I trust Alanna. She brought Luna here because the doctor in her couldn't resist. And she was right. Luna is no doubt my muse. It's the only time I hear music.

I never take my eyes off her. I find my composure and continue playing because this is solely for her.

Each note gets bigger and better. It gets easier. I play for Luna, wishing my music can heal her; wishing it could heal us both.

Her beauty and strength sing to my very soul, and I want her—in every way that I can.

"Help her."

It's him again—my annoying passenger. Or am I his?

I'm trying to, I reply in my mind.

I know how crazy it sounds speaking to the voice in your head which belongs to the man's whose heart gives you life. But this is the first time I've felt sane. This is the first time I feel like we're on the same team.

My fingers ache, but I don't stop until I play the final note, but when I do, it seems it's only the beginning.

"Don't trust her."

Who?

"This is a safe place," says Dr. Greene as he shuffles through some cards.

But I've heard it all before.

The only safe place I believe in is when I'm playing music. And when Luna is nearby.

Today was progress. It was the first day I was able to play.

But when the orderly took Luna away, the music stopped. And so did the voice inside my head.

Maybe I do belong in here.

"I'm going to show you a series of cards, and tell me what you see. It's that simple."

Simple? There is nothing simple about any of this. But I nod, humoring him nonetheless.

He turns over the first card which is a black ink spot of mess. I look at him, wondering if this is some kind of joke. But when he smiles in encouragement, it's evident he is fucking serious.

It doesn't look like anything, but I tilt my head to the side and sigh. "A banana."

He nods with a stiff upper lip, giving nothing away. He turns over the next card which is the same inky mess, but a slightly different pattern.

"A butterfly."

The next card.

I burst into laughter because this is fucking ridiculous. "A circus monkey riding a unicorn."

Dr. Greene peers at me, but when he sees I'm serious, he quickly writes something down. "Very good. How did that make you feel?"

"I don't know," I reply, slouching back in my seat. "Confused."

He scribbles something in his notes. "Confused how?"

"Not sure how ink blotches are going to help me, but hey, whatever floats your boat."

He clears his throat, clearly not impressed with my aloofness. "I've read over your file, and I suspect you're suffering from schizophrenia."

Well, this is nothing new.

"I know you've seen a doctor in the past, but I believe you were misdiagnosed. With the right medication and treatment, I believe you'll be able to live a relatively normal life. You're in the right place to heal. I'll start your treatment immediately and monitor you closely."

"And what about what I want?" I question because what happened to free will?

He adjusts his silver-rimmed glasses. "Well, you're not in the right frame of mind. So we spoke to your parents, who signed off on the trials."

"Excuse me?" I can't keep the bite from my tone. "I'm a grown-ass man. I can make my own decisions. And trials? What the fuck does that mean? These drugs aren't even approved?"

"It's going to be all right. You're in a safe place."

Kicking back the chair, I stand, placing my hands on the edge of Dr. Greene's desk as I lean forward, totally invading his personal space.

"If you say that one more time—" I look at the stapler on his desk, wondering how many staples would seal his lips shut.

He recoils back in his high-back leather seat, clearly terrified. "I just want to help you, Dutch. Your illness has you believing the world is against you. The delusions, the hallucinations, they've grown worse? As have the voices in your head?"

How did he know?

Today was the first day I heard voices. But I'm not crazy. I know it's *him*.

"You don't know what you're talking about. I'm fine. You and everyone in here are the ones who are crazy!"

"No one called you crazy," Dr. Greene says calmly. "And we don't like using that term."

But his tone is patronizing and pisses me off.

"Are *we* done?"

"For now."

He pushes a button, and two orderlies come into his office, ready to throw down if needed. But Dr. Greene shakes his head.

Pushing off his desk, I know the drill and coolly sit into the wheelchair. I salute the doctor as one of the orderlies wheels me away.

I need to get out of here because the more time spent here, the worse things feel. I would rather deal with the voices outside these walls than within. But what about Luna?

"You can't leave her here."

"I know!" I exclaim, and when Merlin ceases pumping his cock from the chair he sits in the corridor, I realize I replied aloud to the mystery voice.

I'm wheeled into the rec room and placed in front of the TV. I'm not strapped in like usual and am surprised when the orderlies leave. Is this a test?

"Yes."

"Who are you?" I ask out loud and no one looks twice because it's just another day in the office to see someone speaking to themselves.

"You know who I am."

"What's your name, asshole? If you're going to annoy the shit out of me, then I should at least know your name."

"Jack."

Not much shocks me anymore, but this does. Did he really just tell me his name?

"Look who it is."

It's Old Timer, sweeping his way toward me.

Memories of seeing him with Noah come back to me, and I curl my lip, disgusted. "Not doing business with your little friend today?"

Old Timer blanches, realizing he's been caught. "You did a real number on him."

"No, I really didn't because if I did, he would be dead. How could you be in business with him?" I make it very clear that I don't trust him because of the fact.

"It's the only way to survive in this place. I've told you that. Has being a smart mouth got you anywhere?" he poses, continuing his ruse of cleaning as he sweeps under the table.

"At least I've still got my dignity," I spit because he's a fucking sellout.

"Has that saved you or *her*?"

The mere mention of Luna has me wishing to rip out his tongue. "Where is she?"

"If you want to help her, do what you're told. As far as I'm concerned, nothing has changed in regard to our arrangement."

"You and your pep talk can blow me."

Old Timer shakes his head, disappointed. "You'll soon learn the rules on the outside don't apply within these walls."

He doesn't linger and sweeps away.

I need out of here and I thought Old Timer was my ticket, but if he's working with Noah, then I can't trust him.

A rally is on the TV. It's of women protesting about abortion rights. I don't understand why anyone believes they have the right to dictate what a woman can do with her body. A woman on the TV smashes a sign over a religious zealot's head.

I fist pump in unity.

"I thought you'd like to sit together for a while." I have no idea what Alanna means until I turn to look over my shoulder and see Luna.

Alanna smiles kindly while I forget my own name. It feels like months since I was last this close to Luna. I was barely alive until now.

But Luna stares straight ahead.

"It's just the effects of the sedation. It'll wear off soon," Alanna explains, reading my concerns. "But I think she'd like to sit with you."

She doesn't dally and leaves us alone, revealing she really is one of the good guys.

It's cloudy out, but the light which trickles in through the window highlights the blonde in Luna's long hair. She really is the most beautiful woman I've ever seen.

I reach out and gently place my hand over hers. She's ice cold. She doesn't flinch, and I wonder what she did to be sedated in such a way.

"Causing trouble again, baby," I whisper, squeezing her fingers gently. "I've missed you."

She doesn't respond.

Her blue eyes are fixed ahead, but no one is home.

"Sing to her."

"Sing what?" But I answer my own question when I hear 'Heroes' by David Bowie. It happened once before and I don't even know why that is—I don't even like Bowie. But just like the name popped into my head when asked who we were, so does the song, so I go with it.

With our fingers still interlaced, I begin to sing, surprising myself when I know the words by heart. When I get to the chorus, something happens—I begin to see the rain, even though it's not raining outside.

I hear the gravel under the tires. I see the headlights of each car I pass by. My singing morphs into the radio as I'm suddenly behind the wheel, tapping along to Bowie. Peering down, I see I'm wearing a football jersey. It's of my football team.

With one hand on the wheel, I reach into the middle console and pull out a joint. Mom would be livid if she found out I smoked pot. But she'd be beside herself if she knew the real me.

She thinks I'm perfect, but I'm not. If she ever found out that I was dealing drugs to pay for my own habit, it'll kill her. I need to protect her because I love her so much.

But that's not the worst of it.

If she knew what I was doing, she'd never forgive me. But she won't tell me the truth, but…*she* will. She knows who he is, and I will do anything to find out who he is.

Shit.

I quickly brush the ash from the leather seat, not wanting to burn Mom's car. She worked hard for it. She's worked hard for everything. I know I seem ungrateful, but I need to know him. Even though he was never there for me, I want to know him. I need to know if he is…sick like I am.

I mean, you've only got one dad…

An ear-splitting crash robs me of air, and I'm flying, careening through the air. I know when I stop, however, I'll be dead. It wasn't an accident…because I know who killed me.

As I take my final breath, I think of her…*I'm so sorry, Mom. I love you. Please forgive me for what I've done.*

I blink back my tears as I claw at my chest. I need to get out of my skin. I want to scream. I want to fight. But a single touch grounds me. It draws me back to her.

With a gasp, I return to the now, unsure what the hell just happened. I was reliving a memory that wasn't mine, but now, I know whose it was—it was Jack's.

The man whose heart is in my chest was named Jack.

Something suddenly shifts between Luna and me.

Looking over at her, I see a single tear trickle from the corner of her eye because she felt it too. We are somehow connected…and I'm going to find out how.

Twelve

Luna

"Do you want help dressing?"

I look at the pretty nurse with suspicion in my eye because I don't know her. I don't see an ulterior motive, however. But regardless, I shake my head.

With unsteady fingers, I fasten the buttons on my blue cardigan. The color matches my summer dress. I don't know whose garments these are, but I woke to them spread out on the end of my bed. Apparently, hospital gowns aren't appropriate attire for an outing in town.

I was thankful the nurse gave me a brush, as I can't remember the last time I brushed my hair. Or wore shoes, for that matter. I can't remember much of anything.

The only thing which stands out is the agonizing pain in my head as my brain scrambled for air. I quickly brush away a runaway tear because I don't want to cry. Well, I don't think I do.

The chatty nurse let slip that there have been rumors in the community about the inhumane treatment of patients. It's all hearsay, of course, she said, but to ensure an official inquiry doesn't take place, the doctors have decided to allow the townsfolk to see for themselves.

"You look lovely," the nurse says as I slip into a white woolen coat.

I nod in gratitude, as speech is an effort I don't have the energy for.

Even though we are allowed to walk, it's clear we must be chaperoned at all times. Just what is this hospital?

"I'm ready." I flinch as I don't even recognize the sound of my voice anymore.

She smiles and we walk out of the room together, side by side.

There are massive holes in my memory, and I feel as if I'm missing vital pieces of the puzzle. I don't remember why I'm here. All I can recall is a deep-rooted pain in my heart like I lost something and know I'll never get it back.

We walk down the corridor and I take it all in because I can't remember being here before. Why can't I remember?

Through the windows, I see a bus parked out the front of the building. There are a few people milling near it. I wonder if I'll recognize anyone. I wonder if anyone knows who I am… because I don't.

She opens the door and the winter breeze slaps at my cheeks. I rub my arms and am thankful I'm wearing a coat, even though I don't know whose it is. It smells like mothballs.

Peering around the gardens, I hope to get a glimmer of

recognition.

I don't.

But it becomes obvious quite quickly that this is a state hospital. I've been committed. But why?

The nurse stays close to me as we approach my fellow patients who have their own chaperones. I take them in, hoping for a familiar face to stand out in the crowd.

None do.

The bus doors open, and we are herded onto it, taking seats in an orderly fashion. The nurse kindly allows me to sit by the window. I happily peer out of it, taking in this life, which is foreign yet familiar to me all at the same time.

It's so surreal.

Although I wish I could remember, a part of me is thankful that I can't, and I wonder why that is.

Lost in a past I can't recollect, I focus out the window, hoping something will help me remember who I am. And when a tall man with blond hair saunters out the doors, I take my time admiring him because I would surely remember that face.

His long hair is slicked back into a low ponytail, showcasing the sharp planes of his handsome face. His jaw is sharp, angular, and his lips look full, supple. Even though he's far away, I know his eyes will be as mesmerizing as the rest of him.

He's in black ripped jeans and a black T-shirt. He's covered in a few tattoos, which just seems to emphasize his 'I don't give a fuck' attitude.

Who is this man?

I should really stop staring, but I can't. He feels…familiar.

When he gets closer to the bus, we make eye contact. Neither of us looks away. A slanted grin plays at his mouth, sending my heart into overdrive. He's quite bold, looking at me openly with those blue eyes. He comes to a stop before me and extends his arm overhead, pressing his hand to my window.

He has silver rings on his fingers. He looks like a rock star.

The gesture touches me deeply. But it also has heat engulfing every inch of me.

He splays his fingers, never taking his eyes off me. It's a peace offering as such, him waiting for me to meet him halfway.

But I don't.

I quickly turn my cheek, looking away.

Guilt overcomes me, which is ridiculous. I don't even know this man. There's no need to feel guilt. But it won't subside. I turn back to the window, ready to accept his offering, but it's too late—he's gone.

He's not gone far, however, because when I hear a whistle, I know shit is about to go down.

"Are we going on an excursion?" says a voice that is dripping with sarcasm and sex. "I hope you packed lunch."

Heart in my throat, I lift my eyes and meet those of this mysterious stranger who is boldly looking my way. He seems pissed off and confused. I think I was the one to cause those feelings in him. I watch as his escort drags him to a seat two rows in front of me and shoves him into it before sitting beside him.

The bus driver starts the engine and turns up the radio as he slowly drives down the driveway.

I'm unsettled and can't stop looking at the man in front of me. There's something special about him.

I can't shake the feeling that he has the ability to change the world, which is absurd.

He turns around; not over his shoulder, but actually rotates in his seat and interlaces his arms across the back of the chair. He rests his chin on them and stares at me. I look behind me in case he's trying to get the attention of someone else, but when it's apparent it's me he's looking at, I swallow past the lump in my throat.

The nurse beside me giggles. "Looks like you've got an admirer…and not a bad-looking one at that."

The man grins, eyes still dissecting me. "Hi."

It takes me a few seconds, but I nod with a stiff upper lip.

Most would get the hint and turn back around, but not him. "How's this weather?" he says with a staged sigh.

I bite my cheek to mute my laughter.

"That's enough. Turn back around," says the orderly near him, yanking him to face the front.

But no surprise, he doesn't listen.

He just continues staring at me and commences whistling a tune which sounds familiar, but I can't quite place it. He whistles louder, which only has the notes inside my head forming music which I can hear—I can hear the voice of a man who I recognize but can't name.

I shut out all other noise and focus on the whistling, and when he draws out a section, a voice inside of me whispers a name which I feel I should know—but I can't remember why.

"Bowie," I whisper, running my finger across my bottom lip.

The man stops whistling and slowly turns back around.

What the *fuck* just happened?

We're ushered off the bus and told to stand in single file. The townspeople stop and stare, attempting to conceal their thoughts with the back of their hands as they whisper to friends. But it's apparent we're not welcome here.

A blonde woman dressed quite fashionably appears. Her large sunglasses take up most of her face, but it's apparent she is really beautiful. Passersby now stare for another reason. I don't know who she is, but she's in charge.

Her attention focuses on the man who I've dubbed Bowie as that was the name which came to me when he was whistling. I don't know what it means, and it frustrates me. Why have I forgotten? I know rudimentary things like how to use a knife and fork and how to talk and write, but in regard to who I am or why I'm here—my mind is a blank slate.

However, when there is a heated exchange between the woman and Bowie, it's obvious I remember how to be jealous.

Even beneath her sunglasses, I sense she is examining him in more than a professional manner. He accepts the challenge, and she is the first one to look away.

When gray clouds loom ahead, my minder opens a large umbrella and stands by me to shelter me from the oncoming rain.

"Have a lovely time," the woman says, sipping from her coffee cup. "But remember, at all times, please stay with your chaperone."

This is her saying in a roundabout way that even though it may appear to townsfolk this is a lovely day out for us, it is, in fact, just another day being told what to do.

No one dares to speak up, and with that, she nods, gesturing we're to have "fun." I notice she walks over to Bowie, but when my minder loops her arm through mine, I have no other choice but to follow.

"Is there anything you'd like to see first?"

"I don't really know," I reply honestly. "I can't really remember what's here."

"Oh, god, I didn't think," she gushes, and I wish I knew her name because it would make this a little less weird. She seems nice enough, but the fact I don't know a simple thing like her name puts a damper on "enjoying" the day.

"How about clothes shopping?"

I smile but know no clothes will be bought because I don't have any money.

We walk into a store and she peruses over dresses and blouses, asking my opinion of them. Looking at her shape, I reply, "If you go for something like this"—I reach for a short orange dress and offer it to her—"it'll help show off your assets."

She appears utterly stumped by what I mean, so I gently position her in front of the mirror. We're both peering at her reflection as I state, "This complements your bust and highlights your shapely legs. Forget dresses that hide your legs. Instead, choose a simple, straight-line dress. This focuses on your assets. And besides, this is completely your color," I conclude, tapping my chin as I wonder if there is a matching belt.

"How do you know all that?" she asks, catching me off guard.

"I don't know," I reply honestly. It came second nature to me.

Was this something I did in the past?

Peering around at the mannequins, I do feel at home. For some reason, I know the cuts of the garments and which body types they suit. Reaching out, I run my fingers through the racks of clothes, flashes of me wearing all different sorts of garments, then to me, on my knees, pins in hand as I take up a hem.

Then another vision comes to me—of girls posing in those clothes before being asked to take them off and pose naked.

I grip on to a nearby rack for support, but a debilitating pain tears at my temples. It takes the air from me.

"Here, sit." I allow my minder to lead me over to a plush lounge and sink into the cushions as I attempt to catch my breath.

I measure my breathing, trying to make sense of what I saw. I'm certain I was involved with something to do with fashion and photography. So what happened for me to end up at Parkfields?

Were the pressures too much?

Frustrated, I punch my fists into the cushion beneath me and soon become aware that everyone in the store is looking at me like I'm some circus attraction.

"That poor girl. She's crazy," a lady whispers to her friend. "They shouldn't be allowed out. It's too much stimulation. I heard it on *Dr. Phil.*"

Oh, fuck her and the pristine horse she rode in.

"What are you looking at?" I scream, glaring at them.

They quickly avert their eyes, embarrassed. But I'm not ashamed of my behavior. "You think I'm crazy? I'll show you crazy."

I snatch a yellow ruffled crop top from the rack, and without thought, I tear it in half. The material is flimsy and rips easily. But it's not enough. I grab any item of clothing I can find and deliver the same fate as I tear the sleeves, pant legs, collars of anything I can find.

I'm hysterical and I've never felt more alive.

Strong arms wrap around my middle, pinning my arms to my sides. I kick and squirm, but I know my fun has ended.

"She just went nuts," says my minder to the guy manhandling me.

I glare at her—traitor.

My feet don't touch the ground as he carries me from the store, but as he passes the lady who called me crazy, I show her what crazy looks like as I kick her in the stomach.

She collapses to the ground in hysterics while I roll my eyes. I barely touched her. What a drama queen.

As I'm carried outside like a naughty child, I laugh maniacally because this is the most fun I've had all day. Onlookers whisper behind their hands, secretly enjoying the show they'll no doubt share with their friends over Sunday brunch.

As we're headed for the bus, I fight with all my might. I don't want to go back on there. I need to think on my feet.

"I need to use the restroom!" I cry, hoping this works.

"Too bad," he gruffly replies.

"Okay then. I'll just go now then."

The threat of soiling his clothes works as he quickly turns direction and heads toward a diner. He doesn't let me down and carries me through the packed restaurant. Everyone stops and stares, but I'm used to it now.

I wink at a man who smiles before his female companion slaps him across the cheek.

A waitress in a turquoise uniform directs my manhandler to where the restrooms are. She covers her mouth, horrified by what she sees. It seems I've caused quite the stir. When we reach the ladies' room, he bursts through the door.

No one is in here.

He shoves me into a cubicle and makes it quite clear I'm to go supervised.

"A little privacy, please." I fold my arms across my chest, but he makes it clear that's not happening.

I take him in and decide to play him like most men because that's what he is, at the end of the day, a perverted, disgusting man who thinks with the head between his legs.

I push out my bottom lip and twirl a piece of hair around my finger. "Pretty please? I can't go with you watching. And besides, where am I going to go?"

His attention drifts to my ample chest.

"I promise to behave. Or not," I add, giving him doe eyes.

It works like a charm.

"Fine, but I'll be right outside the door."

I nod with a toothy smile.

When he leaves, I shake my head, unbelieving how stupid he could be. But as I scope out my surroundings, I realize my escape route is limited to the door he guards. I won't give up, however. There's got to be another way.

And I see it in a small window above the toilet.

I don't have time to talk myself out of this ludicrous idea and stand on the closed toilet lid and pull at the window. It's stuck. But I keep yanking at it until it budges. I've worked up a sweat by the time it's fully open.

Boosting myself up, I peer out and see a dumpster below.

I don't even think twice and slide out the window and into it. I'm surrounded by foul-smelling garbage, but as I look up at the window I just escaped out of, I laugh because it's so worth it.

Jumping out of the dumpster, I look down the alleyway and decide to take off in the opposite direction of the main street. There's no way I'm going back to Parkfields.

I may not remember who I am, but I do remember that being in that place strips all of us of our dignity. With no plan, I mute my footsteps as I run toward what I hope is freedom. When I turn the corner, I try to act composed and blend in with society.

I have no idea where I am. Nor do I have any money or ID.

There's a bus stop down the road. So I decide to wait and hope some Good Samaritan will lend me the money for the fare.

Light trickles of rain begin to fall, and the gray clouds are fast approaching. There's going to be a storm.

Three men in suits stop when they see me, whispering to themselves as they blatantly check me out. I hate that I have to play this game, but I don't have a choice. I need to get out of here, and fast.

"Hey, need a ride?" one of them says.

I don't feel safe getting into a car with them, but as the rain gets heavier, I'm running out of options.

"I sure would, handsome," I say, laying on the charm.

He grins at his stupid friends like I'm some airhead who's looking for a good time. The only good time will be when I steal their car. But first, I need to act the part because this will lower their guard. And that's the time when I can strike.

When I see a frantic orderly up ahead, I quickly dive into

the man's side, pretending to use his trench coat as protection from the rain as I open it up and wrap it around me.

"I've got you, little lady," he says, huddling close.

His heavy-handed aftershave makes me want to puke. But I smile up at him.

"Let's go then."

The three men look like all their Christmases have come at once as they thankfully walk in the other direction of the orderly. I don't relax, however, because to dodge one predator, I've just willingly stepped into the lair of three wolves.

Our pace quickens as the rain gets heavier. The fat raindrops impede my vision, and I follow blindly, but when we turn down a narrow alleyway, I know the car isn't parked here.

I dig in my heels, but the man forces me forward, as do the two other men who are at my back. "Shh, shh. It's a shortcut," he assures me, his black eyes sending a chill through me.

I need to think fast because I know what they plan on doing. I'm in a dirty alley; there has to be a weapon.

The man shoves me face-first against the brick wall, caging me in as he presses his chest to my back. I don't fight him. I need to save my energy.

"Don't rough her up too much, Bosco. We want some too," says one of the men.

I plan on making each one pay, but first, I switch off to Bosco, running his hands over my back and ass, and focus on finding a weapon. The rain pours down around us, but it's not a deterrent for Bosco, who yanks up the hem of my dress.

I'm desperate now because I know I have three seconds until he takes something from me against my will.

"The brick by your feet."

A voice suddenly comes out of nowhere, startling me because it's familiar—I just don't know who it belongs to. I trust it nonetheless and look at the ground. Lo and behold, there is a brick like the voice said.

Bosco rubs his erection over my ass, but I reach out behind me. "Baby, let me take care of you. Let me suck that big cock of yours. I'll let your friends watch," I add because he won't be able to say no. "Then we can all have fun together."

The gang bang suggestion is the clincher and Bosco thankfully lets me go. I don't waste a second and turn, dropping to my knees because I can't risk them seeing the brick. I peer up at Bosco, licking my lips with intent.

His friends slap him on the back, but they're all going down. "Don't be shy."

I lower the collar of my dress, exposing my white lace bra, which is now see-through thanks to the rain. My nipples are erect because it's cold, which makes these assholes putty in my hands as they do as I say.

They lower their zippers and take out their hard cocks. I want to gag, but I know what I have to do. Bosco begins pumping his dick, the rain sloshing in time with the rhythm. I lean forward and take him into my mouth, sucking deeply.

An elated cry leaves him. He grabs the back of my head and forces me deeper onto his dick. He hits the back of my throat, and my gag reflex screams at me, but I keep going. The other men commence jerking off, watching me as I blow their friend, clueless to the fact as I discreetly reach for the brick to my left.

"That's it, sweetheart. Take daddy deep."

Everything about this bastard makes me sick, but I force myself to continue because in just a few seconds, these morons are going to be lost to the throes of passion which is when I'll strike. The moment my fingers brush over the brick, I clench it in my hand.

I pull back from Bosco's cock and peer up at him as I bite down—hard.

I take great pleasure in seeing him turn a lovely shade of red, white, then green when I bite down harder, so hard, I taste blood. He's winded, so not a word escapes him, which allows me to jump up and smash one of the assholes in the face with the brick.

Before his friend has any idea what I've done, I slam the brick into his erection, laughing maniacally when I hear his dick squish under impact. He drops to his knees, howling, while his friend cups his bleeding nose. Bosco is on his side, clutching his bleeding dick, but it's not enough, so I kick him in the face.

His head snaps back, hitting the edge of a fire escape. Blood quickly pours from the wound, the rain washing it down the drain. When Bosco doesn't move, I see his eyes have glassed over.

Oh my god. Is he dead?

This split-second decision costs me dearly as the man whose face I smashed with the brick spins me around and punches me in the face.

A strangled breath gets caught in my throat as I stagger backward, attempting to stay upright. But he doesn't let me as he punches me in the stomach. I drop to my knees, wheezing in air. I taste blood, my own this time.

"You fucking slut!" he roars and punches me in the face once again—harder this time.

I fall onto my back, but I frantically search for the brick I dropped. He stomps on my wrist, it crunches under the force.

"You're going to beg I kill you once I am finished with you." And he makes good on his word as he begins to kick and beat every part of my body.

When I try to fight, he breaks two of my fingers. When I attempt to scream, he punches me in the mouth. But I don't give up. I will die fighting.

And that seems to be my fate when he lifts a silver garbage can and positions it over my head. "Say good night, bitch."

"Good night, bitch."

I didn't say it, but someone did, and with the last shred of energy left, I wearily raise my head to see my attacker being kicked so hard into the wall, pieces of it crumble. Or maybe it's just my imagination as I'm pretty sure I'm on the cusp of passing out.

But through swollen eyes, I hazily see my hero beat each of the monsters to unconsciousness. With his back turned and fists bunched by his sides, the streetlight illuminates him in a way which makes him appear like a superhero.

And when he looks over his shoulder, I see that's exactly what he is—he's here to save me, in every sense of the word.

Thirteen

Dutch

I've sat in this fucking chair, in this fleabag motel, for I don't know how many hours, watching her. But she doesn't stir. She simply sleeps.

She needs to go to the hospital, but I can't take her there. If I do, they'll just call Dr. Norton and return us back to hell. And besides, the car I stole from those motherfuckers will no doubt be reported to the police.

I don't know what happened to Luna, but she's not the same person. She doesn't remember me. I'm doubtful she even remembers herself. What did they do to her?

The whine of the armchair I sit in hints it's about to snap in half if I clench at the arms any harder, but it's either this chair or I go back and beat those assholes to death. It was hard to stop, and it scared me. I've never felt that kind of rage before.

But that voice inside my head just spurred me on.

It encouraged me to hurt them and make them pay for what they did to Luna. I wonder if maybe I am actually crazy. I hate using that phrase, but since waking from my operation, things have been far from "normal."

But being in Parkfields isn't helping Luna or me. I know what will, however.

I need to find out about the man whose heart I have beating within me. I just know when I know who he is, and how he died, all of this will make sense. This started with him. And it'll end with him.

His death wasn't accidental, and although I don't believe in ghosts or the supernatural, I can't deny it feels like he's speaking to me beyond the grave. He seems to like Luna too. But when I take her in, I realize that's all me.

She groans and I launch off the chair like it's on fire and run over to her bedside. Her face is swollen and bruised.

"It's okay. You're safe," I say, ensuring to keep my distance, not wanting to spook her.

She wets her bloody lips and tries to speak, but her voice is hoarse. "Who are you?" she finally manages to whisper into the darkness.

I was right. Her memories have been wiped clean.

"My name is Dutch," I reply, wanting to be honest because this feels like a new start. "And your name is Luna."

"Dutch," she says, turning onto her side slowly. "What sort of name is that?"

I can't help but laugh because it's something I've heard often. "My parents had too much fun on vacation when in Amsterdam because nine months later, I was born."

She tries to smile but begins coughing uncontrollably.

I quickly race into the bathroom and fill a paper cup with water. My hands are still smeared with blood and flesh, so I scrub them clean. When I re-enter the bedroom, I see Luna resting against the headboard.

I offer her the cup, and when our fingers overlap, a small whimper escapes her.

I wonder how far those motherfuckers went with her. Her bra was exposed, her dress ripped, which is why I undressed her as modestly as I could before putting her to bed.

I hate to think what she suffered under the hands of those vile fuckers.

I don't know what to do. I want to be near her, to comfort her, but I don't want to smother her either. So I sit on the edge of the bed.

"Luna," she says after a long moment of silence. "That's my name?"

I nod.

"It doesn't sound familiar," she confesses. "Were we friends?"

"Yes," I reply, keeping the sadness at bay. "You don't remember anything?"

She shakes her head slowly. "Nothing. I get glimmers, but none of it makes sense. Do you know why I was in Parkfields?"

I don't know how much I should tell her. In a sense, her forgetting the past, the pain, isn't such a bad thing. So I decide to leave out the details. Her mind and body are fragile. I want to protect her any way I can.

"You told me you lost someone very close to you. To be committed, you would have attempted to take your own life."

A pained sigh escapes her. "I don't remember that person.

177

Maybe it's better that I don't. What sort of person was I?" she asks, clutching her side as she attempts to sit taller.

"You are brave, strong. You aren't afraid to take risks. You had an opportunity to leave, but you didn't."

"Why didn't I?"

I measure my breaths as his heart begins to beat faster. "You stayed because of me."

"Oh," she finally says, and I'm unable to read her. "Why did you want to stay?"

And that's the question I ask myself every single day.

"I thought I would discover the answers I needed to figure out what's wrong with me."

"And what's wrong with you?"

"*Show her.*"

I don't fail to notice the voice inside me always gets louder and more talkative whenever Luna is around which is why I'm certain she triggers it in some way. I just don't know why.

So, I do as he says.

Coming to stand in front of her, I reach behind my head and slowly remove my T-shirt by the back of my collar. I drop it to the floor, allowing Luna to see the scar down my chest.

The small lamp provides enough light for her to see it and I expect for her to show horror or disgust. But I don't see either of those things. Instead, she pushes back the blankets and crawls on hands and knees toward me.

I don't move a muscle and watch as she comes to rest on her knees on the edge of the bed and gently extends out her hand. The moment her fingers touch over my scar, my skin breaks out into goose bumps.

She seems to be in a trance as her fingers brush over the

scar—up and down. Up and down.

I wonder what she sees because it appears like she is looking through me, through to his heart.

"I can hear it," she whispers, her eyes slipping shut. "Why is it singing to me?"

"I don't know." But I understand what she means because I can hear it too.

This heart connects us in every possible way.

"I was given a new heart because mine was failing me. Most would be thankful for a second chance at life, but since the transplant, my life has changed."

"How?"

"Music was my life. Piano, my mistress, but I can't play a single thing now. This heart has choked the life from me. Ironic, as it was supposed to save me. If I can't play music, then I don't want to live," I confess, and unable to help myself, I reach out and brush a strand of hair behind Luna's ear.

She leans into my touch.

"The only time I hear music, however…is when I'm with you. And the only time this heart ever feels like mine is when you're with me. Without you…I feel lost. *We* feel lost."

The room falls silent.

I expect her to shrink away, terrified of the insanity she hears. And if she does, then I will accept the consequences.

"Why we?"

"Because this heart doesn't belong to me…it's his. It always has been. But in some morbid way, it feels like it belongs to you too."

"How does that make sense?" she asks, placing her palm flat against my chest.

"It doesn't. I don't understand it, which is why I wanted to stay at Parkfields. Dr. Norton thinks I'm experiencing something called heart memory transfer. That his heart is giving me his memories, and those memories—"

"Those memories what?" she prompts when I pause.

Placing my hand over hers, I squeeze her fingers gently. "Those memories consist of violence, anger, and murder."

It's the first time I've said it aloud, but I know, without a doubt, he was murdered. I just don't know why.

A horrified gasp escapes Luna, and a tear trickles down her bruised cheek.

"The man was kind, but he was also hiding a grave secret. He loved someone with all his heart, and that's the only thing that kept him going. He wanted to end it. But he couldn't… because of her."

The more I speak, the clearer things become.

"I need to find out who he is because a dead man holds the answers I so desperately seek. I think I'm reliving this because he needs my help. A heart is the epicenter of a human being, and even when broken, it still is able to love with all the tiny pieces.

"And that's why I need to find all those tiny pieces to make it whole again."

Luna cries softly, but not in sadness. She's crying in happiness. She bends down and places her ear to my chest, listening to the beating of his heart as she's done before.

"I want to help."

Relief overwhelms me because I thought she would be hitting the road come dawn.

"I don't know where to start, but I remember something

from a flashback I had which wasn't mine. I saw the sign for Woodland Waterfalls."

"What's that?" Luna asks, the fatigue heavy in her tone.

"It's the perfect place to hide secrets, which is why I want to start there. But first, will you let me help you get cleaned up?"

I stopped by a pharmacy and quickly grabbed the essentials. I couldn't stay too long as the pharmacist no doubt called the police before I even left the store.

Luna raises her head, and the space between us is mere inches. The chemistry between us is almost suffocating. Eventually, she nods.

I don't give her a choice as I scoop her up in my arms and carry her into the bathroom. I don't know the extent of her injuries because she's caked in dry blood, so I turn on the shower faucet. She's in her underwear, so once I ensure she's steady on her feet as I place her down, I turn my back to give her some privacy.

I don't leave the room, however.

When she hisses, I assume she's standing under the water, washing her injuries away. I don't rush her, and after ten minutes, the water switches off. I offer her the white towel over my shoulder.

"Okay, you can look," she says a few moments later.

Turning back around, I can't hide my shock when I see what was done to her. She is swollen, bruised, and grated raw.

"That bad?" she half teases, tightening the towel around her frame.

I don't reply but lift her out of the shower/tub combo and gently sit her on the edge of the sink. I grab the disinfectant from the bag on the counter and gently commence wiping away the scrapes on her face. She doesn't flinch, but I know it stings.

The entire time, her eyes never stray from my face. It seems like she's attempting to remember me. I hope that she does.

Her wrist and fingers are swollen, and when I ask she move them, she does, which means they're not broken, but they're definitely sprained or dislocated. I wrap them in bandages and hope it helps.

Clearing my throat, I know the real damage is under the towel. And so does Luna.

"Do you want—" I offer her the disinfectant, but she discreetly shifts the towel so I can see her ribs.

They are bruised badly, but I know the worst is yet to come.

She needs them bandaged, but I'm not sure how to do that without her dropping the towel.

"I—" But I don't even know what to say.

Luna fills in the blanks, however, when she lowers the towel, exposing her beautiful breasts. Instantly, I turn my face.

"Can you help me?"

Of course I want to help her. That's all I want to do. So, I turn back around and try to keep my eyes focused on her ribs and nothing else. She's positioned the towel over her lap, covering herself discreetly. I unwrap the bandage and commence wrapping it around her torso.

"What happened to the men?" she asks, breaking the silence.

"They weren't men," I reply, trying to keep the anger from my tone. "But they're alive, if that's what you're wondering."

My fingers clench around the bandage as memories of how I found Luna flood me. I didn't even think twice about it as I beat the ever-loving fuck out of those animals. The voice inside me screamed louder than it ever has, demanding bloodshed.

Once I had beaten them within an inch of their lives, I stole their car keys and carried Luna the three blocks until I found the car which matched the keychain in my hand.

"I should have taken you to the hospital," I utter with regret.

She places her hand over mine, stopping me from bandaging her up. "You're taking care of me now," she says softly. "You saved me from those men. I owe you my life."

"You don't owe me anything."

And I mean it, and that's because in some ways, I feel like I owe her mine.

We both don't say a word, but it isn't uncomfortable. Luna looks at me closely and it feels as if she's attempting to remember me. I wish that she would, but in some ways, I'm glad that she doesn't because the memories that had her committed no longer plague her.

By the time I'm finished bandaging Luna up, she's almost asleep sitting up. She is so beautiful. She may not remember, but the chemistry between us is just as strong. Without thought, I wrap a robe around her and tie the belt around her waist before lifting her into my arms and carrying her back into the bedroom.

"I can walk," she sleepily says into my neck, her warm breath heating my skin.

"I know, but I may as well make myself useful," I tease, laying her on the bed.

She settles against the pillow with a sigh. "You're very useful," she whispers and surprises me as she extends her arm. "Will you stay with me?"

I can't refuse her. "Of course. I'll just get cleaned up."

She nods, her happiness warming his heart.

I shower and dry off in record time. I don't want to put my dirty clothes back on, but I also don't want to sleep beside Luna naked. Reaching for the white robe off the back of the door, I put on the tiny garment and when I peer at my reflection in the mirror, I laugh.

I look ridiculous.

This isn't how I imagined being in bed with Luna for the first time, and I've thought about it—a lot. I just wish it was under different circumstances. Switching off the light, the carpet mutes my footsteps as I make my way to the bed.

Luna is tucked tightly under the blankets, so I carefully pull back the blanket on my side of the bed and slip in. I turn onto my back and interlace my hands under my head, peering up at the water-stained ceiling. We need to grab clothes and other essentials if we're going to hit the road in search of who the fuck my donor is.

Lost in thought, I don't hear Luna shift until I feel her nestle into my side. "Is this okay?" she asks in the darkness.

"Yes."

She wraps her arms around me but surprises me as she slips a hand into the front of my robe and gently runs her fingertips along the scar on my chest. Most would shy away from it, but not Luna. She never has. It's like she finds peace in it somehow.

"I like the way your heart beats," she whispers. "Is that weird?"

"No, because it always seems to beat faster whenever you're near."

Her body tenses at my confession, but I want her to know that whatever she's experiencing, I feel it too. And I want more.

Music has always been my obsession, but Luna is quickly becoming that now. I think that's why whenever I'm with her, I can hear it again.

It's moved over to make room for her, but there's something missing. And until I can get to the bottom of it, I don't think I'll ever be able to play music again.

But for now, these moments with Luna are enough to silence the voices which I wish were filled with song.

Fourteen

Dutch

It's still dark out, but I feel most comfortable in the darkness. It's in the darkness where my monsters live and play. And it's in the darkness where we must survive until I can figure out what to do.

We need wheels, clothes, and money. And we need to acquire all of this undetected. I could call my parents, but when they find out what I did, it'll just convince them that being in Parkfields is the place for me.

But I can't stay there.

No good has come out of that place, and it's only being outside those walls that things have become clearer. Facing my demons instead of convincing myself they'll go away with time is the cure. Not being a medicated zombie. Which is why I need to steal us some clothes and a car.

Sleeping beside Luna felt natural, like everything else I've

186

experienced with her. I want her like a man wants a woman, but I also feel the need to protect her in a way I can't explain. I suppose I can't explain any of this, though.

Focusing on what does make sense, however, I look out the window and zero in on a red Ford Maverick with its window wound halfway down.

Wheels—check.

Turning over my shoulder, I take a moment to admire Luna sleeping soundly. I hate to wake her, but we've got to split before sunrise. I quietly slip into my jeans and boots, but not the T-shirt, as it's covered in blood.

Luna's long light brown hair looks like an angel's splayed against the pillows. She is so beautiful. His heart aches to touch her. Reaching out, I brush away a strand from her forehead.

"Luna?" I whisper into the darkness.

I wait for her to wake and when she stirs, she flinches, still in pain from her injuries. I mentally add more painkillers to the things we need.

It takes her a moment, but when she wakes, a loving smile spreads across her cheeks. "Misha."

Misha?

I wonder why that name holds such importance to her because even suffering this lapse in memory, she seems to remember that name.

I shift so the sliver of light coming in from the streetlight outside the window illuminates my face. I can see the confusion pass over Luna's face and worry overcomes me. Has she forgotten me again?

"Oh, sorry, Dutch. I don't know why I said that."

To say I'm relieved is an understatement.

"We gotta bounce," I say, suddenly losing my train of thought as Luna's attention dallies to my chest. She doesn't hide her appraisal of my body and I like that she's so forward.

She quickly clears her throat as if only realizing she's openly staring. "Of course."

She pulls back the blankets and when I see the robe has parted, exposing her breasts, my cock instantly hardens. Like her, I don't look away. I want her to know if she wasn't beaten black and blue, I would rip that robe from her body and kiss every inch of her delicious flesh.

The image alone has me almost coming in my jeans like a pubescent teen.

Luna gets up and waits for further instruction.

"I've found us wheels. We just need clothes."

She nods, and trusting me completely, she follows me as I quietly open the door. We keep to the shadows, ensuring to blend in. When we pass a blue convertible with the top down, I thank the universe and snatch the brown suitcase from the front seat.

I don't know why someone would leave their luggage out here, but I can question it later because now, I have to hope our luck will continue as I approach the Maverick. Peering around the empty parking lot to make sure the coast is clear, I try the door handle, and when it opens, I exhale in relief that I didn't have to try and wedge my arm inside the window to pop the lock.

Luna doesn't hesitate as she runs to the passenger side as I reach across and open her door. Once inside, I pass her the suitcase, and then, it's the moment of truth. I flip down the visor and when a rabbit's foot keychain falls into my lap, I can't help but feel lucky indeed.

Slipping the key into the ignition, the engine roars to life and when a light flickers on in the room in front of us, I know it's time to go.

The tires kick up gravel as I speed out of the motel parking lot, not looking back at the chaos we just created. Luna quickly fastens her seat belt, but her breathless exhalations hint that she's enjoying breaking the law.

So on that note, I press my foot down onto the accelerator and speed down the empty road.

Animated laughter leaves Luna, and the sound is one that I want to hear every single day. She winds down the window, her hair kissing at her cheeks as it catches the cool early morning air. I can't take my eyes off her as I look between her and the road.

I'm drawn to her, and when she rests her head against the chair and turns her cheek to look at me, our attraction only seems to grow. She looks so carefree and reckless in her white robe, hair loose, and wearing her war wounds with pride.

I quickly return my attention back to the road because my self-control is slipping. But I won't touch Luna when she's injured because when I do, I won't hold back. It's going to be rough, and I need her to feel it too.

When we're far away enough, I pull the car off the road so we can check what's inside the suitcase. Luna opens it, and although it's just clothes and not money, as I was hoping, I'm still thankful. Luna offers me a white shirt and black pants which I accept.

When she decides on a red dress, I give her some privacy to dress and get out of the car.

The men's clothes are a little snug, but they'll do for now. We can at least attempt to blend in without drawing too much attention to ourselves. We do need money, however. I don't know how we're supposed to get that without breaking the law.

We need to keep a low profile, so we can't be robbing any banks.

"Is everything okay?"

Turning, words get caught in my throat when I see Luna standing a few feet away. The headlights light her up like the goddess she is.

"Yes," I finally reply. "Was just thinking about ways to get money. But don't worry, let me take care of it."

"I could go home?" she offers. "But I don't think I know where that is. Maybe things will start coming back to me the farther we drive? I mean, I had to live around here, right?"

She's right.

"It's worth a shot. Let's hit the road."

We get back into the car, and when Luna yawns, I gently touch her arm. "Sleep, baby. I'm not going anywhere."

"Promise?" she whispers, curling into a ball on the seat, her eyes slipping shut.

"With all my heart."

We're here, and I want to be sick.

I've driven down this road before, but now, I'm seeing it through different eyes because I died here. He and I are steadily becoming one person because being here, I feel everything he felt.

The confusion.

The fear.

The pain.

His heart lurches in my chest, and I have to pull over for fear of throwing up. Luna stirs, her eyes slowly opening. The daylight highlights her injuries which just fuels the anger within.

"What's wrong?" she asks when she sees me white-knuckling the steering wheel, attempting to steady my breathing.

"I don't know," I reply honestly. "Keep talking."

What I do know is that hearing her voice calms me.

"It's going to be all right, and you know how I know?"

I close my eyes and focus on her voice and only her voice.

"Because we've lived through worse. Well, I think we have. Being here…I feel so…sad."

I hear her seat belt click and when I feel her settle on my lap, I wrap my arms around her waist. She caresses my face, her fingers openly exploring every inch of me, and I allow it because I need it. I need her.

Soon, my breathing settles, and I open my eyes. Luna doesn't get off my lap, however. She wraps her fingers around the back of my neck and the way she is pressed against me, my dick grows hard. She gasps when she feels my erection, but still, she doesn't move.

"Have we had sex before?"

"No."

"Have we kissed?"

I shake my head.

She wets her lips which does nothing to help my current predicament.

"Why not?"

"I don't know. Being locked up in an asylum is hardly the place to romance a girl."

Her lips twitch. "I suppose you're right. But we're not now."

That's true, but as I look past her and out the windshield, kissing her here for the first time feels so wrong. She reads my hesitation and instantly, I can see she's hurt, taking it as a rejection.

"Luna—" But it's too late. She's out the door, apparently needing some space.

This place just gets worse.

I give her some time and grip the steering wheel, peering out at the road in front of me. A hollowed scream thumps at my temples and I taste blood.

Jack's blood.

Sadness soon overcame me because he didn't want to die. I guess most people don't. But he really wanted to live. His fight for life lingers on my tongue.

Opening the door, I go with my gut and walk to the middle of the desolate road. I don't even know why; I just know that I need to keep walking. Day soon gives way to night, and the road is slick with rain. My boots grow heavier with each step I take until I am hit with what feels like an elbow to the stomach.

I'm suddenly winded.

My legs give out and I collapse where I stand—the spot I suspect is where Jack died.

"Dutch!" Luna's cries feel wrong because she calls out for the wrong man.

I spread my arms out wide and peer into the blackened skies. The air rattles in my lungs as I attempt to cling to this last memory of my days on earth. The full moon comes out of hiding, lighting up the universe and welcoming me home.

Tears leak from my eyes because I'll miss her so much.

With my final breath, a single star comes into view, and I reach up with bloody fingers, making a wish—I wish that she'll be all right.

"Dutch!"

I'm sucked back into my body, and I lurch up, gulping in mouthfuls of air.

"That's it. Breathe." Luna is at my back, rubbing it gently, and her touch makes me feel better. But I still feel so fucking… empty inside.

"They fucking killed him," I gasp, his heart thrashing wildly. "It wasn't an accident. They killed him…*she* killed him."

I don't know how I know it's a woman, but I see it through his eyes.

"Did you know her?" I ask aloud, and Luna soon realizes I'm not talking to her.

Jack isn't talking right now, and I wonder why that is. A blanket of…shame suddenly shrouds me. He knew her and when I peer into Luna's eyes, I gasp for air because it's *her* eyes I see behind the wheel. But that's not possible.

She isn't the one who killed him. Well, I don't think that she is. I don't know a lot about Luna, but I do know that she isn't a murderer. There's no way she'd hurt another person that way. But the heaviness in the pit of my stomach won't subside.

"What's the matter?" she asks, placing her hand to my cheek. "You look like you've seen a ghost."

"I'm okay." I play off my concerns and come to a stand.

Luna senses my detachment once again.

We make our way toward the car in silence, and I don't fail

193

to notice that inside our prison walls, we couldn't seem to stay away from one another. But now that we're out, I can't help but wonder just who Luna really is.

I thought going to Woodland Waterfalls would help somehow. I suppose in some ways it did because I now know the driver who killed Jack was female, and that female could quite possibly be Luna.

I open the window, needing fresh air. It's raining, as per usual, but I don't care. The air allows me to breathe because I suddenly feel claustrophobic. There's no way this is possible. But Jack has gone quiet and I don't know if that's because the mystery is solved and now I'm expected to deal with this revelation how I deem fit.

Or maybe he's just as confused as I am.

The tension can be hacked with a chainsaw and I hate it. I don't understand how we went from being drawn to one another to now me side-eying her in case she's about to grab the wheel and steer us into oncoming traffic.

When I hear growling and realize it's Luna's stomach, I curse myself for not pulling over sooner because of course she's fucking hungry, but too polite to say otherwise. There's no way this woman is responsible for anyone's death.

I refuse to believe it.

I've been driving around aimlessly because I don't know what to do or where to go. We need money. I could hit up a couple friends, but I don't want anyone involved in my bullshit. And going back home is definitely not an option.

Luna has no idea who she is, so seeking out any of her

friends is not in the cards either.

I pull into a parking space when I see a small grocery store. Luna notices me examining it closely. We don't have any money, but we need to eat and I'll be damned if Luna goes hungry.

"You distract the security guard," I order, peering at the middle-aged man inside the doorway. "I'll grab what we need. In and out, okay?"

She works her bottom lip nervously.

"We're going to be fine," I assure her, reaching across and gently stroking her leg.

The ever-present chemistry sparks to life, but we both ignore it this time. Luna reaches for the large sunglasses she found in the middle console and slips them on in hopes to conceal her injuries. She's not complained once about the pain she's no doubt in.

She exits the car before I do, as it seems she wants to be as far away from me as possible.

With a sigh, I shut my door, and we walk toward the store calmly. When the guard sees us, he immediately hooks his thumbs into his leather belt, drawing attention to his gun. This has probably worked on other women before, but Luna isn't just any woman.

"Oh, darling, what happened to that pretty face?" he says and has the nerve to wink at me like we're in some secret boys' club where it's okay to beat on women.

I step forward, about ready to beat *his* face, but Luna grips my forearm discreetly, stopping me. "Silly me," she gushes, laying on the charm. "I wasn't looking where I was going and slipped."

She lets me go and holds up her bandaged wrist with a

damsel in distress look, which is my cue to leave. She can take care of herself.

Basket in hand, I quickly make my way up and down the aisles, grabbing things I need. I turn the corner and bump straight into a young woman. The box of produce she carries tumbles to the floor, sending lemons in all directions.

"I'm so sorry," I say, dropping to a squat to stop the lemons from rolling into the next aisles.

She laughs and doesn't seem to mind as she joins me in retrieving the runaway lemons. Her name tag reads Felicity, and when Felicity's fingers not so innocently brush over mine, it seems my plan to play it discreet just got shot to hell.

"I love your tattoos," she says, smiling.

"Thanks." I try and hurry this conversation up by quickly capturing as many lemons as I can, but Felicity seems content on talking.

"Did it hurt?" she asks, reaching out to touch over the sheet music down my neck.

"I don't know," I reply honestly, subtly recoiling from her touch. "I didn't really think about it."

"Were you high? I heard that's the best way to avoid the pain."

Honestly, being lost to the music which was being permanently inked into my skin was better than any drug because it was my drug of choice, and being without, I'm withdrawing badly.

"There you are, honey."

Peering up, I see Luna, and when I read the look on her face, I know it's time to split.

With a nod, I quickly stand and slip my hand through

Luna's. Felicity doesn't hide her disappointment. We're about to leave, but Luna reaches down to capture a stowaway lemon. She tosses it at Felicity, who fumbles but catches it.

"You know what they say?"

Felicity narrows her eyes, waiting for Luna's punchline.

"When life gives you lemons…make lemonade."

I'm left speechless at Luna's blatant taunt as she leads the way toward the front door. A group of teenagers in front of us are laughing and being obnoxious to an elderly couple. I'm about to show them what obnoxious looks like, but Luna shakes her head.

She reaches for a small bottle of whiskey off the shelf and slips it into the pocket of one of the boys. When we pass the guard at the door, she discreetly says, "I think you may want to check that boy's back pocket. He's trying to steal from your store. But I know you won't let that happen because you're one big strong man."

Her comment is dripping with sarcasm, but the moron doesn't get it.

He adjusts his belt and saunters over to the troublesome teens, oblivious to the real thief who is Luna as she retrieves the stolen basket she clearly left by the door and yanks me outside. I don't have time to question her as we walk briskly toward our car.

The moment I take off, Luna giggles as she rifles through the goods she stole, goods that include a wallet. She opens it up and counts the stolen cash. "It's enough to get us a place to stay for a few nights," she says while I wonder who the hell this woman is.

She opens a bag of Lay's and offers me some. But I shake my

head because my appetite is shot.

She shrugs and chews happily.

The silence continues and honestly, I don't know what to do next. We can't just drive around aimlessly. We need a plan. But I don't know what.

We drive through a deserted area and when a rundown motel comes into view with a strip club called The Big Top next door, Luna leans forward, her eyes alight. This is the devil's playground.

"Stop. Let's stay here."

There is a police car parked around the back, which means this place is where off-duty cops come to blow off some steam.

"I don't think so," I say, gesturing with my chin toward the patrol cars.

"I have an idea."

Her resolve has me going against my better judgment, and I pull the car into the gravel parking lot. Before I can ask what's going on, Luna gets out of the car and makes her way toward the small window where an attendant sits, smoking a thin cigar.

I never take my eyes off her, and although I know this is a bad idea, I'm curious as to what Luna has planned.

She returns a moment later, key in hand. "Room ten."

I pull into a parking spot in front of the room, and we quickly make our way inside. I lock the door and sigh because this is a fucking disaster waiting to happen.

When I hear the bathroom door close, I sit on the edge of the bed and interlace my fingers through my splayed legs. I have no idea what Luna is thinking, which seems to be a common occurrence lately. I rub over my chest because I suddenly feel like I can't breathe.

Each day is worse than the one before it, and I wonder if I'll ever be able to play music again because, at this rate, I don't see myself surviving much longer. I'm losing grip on reality because this life isn't one I want to live.

I must have fallen asleep because I wake staring up at the ceiling. Who I see peering down at me has me launching upright, certain I'm dreaming. But when I look into those blue eyes, I realize this is no dream.

"Luna?"

She grins, and I almost come at the sight.

"What do you think?" she asks, running her fingers through her hair, the hair which she has cut into a bob style and dyed black.

I'm speechless and that's because I'm moments away from throwing her onto the bed and kissing that fucking sexy mouth of hers which is slathered a bright red.

"They're looking for us, so I figured we have to not look like us."

She's right, but I can't focus on anything other than my need to lick her from head to toe. She looks different, and the urge to protect her is still there, but now, I want her how a man wants a woman in every possible carnal way there is.

I like that she looks different. Not that I didn't like the way she looked before. But his heart doesn't seem to recognize this version of Luna, and I like it. She's now mine and not his, which makes no sense.

"Say something," she nervously says, running a hand over her tight black dress. "I just thought—"

But I don't let her finish.

Wrapping my hands around her waist, I draw her toward me. I smell the vanilla soap she used as well as the cherry lipstick she wears. I want to fucking destroy her, in the best possible ways. She's used makeup to conceal her injuries, but I still need to be careful.

"It's a very good idea." I don't fail to notice her ample breasts rise and fall quickly with each hasty breath she takes.

"I have another..." she confesses, tonguing her upper lip. "The strip club...meet me there in half an hour?"

"Why?"

"Trust me," she replies and bends down, placing a gentle kiss to my mouth.

I want more, but she pulls away, leaving behind her cherry-scented kisses. The moment the door closes, I fall onto my back and let out a frustrated groan. My dick is so hard, so I decide to have a cold shower because going into the strip club can only mean trouble.

Showering was supposed to help, but all I can smell is the vanilla soap which Luna used on her body, a body which is wrapped in pure sin. Standing under the spray, I give in to temptation and grip my cock. My hand is a poor substitute for Luna's, but the thought of her jerking me off has me almost coming.

Images of that mouth which she applied a bright red lipstick to has me pumping my shaft faster. I imagine fucking that mouth with my tongue as I grip her freshly dyed black hair and kissing her without restraint.

I then think of fucking her mouth with my dick. Crude, but I think Luna would like it too. I am not a gentle lover. I'm passionate and impatient, but I also like to tease. But with Luna, I know I'd be her fucking slave.

The water acts as the lubrication I need to wildly pump my cock, desperate for a release. Luna is all I think of—her mouth, her laugh, the way she smells.

Jesus fucking Christ.

I remember her perfect breasts. I tried so hard to be a gentleman, but I can't be one a second longer. I need to own her. To mark her. To make her mine. This new look has aroused a monster, and I'm afraid of what happens when it is fed.

But it's not just her looks. It's her. It's everything that she embodies. Her strength. Her convictions. The water sloshes frantically, a reflection that I'm seconds away from coming and it's going to be messy. I think of the many times I felt a connection so deep, it felt as if I knew her in a past life, how sometimes it feels as if we're connected in a way which makes us one.

The thought of being buried deep inside her has me slamming my fist against the wall while, with the other hand, I stroke my cock frantically until I come with a guttural groan. My orgasm tackles me so fiercely, my legs almost buckle out from under me.

His heart beats wildly, but this is the first time it finally feels like mine—my sick beat for Luna and…music.

I hear it. The beat sings to me how it once did.

Closing my eyes, I get lost in the way the water bounces off the tiles and gurgles down the drain. The buzzing of the flickering fluorescents is in concert with the rhythm ricocheting deep within. I tap my fingers against my chest, cocooned in a world I never want to leave.

I begin to string together a piece of music with no start or end. It all flows into one beautiful song.

As his heartbeats subside, so does the music, and before long, I hear nothing once more. But I'm not disheartened this time; I am determined to hear it again.

Turning off the shower, I dry off and dress.

Luna has always been my muse, but it's like I'm seeing her again through different eyes, and with a different heart—*my* heart.

Running my fingers through my wet hair, I exit the room and make my way for the club, unsure what I'm about to walk into. I pay my fee at the door and am hit with cigar smoke and terrible pop music the moment I enter.

Two cops are sitting by the stage, ensuring they make their presence known as they laugh and carry on like fuckheads. No doubt they have runt dicks and use their position of power to get laid.

Luna isn't anywhere to be seen, so I make my way to the bar and buy a drink. The clientele mind their business because they're not here for a chat and the two-dollar beers. The dancers are working the crowd, so I take a seat in a dark corner because I don't want any attention.

Sipping my scotch, I watch the jaded young woman dance around the pole as desperate losers throw dollar bills onto the stage. I've never really understood the hype that comes with strip clubs. Strippers don't want you; they want your money. And they'll say anything to get it.

If you're stupid enough to fall into the honeytrap, then you deserve to be robbed blind.

The music thankfully stops and the lights dim, throwing

the already dark club into almost pitch black.

A microphone tapping sounds over the speakers, followed by a squeal of feedback. Some dicksmoke waddles onto the stage wearing a ridiculous circus ringmaster outfit.

"Here at The Big Top, we like to shake things up a little, and boy, are we about to blow the roof off this fucking place. Please give a warm and wet welcome to our newest member, Poison Ivy!"

'Fever' by Peggy Lee cuts through the darkness which is completely appropriate because that's what I have when the stage lights flick on and I see that Poison Ivy is Luna.

I watch, utterly spellbound, as she uses her body as an extension of the music. Seeing her this way, becoming one with the music, rouses the monsters once again. I can't take my eyes off her as she owns the stage and pole, climbing it with skill.

There's no doubt she's done this before.

The jeweled outfit she wears covers just enough, but the glitter coating her skin glistens under the lights and has me leaning forward, desperate for a taste. She saunters over to the cops, clearly trying to get their attention as she bends in front of them, shaking her perfect ass.

It works because they almost fall off their chairs.

I have no idea what she's doing, as this isn't keeping a low profile. Does she want to get caught? And when she turns over her shoulder, giving me a subtle wink, it seems she is in total control of this situation while I'm seconds away from losing my shit.

The more she gives, the more they want and when the song ends, they stand and wolf whistle, throwing their entire life savings onto the stage.

The club bursts into applause as a man scoops up Luna's hefty earnings in a net. The bald cop offers a hand to Luna to help her down the stairs. She happily accepts.

It takes all my willpower not to spring up and elbow that asshole in the nose for touching my girl. I don't fail to notice my possession over her because Luna *is* my girl. She always has been. And when his hand slides down her back, only to squeeze her ass, all resolve is shot to hell.

I jump up, but a beautiful redhead comes into view, stopping me. She leans forward and whispers into my ear as she slips a set of keys into my hand, "She said you've got twenty minutes to find out who you are and make the call that you're no longer on the run."

I have no idea what she's talking about until I see Luna lead the two cops away to a roped-off area. The beefy security guard parts the red velvet curtain and when she disappears, I realize she wants me to pretend to be them.

Who *is* this mastermind? I know I shouldn't trust Luna because of what Jack "showed" me. She knew Jack. I am certain of it. And I can't rule out the possibility that she was the one who killed him.

It *was* her who I saw behind the wheel. But how trustworthy are the visions of a ghost?

I can deal with that later because now, I must find out the truth.

Nodding in gratitude to the redhead, I quickly make my way through the desperate men and actually sigh in relief when I step outside. Being inside a strip club is like being sucked into a black hole, and when you emerge, you don't know what day or time it is.

I can only hope the cops feel the same way because when I unlock their car, I know there's no room for error. I pick up the walkie-talkie and press the button to connect to home base.

"Reynolds, aren't you off the clock?" laughs a woman on the other end. Her friendly demeanor has me guessing she and the cockhead are friends.

I don't know how Reynolds sounds, but from the looks of him, I assume a cocky asshole. "No rest for the wicked," I reply, covering my hand over the speaker, hoping to disguise my voice. "I'm in the middle of bumblefuck nowhere. Bad line, so I'll make it quick."

"I can barely hear you," she says, which just spurs me on.

"Can you email me the file on that kid, Jack? The one who crashed his car at Woodland Waterfalls. Insurance needs it. Email them at this address please," I say firmly, giving her my email address.

I'm thankful I created a boring email address as a backup because it's come in handy.

I hear her typing away without asking questions. "Sure thing."

That was easier than I thought. I hope my luck hasn't run out when I put the final part of this plan into play. "Can you believe I was out buying"—I see a packet of Marlboros in the middle console—"a pack of smokes."

"The doctor told you to stop!" scolds the woman.

Worked like a charm.

"I know, and I will, after Christmas."

"That's what you always say."

And so does every smoker, sweetheart. But I keep that to myself and continue.

"I know, but you know I don't like to follow the rules."

"Oh, I know," she purrs and confirms that Reynolds is a slimy bastard who probably turns on the charm to any pretty face to get some pussy.

"Anyway, I saw that pair who escaped from Parkfields Hospital. Brought them back so you can file that paperwork and clear it from our system. No point wasting our time on two crazy fucks any longer."

I don't know what the term is, but she does as I hear her typing. "Can I see you later?" She lowers her voice, which means their affair is secret.

Reynolds should not be shitting where he eats, as office romances always end with someone being bludgeoned to death with the copier machine.

"I'll see what I can do." Sounds like some evasive answer an asshole would give.

"Okay. It's all done."

I can't believe it was that easy. But when I think of what Luna is currently doing, I realize there is no easy.

"See you later, baby." I place the walkie-talkie back on the console and exit the car. I don't know what to do with the keys, so I drop them by the front tire in hopes Reynolds thinks he was holding onto something else, like his dick, other than his keys.

I don't go back to the club and it fucking kills me inside. I imagine every vile scenario and multiply that by ten thousand as I enter our room and wait for Luna. I think of the way she danced on stage and how every man will no doubt go home tonight and use her for jerk-off material.

The thought makes me crazy jealous, but it also gets me hot

because I like they want what is mine. The door opens and I turn around to see Luna enter. She closes the door and the fact she won't meet my eyes has me wanting to go back out there and beat Reynolds and his little comrade to death with my bare fists.

She reaches into the pockets of a long white fur coat, which I assume she stole from one of the girls, and tosses handfuls of money onto the bed. This is like a movie where one would lie among their wealth and bask in the riches.

But I know what she did to earn it and I hate to think of the extra services she provided to get it.

"There's enough there to keep us going for a while. Until we come up with a plan," she says, a hint of uncertainty to her tone. She doesn't understand why I'm not happy. "I think I did that for a job before, well, before this."

She's nervous. She's wringing her hands together while I stand impassively.

"Were you able to get into the police car?"

I nod once, arms folded as I think of that motherfucker, Reynolds, and his hands all over her.

"Are you all right?" she finally asks, the tension between us only burning brighter.

"Show me," I say with little emotion.

"Show you what?" She licks her bottom lip, and I clench my jaw in anger.

Did she use that mouth on those undeserving assholes?

This is my fault. I should have thought of another way.

"So help me God, show me what you did to those motherfuckers before I go out there and rip off their arms and beat them to death with them."

207

A stunned gasp leaves Luna.

I know I'm being aggressive, but I can't help it. I'm moments away from exploding. I've never felt this way before. It's foreign to me and I wonder if that's because I've never felt this way about another woman before.

Luna is a danger to me in every way possible and I don't care.

When she reads my resolve, she turns on the clock radio and searches for a station. When she hears Mozart, she leaves it on. My eyes never leave her as she drags a chair to the middle of the room.

"Sit."

I do as she orders.

Mozart sounds soft and when Luna begins to move to the music, I clench my hands into fists on my thighs to stop myself from touching her. She chose this piece, knowing my background, knowing what it would do to me.

Usually, I would be focusing on the changes in the music. But not now. Nothing exists but Luna, and when she slowly removes the coat, revealing a PU leather bra and matching short black skirt, I am her fucking slave.

She never breaks eye contact, watching me watch her as she shimmies out of the skirt. She has on a black silk thong. I have no idea where she got these clothes from, but that's the least of my concerns as she bends down in front of me, showcasing her perfect peach-shaped ass.

She runs a hand up her leg, turning over her shoulder to watch me as she does. She isn't grinding on me or gyrating distastefully. Luna moves like a dancer. The musician in me wants to write a thousand songs for her.

But the man in me has other ideas.

"Come here."

She turns around, allowing me to eat her up from head to toe. The black monster heels she wears just adds to the appeal. She looks like a femme fatale with her black bobbed hair and decked out in her dominatrix attire, and I will happily drop to my knees and lick her feet.

She saunters over, using her body to accent the music. Piano has always roused desire in me. But throw Luna into the mix, and I am done for.

She dances in front of me, her strong muscled body that of a dancer. I wonder just who she is. How can I be so attracted to someone I know so little about? Someone who I don't think I should trust.

But that's always been the issue with Luna—she's never felt like a stranger.

She turns around again and shakes her hips in time with the music. She becomes a note, in step with the beat, and his heart soon resonates with her movements. She moves from side to side, running her hands over her body.

I want to follow each stroke with my tongue.

I love that she has curves and that she embraces what was given to her and fucking owns it. She lowers herself onto my lap, her back to my front, and commences rolling her hips, her ass rubbing over my erection.

I don't touch her because this is her show.

She gives me a lap dance to Mozart and I've never been more turned on in my life. She smells of strawberry kisses, and I want to steal them from her luscious mouth.

No wonder the bed is littered with money. Every man

would happily hand over their entire savings to be near this goddess. However, I wonder how she got the keys to the cop car. Did she see them before the show?

"Did you do more than dance for them?"

Her silence will be the death of me.

"Answer me."

"Why do you care?" she says, giving me a lap dance which she learned from the devil. "You're clearly repulsed by me."

"Excuse me?"

"Every time we touch, you look like you want to run a mile."

I knew she felt rejected, but given the circumstances, it wasn't the right time.

"The cops had no issues touching me, however."

A growl explodes from me, which only spurs Luna on.

"Reynolds, I think his name was, he paid me one hundred dollars to watch me touch my—"

But I don't want to hear it.

Before she can continue, I seize her hips—hard. A gasp escapes her.

"I was trying to be a gentleman. I didn't want to take advantage of you," I explain, my grip on her only tightening.

Her skin is hot and slick with sweat, and I want to lick every inch of her.

"Bullshit," she stubbornly argues, shaking her head. "You don't trust me, do you? I can see it in your eyes. You look at me like you're trying to solve a puzzle. Is that what I am to you? A means to an end? You think I hold some miracle cure to what's wrong with you?"

She turns over her shoulder, and when our eyes lock, we pass the point of no return.

"But maybe you're just fucking crazy, after all."

She's baiting me and it's working.

I am going to fucking destroy her.

I grip her by the throat and force her to stand. I don't care if the angle is painful for her. She's a big girl, and she wants this as much as me. I walk her toward the wall and slam her back into it. She doesn't fight me. She merely challenges me with those wicked eyes.

"You're right. I don't trust you," I snarl, feeling her swallow as I tighten my grip around her throat. "I don't know who you are."

"Join the club," she spits, hatred swirling in her eyes. "But I must be insane to like you!"

"Seems we're just as crazy as the other then."

And those are the last words I intend to speak when I rob Luna of air as I slam my mouth to hers.

She tries to fight me off, but it's weak, and soon, she is yielding to my kisses. I release her throat, only to yank her arms above her head and secure them in one hand. I press my body to hers, keeping her prisoner because I have no intention of ever letting her go.

I'm hard, and I rub my cock against her, wanting her to realize how much I *do* want her.

Kissing her is like a fucking drug and when I suck on her tongue, a whimper leaves her and her knees buckle. I wonder if this is the first kiss Luna remembers—you always remember your first and I plan on being her last because I want this woman more than I need air to breathe.

Regardless of the fact I don't trust her, I know that now that I have a taste, I'll never be able to go back. Her mouth is a heady combination of heaven and hell because she has the power to ruin me, and I'll happily sacrifice it all for just one more taste.

She bites my bottom lip and licks away the sting. Such passion coupled with tenderness reveals Luna feels this too. Our chemistry has always been strong, but kissing one another has only intensified the madness.

Reaching down, I rip the front of Luna's bra, her bountiful breasts spilling free. I don't wait and cup them in my hand. Her nipples are ripe and I circle them with the tips of my fingers. She has a delicious small peach-shaped freckle on her left breast which I want in my mouth.

Breaking our kiss, I do just that.

I circle her nipple with my tongue before licking over the freckle slowly. Her hands are still snared in mine, which frustrates her as she tries to break free. But her desperation is like the most potent drug to me and I continue the onslaught on her hot body.

I cup her breast and take it into my mouth. I lick her nipple, relishing in her needy moans. She rubs her thighs together and the thought of sinking my dick into her almost has me coming. I need to calm the fuck down before I blow it—in every sense of the word.

Before she can question me, I release her arms and drop to my knees before her. The sight is fucking spectacular. Her chest is heaving. Her lips swollen from our frantic kisses.

The only thing separating me from her pussy is her underwear. I want her in my mouth, but there's something I want more.

"Touch yourself," I hoarsely order. "I want to watch."

She rolls her bottom lip between her teeth, a split-second

212

hesitation before slipping a hand into the front of her underwear. No doubt she's wet and needy. She commences rubbing herself, eyes locked with mine as I am still kneeling.

She gasps, moving faster and faster.

I'm hypnotized by this entire show and when goose bumps kiss her skin, the urge to lick each one leaves me hungry for more. Luna reads my desire and removes her hand from her underwear, only to rub her arousal across my mouth with two fingers.

Instantly, I lick my lips, her taste a punch to the solar plexus. The flimsy material of her underwear comes apart easily in my hand as I rip it from her body. She's now naked and I lean back on my heels, eating her up from head to toe.

She's fucking beautiful.

All womanly curves and the muscled physique of a dancer's body, I am lost to everything that is Luna. She is confident and comfortable with her nakedness which has me wanting her all the more.

She grips my shirt into her fists and coaxes me to stand, drawing her mouth to mine. We kiss like frenzied lovers because we both want the same thing. I lead her over to the bed and we fall onto it. She shuffles up, resting her head on the pillows and watches as I undress while on my knees.

I unbutton my shirt and when it parts, she gasps and sits up suddenly. She gently touches over the scar with her fingertips. She's always been mesmerized by it. I wonder if I now know the reason why.

But I refuse to believe that she had anything to do with Jack's death. She told me she lost her son. There's no way she would do that to another mother.

However, his heart has been very quiet since Luna's new look. Does it have something to do with the fact that he no longer recognizes her?

"Why am I so drawn to you?"

"I don't know," I reply honestly. "Yes, the chemistry has always been there between us, but there's something more. You feel it too?"

She nods. "Is that why you don't trust me? You think I've got something to do with this?"

"Yes," I finally say, not wanting to lie to her.

"I guess finding out your secrets may mean also finding out mine." And she's right.

I don't believe in consequences. There's a reason I've always wanted to protect Luna, why I've always felt connected to her, like we've met before.

But that can wait because right now, I need to forget everything and just exist in this moment.

I unfasten my jeans and when my cock springs free, Luna's eyes widen. Glad she likes what she sees. I coax her to lie back down, and when she does, I strip off my jeans and press our naked bodies together. We fit just how I knew we would, and the world sinks into nothingness around us.

I kiss her mouth, her cheeks, her neck; I can't get enough. She reaches down and commences to jerk me off. Her hand on my cock is too much and I almost come.

"Is this okay?" She mistakes my reaction as displeasure.

"More than okay, baby."

She smiles against my mouth before switching positions and rolls me onto my back. She climbs on top of me, her beautiful ass in my face as she takes my cock into her mouth.

I've been blown before, but holy shit, not by someone who I feel such a connection with.

It's like her mouth and body were made for me.

I don't need an invitation and hook my hands under her knees, pulling her onto my face. I take her pussy into my mouth and lick her slowly. Her cries vibrate down to my cock, which only has me fucking her deeper with my tongue.

I grip her ass and spread her wide. I eat her out, encouraging her to grind her clit against my face. She rocks back and forth, my cock still in her mouth as she gives me the best blow job of my damn life. I hit the back of her throat, and she gags but doesn't stop.

She only goes deeper and faster. And so do I.

Her pussy is hot and slick, and as much as I am enjoying this, I want her on me. So I make that happen when I drag her backward and sit her on my face. She moans, positioning her knees on either side of my face as she begins rocking on my mouth.

I grip her outer thighs, encouraging her to fuck my face. I don't want gentle. I want her to fucking break me because I plan on doing that to her.

She's riding my face backward, and with both hands on her waist, I help her move wildly as she clutches my thighs for support. She raises her hips and slams back down onto my face—over and over.

Her cries grow as her body vibrates all over.

She's fucking my face and I love that she takes from me. I want to give her the fucking world. She licks her hand and takes my cock into her palm as she begins to jerk me off again. She runs her thumb over the head of my cock, wiping the precum away as she sucks it into her mouth.

I am done for.

I lift her up, a startled cry getting trapped in her throat, but that soon turns into a whimper as I position her on her hands and knees. The sight of her ass and pussy greeting me is one I will never forget. I come up behind her and tease her pussy with my dick.

"I don't have a condom."

"I don't care." She rolls her hips.

She's ready and so am I, so I sink into her all the way. When buried to the hilt, I don't move. Her whimpers are the sweetest song I've ever heard. Gripping her hips, I keep her still as I pull out halfway, only to slam back into her.

The movement has her bucking forward, but I keep her steady and commence fucking her without restraint. I know she's still injured, but I read her body and she wants me to go hard.

She bounces back on my dick, taking me deep each time, and I want to fucking die because this is pure heaven. I'm far from gentle, but this is filled with passion and love.

She grips the blanket in her fists, and only then do I realize we are fucking on a bed full of money. The thoughts of other men looking at Luna has me fucking her faster, harder. My strokes are almost punishing, but she meets me thrust for thrust, screaming each time I hit her hard.

"I hate that other men were looking at you. Touching you," I confess, threading my fingers through her black hair and yanking her head back.

She arches her neck, breathless moans escaping her parted lips as I fuck her without restraint. "And you don't think I hate

216

it when women look at you?"

Her question catches me off guard, but then I am reminded of the store clerk whose name I've forgotten because no other woman exists to me but Luna.

"You're so beautiful and talented. You could have any woman you wanted. A younger woman who—"

But I don't want to hear it.

"I want you." I draw her mouth toward mine so I can fuck her mouth as well. "I've wanted you from the moment we met. You may not remember, but I do. I belong to you in ways I don't understand."

She moans, her body trembling. "I feel it too. My body, my heart recognizes you. It's like…it's like you're a part of me."

His heart starts to beat uncontrollably, and a wave of emotion overcomes me.

"Please don't leave."

She senses my retreat, a reaction I don't understand.

"I can't," I confess, pushing aside any emotion other than being content with Luna. "We're always going to be one, Luna."

None of this makes any sense, but it does to us.

My response pleases her, and she clenches her pussy around my dick, eliciting a deep-rooted growl from within.

I fuck her so hard, but she takes everything I give, and when goose bumps prickle her skin, I know she's about to come.

"Together forever," she cries, her words clinging to desperation and obsession, and I feel every single emotion that she does.

She comes loudly, robbing me of every last stroke, before collapsing onto her stomach in a breathless, beautiful mess. I grip her hips and wildly fuck her until an orgasm tackles me so hard I almost buckle with the force.

I pull out, coming on her ass.

The beat of his heart is erratic, reminding me of a chaotic piece of music. But I welcome the madness because I no longer hear white noise because music is beginning to fill the void once more.

Once I am done, I collapse beside Luna who is still on her stomach, catching her breath. We lay side by side. She turns her cheek to look at me. She's flustered and a hot mess.

No words need to be spoken because we both feel it—the invisible tether between us has only drawn us closer together and before long, I know we will become one. That may have scared me in the past, but not now.

As my eyes slip shut and I focus on the gentle breaths of Luna, I realize I'm happy. I can't remember the last time I felt this way. Luna reaches for my hand and the moment we link fingers, that happiness is suddenly shrouded by feelings of shame.

And I don't know why.

Fifteen

Luna

I wake alone, but I'm not worried.

He'll be back. He promised he would never leave.

I don't know why it was so important to hear his promise, but I believe him. I also know he feels that we're connected in ways we both cannot explain.

If only I could remember, things would make sense. But it's not from lack of trying. Each time I think I'm about to recognize a memory, it feels as if my mind wipes it clean. I don't know if my brain has gone into self-preservation mode which scares me.

What exactly am I trying to forget?

The door opens, and the moonlight illuminates Dutch like some ethereal god. Although I can't remember my past partners, I am doubtful anyone will compare to him. I am deliciously sore. A girl from the club gave me some strong painkillers, which is why my injuries haven't bothered me.

From the takeout bag Dutch holds, it's evident he went out to get us food. On cue, my stomach rumbles in delight.

He switches on the lamp, the room bursting in hues of warm orange and yellows. He really looks like an angel with that long blond hair and beautiful face. I like this style—always in jewelry and his hair either tied back with wisps free, or loose, which frames that strong jawline.

"I hope you're hungry."

Settling against the headboard, I realize I am suddenly famished. Dutch kicks off his boots and settles beside me. Instantly, a sense of calm surrounds me. He offers me a tall cup of Coke before doing the same with a burger and fries.

We eat in silence, and although it's not uncomfortable, it's filled with thought. I ask the inevitable.

"What happens now?"

Dutch mulls over my question. "I know where he lived," he finally reveals. "The donor. Your plan was fucking genius. The cops will hopefully stop riding our asses long enough for me to figure out something that makes sense."

"So we go to his house and snoop around?"

Dutch nods, chewing pensively. "I need to know who he is and why someone wanted him dead."

I'm suddenly not hungry and push away my food.

"If this makes you uncomfortable, you can stay here. I understand this is fucking…weird. But this is the only thing that makes sense to me."

"And you're certain he was murdered?"

"Without a doubt. His heart confirms it."

"You talk about your heart like it's its own person."

"I know," he confesses, shaking his head. "And in some ways, I feel that it is. It never felt like mine. So I need to somehow figure this out and hopefully uncover what secrets this bastard hides."

I don't want to ask, but where does that leave me? I don't know who I am. How do I solve that mystery? "What was his name?"

"Jack," he replies like they're well acquainted. "I know he played college football. He was messed up with drugs and a bad crowd. I also know he was driving that night to get something for someone he loved very much. I see his death, Luna. He was run off the road by someone he knew. A woman."

His pause leaves me suspicious. "Do you know who that woman is?"

When he averts his gaze, he answers my question.

"Who is it?"

"I can't know for certain…"

"But you have some idea, right?" Panic overwhelms me because I know what he's going to say before he even says it.

"Yes, but that's the one thing I refuse to believe."

"Who?" I whisper, eyes filled with tears.

"When I've had these visions, I see…your eyes behind the wheel."

It's like Dutch has a sudden epiphany, and he clenches his jaw.

"What is it?"

He goes to stand, but I grip his wrist, begging he tell me the truth because I'm at his mercy.

"In a vision, I saw Jack with a woman."

"Like a lover?"

He nods.

"And you think that woman is *me*?"

His silence speaks volumes.

"Oh my god." Vomit soon rises and I throw off the blanket, running to the bathroom.

I throw up the small amount of food I just ate, but I want to purge this entire nightmare from my body.

"Luna—"

"Go away," I mumble, my head buried in the toilet.

He, of course, doesn't listen. He sits down beside me. He doesn't touch me, however, and for that, I am glad. I need to wrap my head around all of this. I don't understand it, but I can't help but acknowledge that this doesn't feel like news to me.

It feels as if I already knew just who Jack was.

"So us meeting wasn't a coincidence? This connection we feel is because we knew the same man?"

I'm afraid to look at Dutch, but I can't hide forever.

Lifting my head, I look at Dutch through new eyes because are we really connected in some sick, macabre way?

"No wonder you don't trust me."

"Luna—"

He tries to touch me, but I shrink away. "No, don't. Until I know who I am…until I know what I did, I don't think I'll ever be okay with us."

Dutch frowns, my comment wounding him. "I understand, but my feelings for you…they're just that. They're *mine*. I meant everything I said to you."

Tears sting my eyes, but I wipe them away. "What god-awful nightmare are we living? Tell me everything you know about me. Please," I add, as I don't want him to sugarcoat anything.

He nods before coming to a stand. He offers his hand, but I don't take it. He hides his offense and leaves me alone to digest what he just shared.

How is this possible?

Coming to a shaky stand, I grip the sink and stare into the smudged mirror. Who the fuck is this person? When I took to the stage, I knew I had done it before. I also knew I had seduced many men before. It all came so easily to me.

Is this what I did to Jack?

This seems too unbelievable to be true.

Splashing water onto my face and rinsing out my mouth, I make my way into the bedroom and for the first time ever, I feel uncomfortable being near Dutch. I sit on the chair instead of the bed. He doesn't say anything, but I can read his heartache—how that word now takes on a different meaning.

He is sitting at the foot of the bed, legs splayed. He really is so stunning. I wonder if my attraction is because the donated heart beating within his chest is of the man I killed.

"Stop it," Dutch says, reading my thoughts. "You're making assumptions from visions that I don't even know are real."

"And if they are? You do realize that means I was screwing the man whose heart you now have. And that I possibly killed him. Oh my god. I can't believe this is happening."

Dutch exhales, interlacing his hands behind his head. He's frustrated. But it's the truth. I'm only preparing us for what might lie ahead.

"You told me you lost your…son, and because of that, you tried to take your own life. That's why you were admitted."

"A son?" The walls close in on me. "I was a mother. I can't

believe I can't remember him. What sort of mother doesn't remember her own son!"

My heart breaks into a million pieces.

"I'm so sorry. This is why I didn't want to tell you. I wanted to save you the pain."

Sniffing back my tears, I try and hold it together because I asked for this.

"It was hospital policy not to use our real names, so we were to choose a name. Yours was Misha. Does that mean anything to you?"

Misha?

I dig deep into my subconscious and wade through the fog in my mind. I try and push against the mental block, desperate to remember something—anything. But I don't. The only time I heard that name was when I called it out to Dutch.

"What happened to me? Why can't I remember?"

"I don't know," he confesses. "There are holes in my memory too. But one day, you came back like this. A stranger in your own skin. Parkfields is a horrible place, filled with fucked-up orderlies and nurses who abuse their power without a second thought. There was one orderly who took a liking to you."

Something comes over Dutch, and it scares me.

"I think he might have something to do with this. But we can never go back there. We're both dead if we do."

"So there's no one there we can trust? Someone who could tell me who I am?"

Dutch ponders on my question. "There may be someone, but as far as trusting him, I don't. But he may be our only chance."

"What else?"

"Your best friend had you committed."

"Some friend," I mumble under my breath. "Maybe if we found her?"

Dutch nods, understanding my train of thought.

"So we need someone inside of Parkfields? How else are we supposed to figure this out? I don't even know my last name."

Dutch stares into the distance, clearly deep in thought. "There may be someone else. A doctor."

"I thought you said they all abused their power."

"She's different."

Of course she is.

I don't say anything, however, because at this stage, we're desperate.

"Let's go to Jack's house tomorrow and see what we find. With any luck, he might start talking to me again."

"We really are fucking crazy," I say with a sigh.

What are the odds? Slim to none this would happen. But I guess it explains why Dutch and I have this inexplicable connection.

"No wonder I like your heart. It belonged to someone I already knew."

Dutch stands and walks out the door without an explanation. When I realize what I just insensitively said, I exhale in frustration.

"Dutch!" I quickly throw on one of his T-shirts and chase after him, needing to apologize.

I find him standing in the middle of the parking lot, face tipped to the heavens.

"I'm sorry. I didn't mean it. I'm just frustrated and confused. I like *your* heart because it belongs to *you*." This still sounds like

225

he's runner-up.

How did we go from being so in sync to this?

He doesn't speak.

He doesn't even look at me.

I don't know how to make this right. I just feel sick inside. Dutch was my safe place. But now, he represents the atrocities I may have committed.

Sadness overcomes me because of who my son was. How did he die? For a mother not to remember her son is a punishment far worse than death.

"Beethoven fell in love with one of his students. He wrote Für Elise for her. She wasn't the best pianist, so he made the notes easy for her to play. However, she didn't feel the same and got engaged to another man. When Beethoven learned of her engagement, he was heartbroken and wrote the rest of the song so hard, she'd never be able to play it."

I listen intently, not sure why he's telling me this.

"The heart makes you do and say foolish things, and I think that's because we're never in control when it comes to love. So there's no need to apologize. It's probably true. You probably only feel something for me because of his heart.

"We are drawn to people for reasons unknown. It may not make sense, but the heart wants what the heart wants. My doctor thinks I am suffering from something called heart memory transfer. I agree that the memories I have aren't mine, but my feelings for you…they're my own."

Tears spill down my cheeks because not once did I take his feelings into consideration. He's suffering too.

"We may be connected to one another because of this fucking heart, but even without it, I know I would still feel the same way I do about you."

He finally meets my eyes, brushing away my tears with his fingers. He then draws them to his mouth and runs them across his lips. "There's so much sadness in your tears. I wish I could take it all away."

One minute Dutch is standing, the next, he's fallen to his knees, clutching at his chest. "Dutch!"

I scoop him up into my arms, but he fights me. "No, leave me. I can hear it."

"Hear what?"

"The music, and it's fucking beautiful. I know what I have to do. To hear it…I have to die."

"You're not going to die," I say, coaxing him to stand and lean against me as I lead us back to our room.

"I die a thousand deaths each time I think your feelings are borrowed. Only here because of this fucking heart!"

He thankfully stops fighting, and when we enter the room, I gently sit him on the bed. I close the door and give him space because I don't know what to do.

Maybe we're both fucking crazy. Maybe we really do belong at Parkfields.

"Tell me what to do," I beg, my back to the door.

"Kill me," he morbidly replies, his long hair shrouding his downturned face.

"What?" I gasp, horrified he would even suggest such a thing. "I would never."

"If you want to help me, then kill me." He slowly lifts his head and the pain I see breaks me. "I am already dead inside. To be robbed of the only thing that made life worth living is punishment."

"When do you hear it?" I ask, needing to think fast.

"When you're with me. Or when this motherfucker is at risk of me cutting it from my chest."

"Well, I'm here now." Pushing off the door, I don't rush and walk toward him.

He watches me with interest, but I can see that he doesn't hear a thing. I think over what he said and decide to try something. It seems me and danger is what Dutch needs to hear music, so I wonder what happens when I combine the two.

I straddle him gently and press my lips to his. The ever-present spark burns brightly, but it's not enough. His kisses are halfhearted. He needs more. To silence the demons, we need to feed them.

With our mouths still locked, I wrap a hand around his throat and squeeze lightly. A moan leaves him, and I feel him grow hard. He likes it.

Squeezing harder, I begin to rock against his erection. I never break our kiss. He doesn't touch me. He leaves his hands by his sides and allows me to use him how I want. The harder I squeeze, the more frantic our kisses grow.

I don't want to hurt him, however, just as I loosen my grip, he latches on to the back of my hand, begging I don't stop. So I don't.

I cup his throat, and he gasps for air as I continue to assault his mouth with mine. The power I wield is a dangerous mix of desire and control, and I'm surprised at how comfortable I feel. I squeeze over the pulse at his throat and feel his heart beating erratically.

We are straddling a very dangerous line because Dutch's heart is still at risk. His scar is still healing. He's not fully recovered, but does one ever really recover from something like this? I would never hurt him, but what's pleasure without a little pain?

"Harder," he orders breathlessly, slipping a hand under the hem of my T-shirt and rubbing over my bare sex.

I do as he says, but I need him inside me.

Brushing his hand away, I frantically tug at his jeans, and when his dick springs free, I don't waste a second, and even though I'm hardly ready, I sink down onto it. We both moan at the connection.

I yank off my shirt because I want nothing between us, and begin to rock wildly, lips locked and grip tightening around his throat. I bounce on his lap, taking him deep each time I come back down. It's heaven wrapped in sin.

Dutch's breathing is labored, and I worry it's too much. I don't stop, however.

I cross my ankles around his lower back so I'm able to ride him with ease. His cock throbs inside me and it's evident he gets off on rough play. I don't know if I liked this "before," but I do now.

"Fuck," he curses, gripping my hand and forcing me to press down even harder.

I feel like I'm strangling him, but he won't let my hand go. He lifts his hips, impaling me onto his dick mercilessly. My breasts bounce between us and I know he likes them because his gaze shifts between them and my eyes.

This is raw and carnal, and regardless of whose heart he has, it's his heart I want. I want him.

When his eyes slip shut, and he arches his head back, I feel the flow of energy pass through us.

He hears it.

I can see him get lost in a world where only he belongs.

I don't stop, and when I feel the familiar burn swell in my belly, I rock my hips faster. I don't know where he ends, and I begin. We're so close, yet not close enough. I want him to come first, but I can't stop and I come so hard I lose my breath.

Dutch is still pumping his hips and only when his eyes pop open and he pulls out, coming all over my sex, do I release his throat.

He gulps in mouthfuls of air as I lower my ear to his chest and listen to his heart. The rhythm has always soothed me.

"That was incredible," he pants, wrapping his arms around me. "I heard it again. Something isn't lost if you know where to look."

He kisses the top of my head before gently coaxing me off his lap. He stands, only to return a second later with some tissues to clean me up.

I lay on the bed and watch with interest as he retrieves the small notepad and pen on the dresser and sits down on the floor. He closes his eyes and his fingers begin to tap out a tune that he can only hear.

I am lost in his world, totally mesmerized by a true artist in his realm. I wonder what he hears. He begins scribbling notes onto the paper, nodding in time with the beat in his head. I hope to be there the day he sits behind a piano and plays this piece because I know it'll be a masterpiece.

Anguish and torment are what makes a true artist. They use art as an escapism. You can't fake that. And Dutch's pain only seems to grow.

I settle against the pillows and fall asleep, wondering when this pain will end.

Sixteen

Luna

W e're driving in silence once again. It seems we can't escape it these days.

I have no idea what faces us today, but I suppose I never do. The farther we drive, the more anxious I become. I don't know why, but I can't help but feel today is going to change everything.

I suspect Dutch feels it too because he's not his usual self.

This entire situation is something out of a horror movie. It doesn't make sense, but in some weird way, it doesn't feel foreign. It's like I've been here before.

We drive through a beautiful neighborhood. It's apparent Jack was from a family who could afford luxuries in life. But in the end, it didn't matter. It didn't save him.

Dutch is driving slowly, peering at the house numbers, and when we arrive at a lavish double-story home, he pulls up by

231

the curb.

"This is it."

We both take a moment to look at the home, which I hope holds the answers we seek. A sense of nostalgia suddenly overwhelms me. Tears gather in my eyes.

"Did you want to wait here?" Dutch gently rubs over my leg, sensing my emotions.

I want to go, but I don't think I can. My actions have proven that I'm not afraid of taking risks, but this feels different. I can't help but think this is because I've been here before. That this place holds memories—good and bad.

"I'm not sure why I can't go in."

"It's okay. I won't be long." Dutch leans across the middle console and kisses my cheek. It's comforting.

I watch as he exits the car and makes his way to Jack's home. He doesn't rush, but I guess he's as anxious as I am. He knocks on the door and waits with his hands in his pockets.

I can't take my eyes off him and when the door opens and a woman with long brown hair steps out onto the porch, nervous energy mounts, winding me.

Folding in half, I grip on to the dash to ground myself. Is this Jack's mom? Sister? Do I know her?

I examine her closely in hopes of recognition hitting me. It doesn't.

She listens intently as Dutch speaks and peers over at the car. I feel like shrinking in my seat. I shouldn't judge a book by its cover, but I don't like her.

She goes inside, and when Dutch follows, I begin to doubt my decision that I didn't go with him. My anxiety peaks. What are they doing?

My leg bounces because I can't keep still. I can't shake the feeling that something horrible is happening, and I'm stuck in the car because I'm too afraid to find out what that may be.

One minute becomes two, and just as I'm about to open the door and see what's going on, Dutch reappears. The woman follows, offering him something. He peers down at it, not looking away for a long time. He places whatever it is into his back pocket.

My stomach drops and I want to be sick as she steps into his arms and hugs him tight. His arms are rigid by his sides. He looks uncomfortable but doesn't push her away.

When she finally lets him go, she wipes at her eyes.

Dutch nods after a minute of her talking, and then he walks away.

The lady stands on the porch, staring at me. Even though we are far away, it's evident she is looking at me. Why?

Dutch's door opens, and he gets in but doesn't speak. I give him the space he clearly needs even though I want to ask a million questions. I see he has a photograph in his hands. What did he put into his back pocket?

"Is that him?" I ask, even though I know the answer.

Dutch stares out the windshield, tapping the edge of the photograph against the steering wheel. His silence scares me.

"Is everything okay? Did she know him?"

Dutch nods slowly, his jaw clenched.

Before I can hound him for answers, he offers me the photograph which is turned over. I accept it with shaky fingers. This needs to be quick, like a Band-Aid. But I'm afraid.

Dutch won't look at me which just heightens my anxiety.

Taking a deep breath, I turn the photograph over and who

I see has tears streaming down my cheeks.

I don't recognize him, but my heart does. He has kind eyes and a beautiful smile. But behind that smile, I sense sadness, like masking a secret which has the ability to change the world.

"This is Jack?"

There's a pregnant pause before Dutch replies. "Yes."

"Jack," I whisper, fresh tears falling. "You were loved."

I don't know why I said that, but I feel it's the truth. I run my fingertips over the photograph and am once again blanketed in sadness. I don't speak when Dutch starts the car and drives away. I can't let go of the picture, and I know without a doubt, I knew Jack.

I just don't remember how.

"Who was that lady?"

Dutch keeps his eyes on the road, but the hard set of his jaw reveals his inner turmoil. "His mom."

I wait for him to continue, but he doesn't. His silence leaves me anxious.

We drive for what feels like hours because the uncomfortable tension between us just continues to grow.

"Did you find anything out that will help?" I finally ask, breaking the silence.

Dutch nods but doesn't share what.

I give him the space he needs and we drive in silence until Dutch takes a turn down a dirt road. I have no idea where we're going. There's a lookout point ahead. Dutch pulls over and parks the car. He gets out but doesn't ask if I want to come.

I wonder what Jack's mom said.

I watch him through the windshield as he walks to the cliff edge and peers into the distance. Why does he carry such sadness?

Opening the door, I walk toward him cautiously, making sure not to crowd him as I come to a stop beside him. "Talk to me. Please."

His hands are dug deep into his pockets and he looks to carry the world upon his shoulders. "She didn't tell me her name, but she told me what I already know—Jack was a good driver. There's no way it was an accident."

Is this why Dutch is quiet? Does this confirm the voices he hears are real?

"She said Jack was messed up on drugs, and to support his habit, he was dealing. She tried to help him, but he was too far gone. She knew he needed help. But he wouldn't let her. He said he was fine and dealing with it. She believes someone he knew ran him off the road that night."

"But why?"

Dutch won't look at me. "She doesn't know, but assumes it's got something to do with the life he lived."

"Did you tell her he is your donor?"

He nods. "I told her everything, thinking she'd throw me off her porch and call the cops. But she didn't. Instead, she said it didn't surprise her because Jack was as stubborn in life as he is in death. She asked if I would help her find out who killed him."

I blow out a long-winded breath.

I can't help but feel Dutch isn't telling me everything.

"Did she mention anything about…me?" I don't even know how he would broach that topic, but he definitely isn't sharing everything.

"No. She didn't mention anything about a woman in Jack's life. She said he was very secretive when it came to his personal life."

"So what do we do now? You're no closer to finding out the truth."

Dutch sighs, and for the first time since I can remember, I sense defeat. "I told her I'd be in touch. It's a lot to process right now."

"Of course."

"Does any of this feel familiar? The house? The woman?"

I shake my head. "I wish it did. It's so incredibly frustrating. Have you heard anything?"

I don't need to clarify what I mean.

Dutch attempts to walk away, but I grip his wrist, stopping him. "What aren't you telling me?"

"This is so fucked up, Luna," he says, finally meeting my eyes. "It doesn't feel real."

And he's right.

None of this feels real. The only thing that does are my feelings for him.

"I don't know what lies ahead, but I need you to know something. I need you to kno—"

He doesn't let me finish, however, as he slams his lips against mine, silencing me. This kiss is far from gentle. It's laced with obsession and an urgency which I don't understand.

I bite Dutch's lip, tasting blood.

A strangled moan gets caught in his throat before he threads his fingers through my hair and pulls hard.

Will I ever stop wanting him?

Just as I rub over his erection, he pulls back, shaking his head. "Not here. I want to show you something."

I can't hide my disappointment, but my curiosity gets the

better of me.

We walk back to the car, a million thoughts racing through my mind. Things have definitely shifted between us, and I worry Dutch will never look at me the way he first did when we were on that bus. I can't shake the feeling that he's hiding something from me, and I'm afraid of what it might be.

We drive in silence once again—our forever passenger.

I come to realize that although Dutch is wary of me, I, too, am putting my entire faith in him as well. I'm accepting everything he says at face value because I trust him.

But should I?

Something so beautiful has suddenly turned ugly, and I hate it. If only I could remember. I can't help but wonder why I can't. What is my memory trying so hard for me to forget?

I'm not sure when day turned to night, but when Dutch pulls over, the skies are twinkling with dots of light. I'm not sure why, but I feel most at home in the darkness. I wonder if I always felt this way.

"What are you thinking?"

I want to be honest because at this point, I have nothing to lose. "I thought by now, I would have remembered something, but it's like my mind refuses to remember because of the things that have happened…because of the things I've done."

A heavy sigh leaves Dutch.

"I know you said it's dangerous, but I don't see there being any other way. You said there was someone at Parkfields who might be able to help?"

"I don't know that he will."

"We have to try," I press, refusing to take no for an answer. "I don't care what I have to do. I can't live this way anymore."

Dutch still won't look at me and I hate it. "I don't know what you'll have to sacrifice to get what you want."

His ambiguous comment is laced with an undertone of worry and sadness. Something dire looms—I just don't know what.

"I don't care anymore. I have nothing to lose."

And I mean that in every sense of the word.

Dutch nods before getting out of the car without a word.

I hate this. I hate feeling powerless because that's what I am. I'm relying on him for everything which I shouldn't because we met in an asylum, for God's sake. Dutch is hearing voices from a dead man whose heart beats within his chest. And me, I might have killed that man.

There is nothing normal about this entire situation. Maybe we're just as crazy as the other.

When I peer out my window, I see Dutch walking toward a church. Instantly, a bitter taste lingers on my tongue. I guess I wasn't a devout Catholic.

I exit the car, curiosity once again getting the better of me as I follow Dutch into the small bluestone church. I'm surprised the doors aren't locked, but when I see Dutch walk confidently down the aisle, it's apparent he's been here before.

Must be nice to remember...

I stop in the middle of the aisle, watching Dutch as he makes his way toward a white piano. He stops in front of it, and I can see he's deep in thought. Reaching out, he places his palm on the top of it, before running it across the gleaming surface.

I watch, utterly mesmerized as Dutch goes to that place he usually does when music is involved.

It's beautiful.

"I was a choirboy here." Explains why he knows the layout so well and also the crucifix necklace he never takes off. "I always knew piano was my destiny, though. My parents thought if they introduced me to other aspects of music, I'd stop obsessing over the piano.

"It didn't work. I've always felt music understood me better than any human being could. Music could speak for me when I couldn't. That's why I need it back. To not hear it…I may as well be dead. It's like Jack's voice has replaced the notes in my head."

I don't speak because this feels like Dutch purging all the secrets that plague him.

"The music stopped the moment I awoke from my operation and the only time I hear it…is when I'm with you," he confesses, finally meeting my eyes. "That means something. I knew it from the first moment I saw you."

My heart swells.

"Being without music is like being without breath and each breath I take feels borrowed, like my time is running out. So, I need to show you something just in case this is the last time."

"The last time for what?" I'm afraid to ask, but I need to know.

Dutch stares at me, nothing but sorrow blanketing us both.

"Why do I feel like this is goodbye?"

A heavy breath leaves him before he takes a seat behind the piano.

I don't dare move.

He strokes the piano as he would a lover—I know how that feels firsthand. I wonder what's about to happen because Dutch said he hasn't been able to write since the operation. But when he places his fingers on the keys, it seems something has shifted because music fills the silence and nothing else exists but this.

Dutch's eyes are closed, but the piano, the music is an extension of him. He doesn't need sight. He has a heart, and although he doesn't think it's his, this proves that it is. Each beat of Jack's heart gives Dutch life and that life gives birth to the most beautiful music.

Dutch is a true maestro, and this is the only time I've ever seen him at peace. I get it now. I understand why he so desperately needs to solve this mystery because it's killing him inside. Each silent note is driving him insane.

The music builds, evoking emotions in me which I can't control.

I feel happiness.

Sadness.

I feel love.

I'm transported to Dutch's world, and I never want to leave.

He bends the notes to his demands, his fingers almost too fast to see. It's effortless for him. This is where he feels at home. I wonder what happened for him to hear the music once again.

When the melody slows and the upbeat tempo is replaced with heaviness, I slide across a pew and sit. Dutch's head is bowed, his dirty blond hair shielding his face. He's beautiful, and that's when an epiphany hits—I love him.

I love Dutch with my entire heart and soul. It doesn't make sense because he's nothing but a stranger to me, but I know there's more to this, and I plan on uncovering what that is.

The notes slow, a sickened beat which suddenly is reflective of a broken heart barely beating. Tears swell, and I allow them to fall because I know this is the end.

I just don't know what happens once he plays the final note.

Dutch's fingers punish the keys with a delicate wound, and when the piece of music erupts into chaos, I realize this is his life in music. An echo of his journey that no words could ever explain. It's gruesome and raw—it's a masterpiece.

It suddenly ends, cutting me off from a world that I never want to leave.

Dutch is breathless, taking a moment to return from wherever he went.

"It's not finished," he says. "But each section was written in my head when I was with you. I didn't know what it was at the time, just notes floating in white noise. But each time I'm with you, Luna, it feeds the silence, and I can play."

I don't know what to say.

He finally lifts his chin and locks eyes with me. I die a thousand deaths.

"Come here."

I don't even think twice as I stand and make my way toward him. The air sparks with an undercurrent which is sure to burn us alive. I don't know who lunges for who first, but our mouths, our bodies soon become one.

We kiss one another with fire and passion as I wrap myself around him, but it's still not close enough. I know change is on the horizon, and I'm afraid. I can't help but feel this is the end for us.

Tears spill down my cheeks, flavoring our union with a salty kiss.

Dutch pulls away, only to lick at the tears on my cheek, like he wants to make my pain his own. It only has me wanting him all the more.

He walks me toward the altar, and when my back hits the

marbled slab, he spins me around. He coaxes me to lean over. I go willingly, anticipating what he has planned.

He lifts the hem of my dress, running his hand over my ass. "I don't think I'll ever finish that song," he reveals, sliding his hand to the front of my underwear.

He commences rubbing over my sex while I bite my cheek to smother my moan.

"And that's because I don't want our story to ever end. To compose, I need pain. I use it to feed the depravity inside me. I think that's why I couldn't hear the music when I woke up. I was fixed."

He scoffs, apparent that he doesn't believe there's such a thing.

"A new heart meant I could do all the things I couldn't before. I could live a normal life. But now I see, I don't want normal. I never did. The danger to living is what drove me to write. Knowing that each beat of my heart could be my last is what pushed me to compose my best piece of music before I ran out of time.

"But when that was taken away, I didn't see the point of urgency because I had my whole miserable life ahead of me. But I don't want that. Maybe I'm just one fucked-up, tortured artist who needs chaos to survive."

He slips his hand inside my underwear, setting my body alight when he sinks two fingers inside me. He begins moving those wicked fingers with skill that leaves me a breathless mess. My body knows him well and is greedy, always wanting more.

"Music has always been my first love, and I just accepted that I'd never connect with a human the way I do with music. But then I met you."

I move my hips in time with his fingers, gripping the edge of the altar in fear my legs won't hold me up.

"I've never wanted anyone the way I want you," he confesses, bending down and licking the side of my neck slowly. "You sing to me, Luna. Your mind. Your taste. Your heart. Every artist needs a muse, and you're mine, and that scares the living shit out of me."

"Why?"

"Because I've become addicted to the feeling. I've become addicted to you, and when you leave, I don't think I'll survive it."

"I'm not going anywhere."

But it suddenly doesn't feel like it's my choice.

"Dutch—"

He doesn't allow me to finish, however, because now, we both want to forget—just for a little while anyway.

He slides my underwear down my legs and when he coaxes me to spread my legs, I lean my cheek against the cool marble of the altar, surrendering myself to the man who has captured my heart and soul.

Dutch kisses up the back of my leg, before those kisses lead across to my ass. He licks and sucks, his tongue sending my body into overdrive. He doesn't shy away from kissing every single part of me and when he spreads me wide and licks a place which has me blushing, I shudder and moan at the thought that he owns every part of me.

He grips my hips and encourages me to buck onto his face as he fucks my back passage with his mouth and tongue. Everywhere he touches sets me on fire, and I want him forever.

This is worship as I feel nothing but love through his touch.

As he's tonguing me deeply, he slips two fingers into my sex. I've never felt so full. But I want more.

"Fuck me," I demand without apology.

Dutch moans, clearly turned on by my aggression. He stands, and when I hear him unfastening his jeans, I brace myself because the first time he enters me always takes my breath away. He doesn't tease. He knows I'm ready for him.

He grips my hips and slides into me. We both groan because nothing else feels this good.

I hold on to the altar as Dutch commences fucking me relentlessly. It's what I want. What I need. In this place of worship, we become one. He pulls out, only to slam back into me—over and over again. I love when he loses control this way.

Peering up, I look at the wooden crucifix hanging in front of me. I am desecrating this place of worship without apology and in some ways, the rebellion adds to the pleasure. Doing something bad feels so good, and what Dutch is doing right now feels fucking incredible.

"This gives me life," he pants, and his comment touches me in ways he'll never know because I know how much he doesn't want to live. "Always remember that."

I don't know why, but there is an air of finality in his tone.

I remember what he said about needing pain to thrive, and I want to deliver this to him if this is the final time.

Reaching for a small gold crucifix on a pillar, I move my hips, and when Dutch slides out of me, I turn around and hoist myself onto the altar. Before he can ask what I'm doing, I yank off his shirt and with the sharp corner of the crucifix, I slash it across his left pectoral, drawing blood.

He drops his chin, peering at the cut I just created. As blood trickles from the wound, an animalistic urge overcomes me and I follow instinct and lean forward and lick the trail of blood. Revolting to some, but not to me because his blood is mine.

With his blood on my lips, he slams his mouth to mine, kissing me with such longing, I would happily give my life to forever be lost in time. He doesn't break our kiss when he drags my hips forward and enters me swiftly.

I moan into his mouth because nothing compares to this.

He fucks me with passion and love, and although this is rough and hard, it's filled with an undying obsession for the other.

He pulls away and yanks my hand toward his chest. "Again."

I do as he demands and cut his chest, but this time, I score his flesh with my fingernails. He hisses as I scratch over the cut I made with the crucifix, drawing more blood.

The same look comes over Dutch, the one he gets when he gets lost in the music. I bend down and bite his chest, licking away the sting with his blood lingering on my tongue. He sinks into me so deeply, I can scarcely breathe.

His strokes are almost punishing, and when his eyes slip shut, I know he's composing an ending to this beautiful affair. I can't sit up any longer and collapse onto my back, but that's not a deterrent for Dutch. He continues working me into a legless mess.

Arching my neck, I spread my arms out wide, mimicking the Lord on the crucifix. I let go and allow this man to possess me because I belong to him—I always have. I don't know what tomorrow holds, but I can face anything as long as I have Dutch by my side.

He grips my hips and drives into me so hard my body

propels up the altar, leaving my back a hot mess. But I don't care. This is what love entails—it's messy, and it's about surrendering to the one you choose.

And I choose Dutch.

Whatever is ahead, I need him to know that I want him, regardless of the sins we committed.

The familiar burn swells in my belly and I close my eyes, the intensity of my orgasm robbing me of air. He keeps working me over until I cry out, tears of pleasure rolling down my cheeks. I get lost in his smell, his labored breaths, and this feeling of being united with the one you love.

And I want him to know it.

"I lo—"

He doesn't let me finish, however.

He slams his mouth over mine, swallowing my unspoken words before I feel him pull out and spill his seed over my sex. I want to bask in him forever as he slumps forward, blanketing me with his body. We stay interlocked, in no hurry to disconnect because it's always quieter when we're together this way.

"It's almost finished," he says, and I know he's talking about his song. "But it'll forever be changing. And that's because I'll always wonder if I did the right thing."

He kisses my neck before pulling away to get dressed.

He offers me my clothes, but there is something wrong. I suddenly feel so exposed.

I jump down from the altar and quickly dress. "What's wrong?"

Dutch runs a hand through his snarled hair, his cheeks billowing with his pent-up breath. "Please forgive me, Luna."

I don't know what he's apologizing for. "You're scaring me.

Look at me."

Instead, he drops to his knees and peers up at me with desolate eyes. "I just wanted to help you. But I think I've made a mistake."

"W-what are you talking about?"

He never gets a chance to answer me, however, because when I hear someone's heels stabbing at the floor, a flood of memories hits me and leaves me gasping for air.

I've heard this before…I remember.

Suddenly, I hear the click…click…click of heels echoing down the corridor. The sound sends chills down my spine.

I don't know what to do. I fruitlessly tug at the straps, but they won't budge. "Tell me what to do!"

"We've got to go. Now! She can't find us down here."

His terrified tone reveals whoever she is, is the person responsible for doing this to Bowie.

"Should I stay and fight?"

There's no movement. He simply stares straight through me.

"Or will that make things worse for you? Do I hide and watch, and when the time is right, strike?"

That sounds like the coward's way out, but I have no weapons and no way to get us out of here safely.

"We've got to go!" Old Timer repeats, but he can wait.

"You want me to go?" I ask Bowie, clutching his cheeks, and when he blinks once, a sob gets caught in my throat.

Even stuck in a medicated nightmare, he's trying to save me. And this is the only way I can save him.

The life is sucked back into me as quickly as it left and when I peer down at Dutch, I remember him. "Bowie?"

His mouth parts because he sees it too. "You remember?"

Tears slide down my cheeks because I don't remember everything, but I remember *her*.

"I'm here to help," Dr. Norton says as she approaches us. But she doesn't help anyone but herself.

"You're the one who did this to me, aren't you?" I snarl, locking eyes with her and wishing to slap that smug smirk from her face.

A gasp leaves Dutch. He didn't know, but I can see that he believes me.

"You're confused. We will get you back to Parkfields and everything will be all right."

Dutch looks at me, really looks at me, and realizes I'm telling the truth.

He springs to his feet, shielding me with his body as three orderlies follow behind Dr. Norton. When he sees one man, in particular, he reaches for me and presses me into his back.

"Why is he here?" he demands, and I know this man has done some horrible things to us both. "You promised she wouldn't be harmed. You fucking lied!"

Dr. Norton smiles, but there's no warmth behind her eyes. "I'm going to take care of you both."

"Over my dead body!" Dutch only pulls me in tighter.

"That can be arranged."

"Noah, enough!"

Noah?

"I give the orders. You obey. We clear, crazy bitch?"

Images and voices flash before me so quickly I think I'm going to be sick. It's like I'm on a merry-go-round that is moving in fast-forward. I can't make sense of any of the images, but what I see makes me want to run.

"How could you do this?" I twist out of Dutch's arms, feeling nothing but betrayal.

He turns around, trying to touch me, but I take two steps back.

"I trusted you. And you called *her*? She's a monster. She—" The wind gets ripped from my lungs when an image of her having sex with a man who resembles a corpse smashes into me so hard, my knees buckle and I hold on to the altar for support.

That image is soon replaced with another of her having her way with a comatose Dutch. "Oh my god," I gasp, holding back my vomit. "Do you fuck all your patients?"

"We'll be all right again. I love you, Jonathan. Please come back to me."

That's what she said to Dutch. She called him Jonathan. I don't know who anyone is anymore.

"Luna." Dutch reaches for me, but I recoil backward, shaking my head.

"Stay away from me! I don't know who you are! Your name is Jonathan?"

"*What?* No," he replies, raising his hands in surrender. "What I've told you is the truth. I swear to you. My feelings for you are real."

"How can I believe you?" Tears fall down my cheeks because the one person I trusted has betrayed me and I don't even know why. "Why? What happened at that house?"

I don't need him to draw me a diagram. Something shifted the moment he entered Jack's house. I then remember he put something into his back pocket.

"What did she show you?"

Dutch's guilt has me launching forward and reaching for

whatever he has stowed away in his pocket. It's a photograph.

"Luna, don't," Dutch pleads, but this just spurs me on all the more.

I turn the picture over and who I see has me dropping to my knees.

It's me and a young man whose eyes I've seen before. They are kind and provide me comfort which breaks my heart because I miss it so very much. We are hugging and there's no question that we know one another well.

"Jack," I mumble under my breath, running my finger across his face.

But this name feels wrong, like this name isn't his. But it must be because he looks familiar and it's me with him in this photograph.

Nothing makes sense.

"What did she say to you?" I ask Dutch, lifting my eyes to meet his.

He's torn, and I know that's because whatever he's about to say will change me forevermore.

"That woman, her name is Joy…she's your best friend," Dutch reveals, walking toward me slowly, as he would approach a rabid animal. "Jack was her son. You were neighbors. You helped raise Jack. You loved him like your own."

Dutch swallows past the lump in his throat because this doesn't end in a happily ever after.

"She doesn't know when you and Jack…started seeing one another. But she suspects when he was seventeen. That's when he started to change. He got mixed up with a bad crowd. He stopped being the son she knew.

"She knew he was hiding a secret. That he was seeing a

woman, but when he ended things, she didn't handle it well. She became infatuated with him, he shared with his mom."

I can't breathe. I don't want to accept this as truth, but what she says confirms what Dutch has told me. It confirms what he's seen; what he's felt.

"She said you became obsessed when Jack tried to live a life away from you. He went away to college to play football, and that's when she noticed your behavior changing too. You hardly left the house, and when you did, she said you didn't acknowledge her.

"She tried to help you, but you didn't want help. You told her there was no reason left to live if you couldn't have the man you loved. You never told her it was Jack, but she soon discovered it was him when she walked in on you and him.

"She said the way you touched him, the way you looked at him, was that of a lover. Jack never told her it was you when she asked. She said he was trying to protect you. But he did tell her he was trying to end a relationship, but the woman wouldn't let him go.

"He was scared for her. It was apparent he loved her very much. But it was done."

I wade through the sludge in my mind, desperately trying to connect to these memories, but I can't. There's nothing but white noise.

"She said the night of Jack's accident, he went to the pharmacy to get some pills for Joy. He was only supposed to be gone for twenty minutes. But when someone knocked on her door, she knew something terrible had happened.

"The police ruled it an accident, but—"

"But what?" I coax when Dutch pauses.

"But she thinks he was murdered...and she thinks you were the one who killed him."

Bile rises and I want to be sick because this is what Jack "showed" Dutch.

"She believes in a fit of jealousy, you ran him off the road because if you couldn't have him, then no one could. He started seeing a young woman, Trista. You hated her. Joy never understood why, but she started piecing it all together. She had you committed for your own safety because she'd rather that than the police investigate and confirm her worst fears."

Tears roll down my cheeks. I am a monster. And I'm also a murderer.

I don't want to believe it, but everything Dutch says confirms what he felt before he spoke to Joy. How would she know this if it wasn't true?

"And you believe her?" I whisper, begging Dutch tells me this is all a bad dream.

His silence is all the answer I need.

"It's your eyes I see behind the wheel," he confesses with nothing but sorrow. "I don't know what that means, but Jack, his heart, it's always recognized you. I don't want to believe it, but—"

Dr. Norton decides now is the time to intervene. "I know this is a lot to stomach, but here, this might help."

She offers me a folder. No guessing what's inside.

I sit on the floor cross-legged, placing the folder in my lap. I don't hesitate and open it. What I read tears my heart into two because it's all here in black and white. My name is Luna Huxley and Joy McNelly is, in fact, my best friend, the best friend who committed me after I lost my mind and tried to kill myself.

The doctors have diagnosed me as a paranoid schizophrenic, and to cope with the loss of Jack, I fabricated this entire scenario in my head that I was Jack's mother. They concluded to deal with what I did, I believed the world I created in my head was real.

I became Joy, in a sense. That the grief I felt was because Jack was my son, not my lover, the lover who I killed.

The white noise is soon replaced with one single word. A name.

"Misha."

Recognition passes over Dutch. He's heard me say this name before.

"That's what you called Jack," Dr. Norton explains calmly. "The doctors believe it was easier for you to disassociate yourself with what happened. Misha was a famous violinist you loved to listen to."

"No," I cry, shaking my head, refusing to believe her.

But the paperwork in front of me proves otherwise. My file confirms everything Dr. Norton and Dutch has said.

"Why can't I remember?"

"The mind can play tricks on us, Luna. There's nothing to be ashamed of. I just want to help."

Dr. Norton appears genuine, but how can I accept this as truth?

"The world you've created in your head has helped you cope with your loss. It's a lot nicer in there than it is out here. No one can blame you for wanting to believe in that world. But it's time you joined us here, in the real world. Don't you want that? Don't you want to get better?"

I don't know what I want.

I think about all the things Dutch told me and I hate that it coincides with what's in this file. Closing my eyes, I try and remember. I wade through the heaviness and try to remember the man whose eyes haunt me in every possible way.

I focus on him and the way his heart has always sung to me. I'm met with a solid wall, like my mind refuses for me to penetrate to the other side. But I persevere and when I'm blinded by a bright light, I get lost in the memories which I wish would remain forgotten.

I hear David Bowie. I smell the unmistakable scent of marijuana. I see Jack behind the wheel. I see him because I'm there.

"No!" I scream, covering my ears to block out the horrible sounds.

The car crashing. Jack's labored breaths.

This is my fault. I know I was the cause of his death. I can feel it spread like wildfire through every inch of my body.

It's true. All of this is true.

No wonder I can't remember. Who the fuck would want to remember this?

"It's true?" I say to Dutch. "Your heart…*his* heart, it's true, isn't it?"

I know it sounds crazy, but it makes sense to Dutch and me. This entire time, Dutch felt like his heart was leading him toward the answers he so desperately needed, but now that we've got them, I wonder if his heart has confirmed what we know to be true.

"Luna—"

"Just answer the fucking question!" I exclaim because I need to hear it. I need him to say the word which will seal my fate forever.

"Yes."

There's no closure. I don't feel like a weight has been lifted from my shoulders.

All I feel is empty.

"It's going to be okay, Luna," Dr. Norton says softly. "We'll get you back to Parkfields where you'll be safe."

She gestures over her shoulder to the orderlies who approach me with caution. But I won't fight. I've got nothing left to fight for. I deserve to rot in Parkfields for all that I've done.

The orderly, Noah, helps me stand, and when Dutch tries to come to my aid, Dr. Norton grips his wrist, stopping him. I'm thankful that she did because I don't deserve his kindness, not after what I did.

I'm led down the aisle, my life spiraling before my eyes. I don't know who I am. I don't know what's real. All I know is that I created a make-believe world to escape a monster, and that monster is me.

Seventeen

Dutch

What the fuck have I done?

I rip away from Alanna's hold because there's no way Luna is doing this alone. "Let her go," I order, glaring at Noah, who simply smirks happily.

I can see it all over his smug face—he's won.

"I'm going to take real good care of her," he says under his breath.

"You motherfucker!" I launch for him, prepared to rip off his head.

Two orderlies stop me, however.

"Dutch, enough," Alanna says smoothly. "We spoke about this on the phone. You've done the right thing."

Have I, though? Because this feels like anything but the *right* thing.

I didn't want to believe Joy, but the evidence was there. Her story confirmed everything I knew to be true. It confirmed everything Jack told me. And when she showed me the photograph of Luna and Jack, it was the proverbial nail.

I called Alanna, asking to corroborate what Joy said. She did.

She told me Luna was a paranoid schizophrenic and concocted this entire alternative universe to deal with what she'd done. Joy had a choice—have her committed or press the police in hopes they would reopen the investigation.

Her loyalty to her friend won out in the end.

The evidence is all here, but there's one bothersome factor which has me refusing to believe it all—Jack.

He's not said a word.

The son of a bitch hasn't been able to shut up since I woke up, but now that we're faced with the "truth," he's decided to take a vow of silence.

I thought once the mystery was solved, there'd be something, anything, but I hear nothing…and that's what bothers me.

There's something wrong—I just don't know what that is.

"I want to go with her," I press, but Alanna shakes her head.

"She needs to do this alone. Luna is very sick. The hallucinations she had will only get worse if she doesn't cut ties with a life she believes to be real."

"You mean I can't see her again?"

Alanna nods.

"You never told me that," I say with bite.

"Would you have agreed to this if I had?"

I appreciate that she had Luna's best interests at heart, but what the fuck. "You lied to me. How is her doing this alone good for her?"

257

I look at Luna. She's broken, and it's my fault.

"We need to…reset her," Alanna explains, and again, I know she only wants to help, but Luna isn't a fucking clock.

"Reset her?" I question, disgusted. "She's a human being, not a fucking science project."

"And this is why you can't see her. You're too close to this. Whether that's because of Jack's heart or your feelings for her, you will only hinder any progress she can make to live a normal life. I only want to help you both. You came to me with the notion that your donor heart was the reason you couldn't play music, and I never once doubted you, did I?"

She's right. She's only tried to help.

"So what if what you told me is in fact real. Are you drawn to Luna because the heart you have belonged to the man she once loved? The man she may have harmed?"

Luna sniffs back her tears.

"None of this makes any sense, but what you told me has correlated with Jack's life. I'm a doctor. I don't believe in fantasy, but this is very hard to ignore. I ask you to trust me. Now that you know the truth, I hope you have some sense of peace and can move on with your life.

"I still would like to observe you. Just for a couple days," she adds when she reads my distaste at the suggestion.

But if that means I'll be able to be close to Luna, then yes.

"So you believe me?"

Alanna simply smiles. "This isn't about what I believe. It's about you living the life you deserve. Don't you want to play music again?"

"Of course I do."

"Then you need to overcome whatever emotional blockage

is stopping you from doing so."

She's right. But I hate that she brought Noah here when she knows I want to murder him with my bare hands.

A memory suddenly smashes into me of Noah and his asshole friends defiling a patient. Things are sketchy and I can only remember bits and pieces, but I know I saw Noah filming his bastard friends taking advantage of someone who needed their help.

"He is a fucking asshole," I spit, eyeing Noah. "I saw him doing disgusting things to one of your patients. Why haven't you fired him?"

"Here we go again." Noah has the balls to roll his eyes.

"Let's just get you back to Parkfields, and then we can talk about it."

Run…

I don't know whether I'm relieved or fucking pissed off this asshole has decided to talk *now*. These words of wisdom would have been useful hours ago.

Nothing slips past Alanna. "You know the voices aren't real. They're just your mind playing tricks on you."

"He sounds fucking real to me!"

Luna finally makes eye contact with me and that's because she believes me. "What did he say?"

I beg he says more because I can't trust one single word. Is he telling me to run away from Luna? Or is he warning me of what's ahead for us both if we don't flee?

Why has he chosen this exact moment to speak?

On cue, his heart starts beating quickly and I'm short of breath. I buckle in half, almost losing my footing.

"Dutch!" Alanna and Luna cry out at the same time, but I

can only focus on the pounding of Jack's heart.

There is only one way to make this fucker talk to me. Whenever his heart is in danger, I hear music. So maybe, if I straddle the line between life and death, he'll sing like a fucking canary.

I need to think on my feet. The only way I can get him talking is if he believes he's in real danger. But another idea soon hits.

Luna has always been our muse. So what if *she* was in danger? What would he do to save her? If they were really lovers, then he would do anything to keep her safe.

It makes sense why she's inspired me to play. His heart has always recognized her. So it's time I test just how deep their love ran.

"I'm okay," I assure Alanna, hoping she doesn't see through my ploy.

I wish I could let Luna in on what I have planned, but she needs to be genuinely scared for this to work—not that I'm certain it will.

Alanna nods, watching me closely for any signs of deceit.

"You're right. Let's go. I'm done with this."

The disappointment on Luna's face is clear. It's almost enough to have me forgetting about this, but I need him to talk and I don't know how.

Alanna stays close to me as we walk down the aisle. She doesn't trust me, and she shouldn't because the moment an opportunity presents itself, I plan on taking it.

We step outside, and the dismal weather reflects the current mood. The light drizzle soon becomes a heavy downpour. We're escorted to a white van, and I hate that this entire ordeal is a fucking stereotype. Noah grips Luna by the arm and drags her toward the back doors.

His heart begins beating faster when headlights appear in the distance. They're two small dots on the horizon, but they may as well be beacons of hope because I have an idea. I clutch at my heart again as if needing to catch my breath.

The rain doesn't relent and seems punishing as it continues to fall with force.

I bend down, discreetly looking between Luna and the approaching car. The sounds of nature are suddenly amplified and the music returns. It's becoming easier to hear and I wonder if that's because Jack is calm.

That provides me no comfort because his harmony is Luna's battle. I don't care what she did. It doesn't change my feelings for her, feelings that just continue to grow. Even though this is the "right" thing to do, it feels like anything but.

But maybe we're just as fucked up as the other.

Noah shoves Luna when she doesn't move because she's trying to see if I'm okay. "Let me go!" she screams, yanking from his hold.

Her words are caught in the rainstorm, but I can hear her concern, which is why I need to do this. We hurt the ones we love, and what I feel for Luna is something like love. I say that because this extends past love.

The car gets closer and closer and just as Alanna bends low to offer me help, I do something despicable and grip her by the throat before tossing her aside. She slams into a wall, the impact winding her and ensuring she stays down for a while.

The two men run to her aid, just as I knew they would because I think Alanna uses her looks to get what she wants.

Noah, however, has other ideas and shoves Luna to the ground. She skids along the wet cement, which incites my rage.

I charge for him, focused on nothing but ripping off his fucking head. He, too, comes running for me, but the anger inside me is no match and I punch him square in the jaw. He falls to the ground and I don't wait a second as I stomp on his kneecap, breaking it in one brutal snap.

His howls rival the pouring rain, and as much as I want to continue beating Noah until he is one with the pavement, I need to put this plan into play before it's too late. I run to where Luna is trying to stand, but the rain and the fact she got the wind knocked from her is making it hard to move.

Grasping her arm, I yank her up and drag her toward the road. She doesn't fight because even after everything I've done, she trusts me. The car is approaching us and as Luna's eyes widen, I slam my mouth to hers.

If this is to be our last few moments on this godforsaken planet, then let it be in the arms of the woman I love.

She threads her fingers through my hair, pressing her body against mine and kissing me back with as much intensity. She doesn't care we're standing in the pouring rain, kissing like our lives depend on it, because they do.

She bites my bottom lip so hard it draws blood. "I hate you," she mumbles against my mouth, pulling my hair.

"You should," I reply, rubbing my erection against her. "But you're about to hate me even more."

Before she has a chance to ask what I mean, I spin her around and press my forearm over her throat. She squirms, trying to break free, but with her back to my front, I tower over her. We're blinded by the rain and headlights.

"Dutch!" she shrieks, clawing at my arm.

Her panic breaks his heart, and he begins rattling at the invisible bars on our cell.

"That's right, you son of a bitch!" I roar, pressing over Luna's throat harder. "Talk! Tell me what to do! You want me to save her? Tell me how!"

A thousand guttural screams echo in my head so loudly I want to dig out my brain. But the more frightened Luna is, the louder he screams.

"Dutch! No! Please d-don't do this."

But I ignore Luna.

"You want her to die? Then fucking fine! You want to be a chickenshit little pussy when she needs you the most? No wonder she fucking killed you!"

The rain distorts the headlights, but the blaring of the horn alerts me that in seconds, this will end for us both, and the serenity I feel gives me comfort, which I never want to let go of.

"Talk!" I scream into the blackened sky, pressing over Luna's windpipe as she gasps for air. "If you ever loved her, tell me what you could never do. Tell me how to save her!"

Everything is amplified, and nothing exists but music…just how it's supposed to be. I get lost in the sounds because, my God, it's beautiful. It's like before, before this heart took over my life and ate away at my soul.

I see it…I see her.

Jack shows me her. He shows me how he loved her and she loved him. My eyes slip shut as I get lost in his memories as I become him.

Joy was right. Luna loved Jack with her entire heart. It's no wonder we connected the way we did. The odds are slim to none, finding one another in a twisted fate. I accept that Luna knew Jack, that she would die for Jack because…

The lights are suddenly blinding, and I can't breathe. All that exists is the music. That's all I ever wanted…but what have I sacrificed in order to hear it?

"You wanted the truth, asshole, fucking choke on it!"

Jack's life flashes before me. Every single moment flickers before my eyes in seconds and I see it…I see Luna and Jack together.

But it's wrong.

No…

The memories make me want to vomit as Jack hangs his head in shame.

I shove Luna to the safety of the sidewalk because this is the last thing I can do to beg for forgiveness.

I hear the impact before feeling my entire body go numb. But not before Jack says one last thing before the final curtain call…

What the *fuck* have I done?

Eighteen

Luna

Everything is so muddled.

The doctors said I'm lucky to be alive. But I'm not so sure I want to be. I don't understand any of this.

Dutch dragged me into the middle of the road, talking to his imaginary friend, and I don't know why. I'm certain we're both as fucked up as the other, and I have no reason not to believe all the horrible things I've done.

I thought we'd be okay. I really did. But when Dutch pushed me to safety, I hit my head, and I woke here, in Parkfields—my home for God knows how long. The only thing that made this thing bearable was Dutch, but he's gone.

Tears spill from the corners of my eyes, and I would wipe them away, but I can't because I'm restrained to the bed. But this is my life now. Dr. Norton says it's for my own good. I was wrong about her. All she wants to do is help.

265

All she wanted to do was help Dutch, but it was too late for him. The voices, or rather, the voice inside his head, is what drove him to take his own life. I still don't know why he did what he did. What was he wishing Jack to say?

We have all the evidence we need in black and white.

I've read over my file. I know what I did. Joy has even come to visit. I don't know how she could forgive me after everything I've done. But that shows what a good person she is. I think back to our conversation and how she felt so familiar.

"You don't remember anything?" Joy asks, and all I can do is shake my head. "You loved Jack very much."

"How can you forgive me for what I did?" I burst into tears but wipe them away quickly because I have no right to cry.

"We've been friends for a long time, Luna. You're all that I've got left."

Joy is a bigger and better person than I am because if I were her, I would want to murder the person who took away my son.

For the next few hours, she explains who I was and the events leading up to Jack's death. I know that what she says is the truth because although I don't remember it, it feels familiar. She explains I concocted a world where I was her and when she explains how Jack was in the hospital bed, hooked to the endless machines, a memory flashes before me—my ear pressed to his chest, listening to his heart just how I did with Dutch.

It all makes sense. I was always missing pieces of the puzzle and that's because my brain went into some self-preservation mode and concealed the truth.

"Don't worry about anything," she says, producing some paperwork. "I'll take care of everything. This is just to say you appoint me to be the executor of your affairs until you're…better."

266

She offers me a pen and I sign on the dotted line without reading it and when I do, a bright light blinds me as I remember—I watch the rise and fall of his chest and memorize every single breath.

I come to a shaky stand and forget where I am as I climb onto the hospital bed and press my ear to his chest. I listen to the tender rhythm of his heart, the heart which was always too big for this world.

"Oh god," I cry softly. "I remember. You're right. I did do all the things you said I did. I fabricated this entire world, living in a fantasy, thinking it was real."

Joy wipes away her tears. "You're going to get better. No matter what happens, I'm always here."

We hug for an eternity and her smell transports me to a time when things were simple, when we were laughing and none of this despair plagued us both.

An orderly appears. Visiting hours are over.

"Could you bring more photos? Or maybe some of my belongings. It might help me remember."

Joy nods. "Of course. I'll be back next week. Until then, you just focus on getting better."

She lays a kiss on my forehead before leaving me alone to deal with this hell.

I don't know when that was because time all morphs into one never-ending cycle of chaos. The medication I'm on just makes me want to sleep. But maybe that's for the best. Although, I can never escape his eyes, no matter how hard I try.

"All ready for your session?" A nurse whose name tag reads Beth smiles.

I don't know why she phrased it as a question because it's

not like I have a choice in the matter. But I nod nonetheless.

She unfastens the restraints around my wrists and ankles, humming under her breath. On any given day, I wouldn't mind, but today, the humming grates on my nerves. Images of Beth's brain matter soiling these white floors as I run over her head with my wheelchair suddenly flash before my eyes and an inappropriate laugh escapes me.

Beth looks at me, brow raised, no doubt wondering what I'm laughing at, but she doesn't say a word.

Once I'm strapped to my chair, she wheels me toward therapy, still humming that fucking tune. The wheels squeaking over the linoleum and the flickering of the fluorescents is akin to nails being dragged down a blackboard.

I want to cover my ears, but I can't, thanks to fucking Beth. What's wrong with me? Why am I so angry?

Once inside the room, I'm wheeled to where a few others sit. Beth locks my brakes, not that I can go anywhere, and leaves me to deal with this shitshow that is therapy. I don't like therapy. I wonder if I did before.

But I would rather down a stomach full of pills again than be subjected to Jade's mumbo jumbo.

Once a few more prisoners are wheeled in, Jade dings her "serenity bell," as that's supposed to give us inner peace or some bullshit. The rage I feel begins to mount, and I can't stop it.

Suddenly, the air is ripped from my lungs and déjà vu hits because I've been here before.

"I thought this was a safe place, Doc?" Bowie counters, *arching a challenging brow. "I thought anything can be changed by asking the right questions?"*

His tenancy, it reminds me so much of…

And then I'm sucked back into the now.

So much of who?

Squeezing my eyes shut, I focus on nothing but that gaping hole in my memory, desperately trying to remember. But it feels like I'm standing at a cliff's edge, peering down into a blackened abyss.

Why can't I remember his name?

The harder I try, the faster my heart beats. It suddenly feels like I'm running a marathon, a race for my life.

"Remember," I mumble under my breath, rocking back and forth.

"Are you all right?" someone asks, but I can't answer. I can't think. All I see are his eyes. Jack's eyes, but they're not his.

A debilitating force smashes into me, and if not strapped to this chair, I would have collapsed onto the floor. But my body doesn't want to be alive, and I begin to convulse so violently I taste blood as I bite down on my tongue.

Panicked voices all morph into one, but none of them make any sense because I'm caught in a vortex, and down the rabbit hole I go.

"I'm already gone. But I can live on. Every beat of my heart helps another live."

"I lost my reason to live."

"When will they stop drugging him like this?"

Endless conversations slam into me over and over again, conversations I don't remember having, but I know that I did. I just need to wade through the heaviness because the truth is within reach.

"You're going to be all right." Frantic fingers feel for a vein in my arm, but I don't want to be sedated. Not now, not when

I'm so close.

My teeth are clenched so tight I'm sure they're about to shatter. But I don't care because none of this matters. The only thing that does is finding out his name.

The world begins to move, and I realize that's because I'm being wheeled away.

"We were talking about getting a place together. And we often spoke about the future. He wanted to have a big family. We had so many plans. But now…now he's gone."

"I love you. Please live…live for me."

They won't stop.

All I can hear are voices, voices which are the key to uncovering this all.

I want to scream.

I want to claw off my skin.

I want to rip out my heart.

The chaos is blinding; it's deafening.

"Get her onto the table." That voice, now that voice I remember.

She's the one who told me I was insane and being here was for my own good. And I believed her. I mean, she is a doctor, after all.

She's the one we looked to for guidance. She's the one we trusted.

Oh god…vomit rises and I gag on it.

"I'm trying to help you. I'm trying to make you better so you can play music again. I know that if you can do that again, everything will be all right."

"I'm going to make you better. It's going to go back to how things were."

She isn't helping anyone but herself.

"Luna? Can you hear me?"

My eyes are pried open, and a bright light is shone into them, blinding me. However, even though I'm blinded, it's the first time that everything is crystal clear.

She kisses him passionately even though he is non-responsive. But she doesn't seem to mind if the moans coming from her are anything to go by. She unlocks his restraints, and when I hear the water sloshing, I charge forward, ready to rip off her hand.

I remember…I fucking remember.

"Have it your way then because after I'm done with you, you won't remember a thing."

It's because of Dr. Norton that I can't remember a thing.

I blink past the light, finally seeing the truth, and it burns. Focusing on the doctor, she sees it—she knows I remember and that she's a fucking liar.

"You…bitch," I snarl, a surge of adrenaline giving me the strength of a hundred men as I fight against the men holding me down.

I'm jabbed in the leg with something, but it doesn't slow me down.

"Where is he?" I scream, saliva running down my chin.

Dr. Norton ignores me as she wheels over a machine.

"I said, where the *fuck* is he?"

"The hallucinations are back," she says to an orderly like I'm not here. "I really thought she was getting better."

"Her world is better than facing the truth, Doc."

It infuriates me further.

"Where is Dutch?"

The orderly attempts to shove something into my mouth,

271

but I'm too fast and bite his hand.

He pulls away, hollering. Good, I hope I drew blood.

Dr. Norton suddenly appears overhead. I arch my neck to look at her. She's upside down, which seems like the perfect image for this messed-up situation.

"I told you," she explains softly, but it's patronizing. "He's dead, Luna. He died because of the voices inside his head. He was very sick. He had hallucinations, just like you. What he was claiming, to hear the voice of his donor, it's not real. His mental illness took his life in the end. But I won't let that happen to you."

I don't want to believe her. Dutch wasn't insane. Together, we made sense. It was us versus the world.

"He's not dead!" I refuse to believe it. Surely life isn't this cruel.

"He *is* dead. I am so sorry. But if it gives you any solace, his last act was to save you. The love you shared wasn't conventional, but it made sense to you both. A unique love."

"Stop it!" I shake my head violently, refusing to believe her. "You're lying! He wouldn't leave me."

Dr. Norton places cool paddles on the side of my head, and as I scream, a nurse shoves a guard into my mouth, forcing me to bite down.

My eyes are locked with Dr. Norton's as she smiles sweetly, so sweetly, I want to be sick.

"I'll take care of you. Everything is going to be all right."

Tears run down my cheeks when I realize this is now my reality, a world where Dutch no longer exists. I finally surrender, the electrical current burning me alive from the inside out.

When the buzzing ends and the current ceases, I see myself

lying on the table because I'm floating above myself. I'm no longer a part of this world.

Dr. Norton checks my pulse and nods at the nurse, who pales when she says, "One more time."

My body convulses, but I don't feel a thing.

I am numb.

This is my world now, but before I close my eyes, I hear the words which have me clawing at the dirt which covers my grave.

No, this isn't the end. It's just the beginning because I remember his name…the name which forever will be my reason to fight.

Misha…

"It's a unique name for a very unique man. He will honor Misha because his heart is theirs. It's because of Misha that Dutch can live."

So, now the question is…who the fuck is Misha?

Nineteen

Dutch

I want to scream, but I can't because I'm gagged.

I want to move, but I can't because my wrists and ankles are tied to the bed.

Where the *fuck* am I?

Squinting, I peer around the starkly lit room because it's so goddamn white in here, it hurts my eyes. I'm not in a hospital, but the room is definitely hospital-like with the machines and that sterile smell that burns your nose.

However, I can also smell lavender which seems completely out of place.

Peering overhead, I see I'm hooked up to an IV. Someone is trying to keep me alive, so that's a bonus—I think.

My eyes adjust to the lights, and when I see I'm not alone, I don't know whether to be relieved or terrified.

Someone lies in a single bed across from me. I don't

know if it's a man or woman because their face is covered in bandages—total mummy style. They're also hooked up to an IV, but no heart monitor like mine, which reminds me of that motherfucker Jack.

The last thing I remember is standing in the middle of the room and his voice whispering something which changed the course of everything.

"It's her eyes you see because…I'm her son."

I wanted there to be some mistake, but I knew there wasn't. *This* made sense because it was the truth.

Jack wasn't his real name. It was the nickname his football friends called him after taking down a giant on the field, earning him the name. His real name is Misha and Luna is his mom.

It was like a moving picture before my eyes of Misha's life from the moment he was born to the moment he died, and who was behind the wheel wasn't Luna…it was Joy.

Joy was the one who ran him off the road that night, but he doesn't know why. Yes, they were lovers, and when he ended it, she became a little unhinged. But I could feel his confusion. He doesn't know why she's doing what she is to Luna.

He showed me their affair. She seduced him young. He thought it was real, but he believes she was drip-feeding him information that he would kill for—he wanted to know who his dad was.

Joy would give him snippets of information, but never enough for him to ever find him. When I asked the inevitable, why was he so desperate to find out who his father was, he said he needed to find him and see if he heard the voices too.

Misha got into drugs as self-medication to help block out the voices. He then realized he had an addictive personality which led to harder drugs which then led to dealing to feed his habit. He was a functioning addict.

And Luna had no idea her son was in trouble. He didn't want to tell her because he didn't want to worry her. He really loved her, but he didn't need to show me that—I've felt it with every beat of his heart.

Joy lied to me. She took on Luna's life and made it her own, making me believe her, and I did because…

Fuck…

Realization hits because I need to get the hell out of here.

Tugging at the restraints is useless because my left leg is in plaster. I guess that's what happens when you're hit by a car. And my arms are black and blue. I don't even know how long I've been holed up here.

I spit out the gag in my mouth.

"Psst," I whisper to the person in the bed. "Can you hear me?"

They don't move.

"Hey!" I say a little louder in case they're asleep and not in a coma.

Still nothing.

They're not going to be any help.

I'm helpless because I'm not going anywhere without assistance. I could try and scream for help, but I think the person who brought me here intended to keep me here.

"Do you know who keeps us here?"

Nothing.

"It's like I'm talking to the dead," I mumble to myself.

I need to think of a plan quickly because I need to find Luna and beg for forgiveness and then I need to tell her the truth—

that she isn't a murderer. That Jack is in fact Misha, and that Misha is her son. I didn't connect the dots because I expected Luna's son to be younger, which is my bad for assuming.

Now we're both caught up in this fucked-up mess because I was an idiot.

This entire time, I questioned both our sanities because how we met and what happened is fucking insane, but what's even crazier is the fact I can hear a dead man whose mother I am madly in love with.

And I am. I love Luna so fucking much and that's with *my* heart, not his. I need to find her.

"Hello?" I ask in case my roommate has decided to join the land of the living.

They haven't.

I can't go anywhere which means I need to rely on the person or persons who hold me here. And on cue, I hear the sharp echo of heels on linoleum. A haunting whistling soon follows.

This is how every horror movie starts.

My eyes never leave the doorway which has no door on it as I expect the antichrist to enter. But when I see who it is, I exhale in relief.

"Alanna, oh thank fuck, it's you."

But she continues to whistle, ignoring me.

The hair at the back of my neck stands on end because something is very wrong.

Alanna doesn't even acknowledge me but instead walks over to the bed of my roommate. "How are you feeling today?"

They give her the silent treatment too. But that doesn't deter her in the slightest. She reaches for the stethoscope around her neck and checks the vitals.

"Alanna?"

"You're doing better," she says to her patient. "Soon, you'll be back to your old self. I've stuck to my diet. I've not eaten a thing I shouldn't."

What the fuck is going on?

She recommences whistling and begins slowly unwrapping the bandages from their face. She's blocking my view, so I can't see, but I sure as shit can smell and what I smell is the unmistakable stench of decay and death which no lavender can mask.

I gag on the putrid smell, but Alanna isn't bothered. She really takes her job seriously.

"Ah, Doc, can we open a window in here? It fucking stinks. No offense."

"Soon, we'll be together, Jonathan. I've done all of this for you."

Suddenly, the walls close in on me and my heart squeezes because finally, it's mine.

"*Stay away from me! I don't know who you are! Your name is Jonathan?*"

That's what Luna said to me. She thought my name was Jonathan. There's no coincidence that Alanna just called this dude that name.

"Who the *fuck* are you?" I snarl, demanding answers and demanding them now.

Once Alanna is done unwrapping her gift, she stands back and covers her mouth. "You're just as handsome as the day we met. Do you remember? You were playing at a recital. It was my favorite—La Campanella."

Oh my motherfucking god.

Alanna has said this before. In her office. I remember.

"You were unlike anyone I've ever heard before," she says in *a faraway voice, her fingers continuing to explore my skin. "La Campanella is one of my favorites."*

I arch a brow, confused. "I didn't play Liszt at that recital. It was Bach. Are you sure it was me?"

My question snaps her from wherever she just went.

She shakes her head and removes her hand from my chest so abruptly, she almost falls on her ass. "Oh, sorry. I got the names mixed up. Sometimes, I like to think I'm a classical music expert."

Her fingers tremble when she brushes a piece of hair behind her ear. A surgeon's hand should never tremble and the perfect scar down my chest is proof of that.

Something is wrong…but I don't know what that is.

I didn't know what was wrong, but now I do.

"Alanna! Fucking turn around and look at me! What the fuck is going on?"

I am done with her games. Something is rotten—fucking literally.

"I knew you'd be a perfect fit," she says, her back still turned. "The moment I read over your file, I knew you would be perfect."

"Perfect for what?" I scream, straining my neck to see who lies in that bed.

She reaches into the pocket of her white doctor's coat and when Moonlight Sonata starts playing, I know things are about to take a macabre turn. She steps away, allowing me to see Jonathan…

I don't even know if what I'm seeing is real. Maybe I *have* lost my fucking mind because this is something out of a horror movie. I am robbed of words and music is once again my savior, filling in the silence.

Alanna walks over to a partition while I divide my attention between her and Jonathan. "We were supposed to be married. But my Jonathan, he loved me with his entire heart, so much so, it stopped working. But unlike you, Dutch, there wasn't a donor who could give him his heart. But I'm a doctor. It's my job to make people better. And I refused to allow my Jonathan to die. No."

She wheels away the partition, and what I see just adds to this fucking morbid show. "This is my wedding dress. I got it made especially for me. I know they say it's bad luck for the groom to see the dress before the big day, but—"

"But your groom is fucking dead, Alanna! So I think you're good."

Jonathan smells like a corpse because he is, in fact, one.

I don't know how she's preserved his body, maybe a fuckload of formaldehyde because this motherfucker is embalmed like a mummy. Tufts of stiff hair stick up in all different directions, and his skin is a wrinkled, sickly yellow.

His cheeks are gaunt, and his teeth are exposed, twisted into a ghoulish smile. The rest of his body resembles a prune, but Alanna looks at him like he is the most handsome man in the world.

Love is really fucking blind.

"Why am I here?"

Alanna giggles, and if hell had a doorbell, this would be its sound. "Because, silly, you're going to make my Jonathan live again."

"How the fuck do you propose that because, in case you missed the memo, he's fucking dead!"

She storms over and slaps my cheek. "Don't you say that! He's not dead."

"Sweetheart, he's not sleeping. He is D-E-A-D!" I spell it out for her in case she needs further confirmation that she is treating the corpse of her dead fiancé like he's on a sabbatical.

Alanna pulls back her shoulders and takes a breath, composing herself. "I really didn't want things to turn out this way, but you are so similar. You look the same. You play piano."

"That's hardly the same. That's two out of a billion things. We are not the same. You're the fucking crazy one!"

She ignores my outburst and strokes over her white wedding dress on the mannequin with love. The face looks like a five-year-old had access to her mother's makeup. A spotlight beams over the top of it, like it's the answer to her prayers. She then walks toward a small silver cabinet and reaches for the key she wears around her neck.

I always wondered what that unlocked. Now, I'm not too sure I want to know.

She unlocks the doors and when she opens them, I blink once because this is a fucking dream.

A glass case sits on the shelf and inside, inside that motherfucker, in a watery solution, is a heart...no guessing whose heart it is.

"I tried to use your heart. I'm not a bad person. I wanted you both to live. The world needs your music. But it didn't work."

"You think?" I quip, lip curled. My poor fucking heart. "You can't perform surgery on a dead person!"

I can't help it. I shouldn't be baiting her but what in the ever-loving Frankenstein hell am I witnessing?

"This will work. It must. I'm not getting any younger. It was our dream to have a family."

Bile rises.

"So, let's get this straight, you want my heart to give to Jonathan?"

"No, silly," Alanna says with a smile.

I exhale because this is just a big misunderstanding. But when she opens a drawer and produces a hammer, I realize there is no misunderstanding.

"It's not your heart. You told me that. It's his. Misha's. You told me you didn't want it. That you'd cut it out if you had the choice. So, I'm giving you your wish. I need you to be strong, however. I can't do this with you injured. So I'm nursing you back to health until I can make it all better."

"And what's better in this scenario, Alanna?"

She strokes over Jonathan's cheek with love and tenderness. "You get your heart back and Jonathan will take Misha's. It's a perfect match."

"In what universe is that a perfect match? Why didn't you just give Jonathan, Misha's heart!" I scream, enraged beyond belief.

"I wanted to help you both, but I knew if your heart wasn't a match, then you'd be the perfect host."

"Oh my motherfucking fuck! A host? And you think Luna and I are crazy! You're fucking insane."

"Oh yes, perfect little Luna. This wouldn't be so complicated if it wasn't for her."

I grit my teeth together. "She has done nothing wrong, you

fucking psychopath!"

Alanna takes the insult with grace and I soon see why that is when she walks over to my bed. "If it wasn't for her, you'd maybe see what a big happy family we could be."

"What the fuck? You think I'd want a gang bang with you and McStinky over there? Hell to the fuck no."

Does she honestly think we could kick it as a throuple? Or that I would be runner-up if her already dead fiancé rolled over and died—again? Or does she think I'm Jonathan?

I don't know what the fuck is going on, what I do know is that I want off this ride.

This entire time I trusted a fucking nutjob. I doubted Luna, and wherever she is, she believes she's done all the horrible things I told her she did.

"How is Joy involved in this?" I ask because it's apparent these two conniving witches are in cahoots.

"I can't tell you all my secrets, but soon, all will be revealed. But now, I know you're going to try and find Luna. And I can't have that happening. She thinks you're dead, and soon, she'll forget about you."

"Why don't you just fucking kill her then!" I spit, tugging at my restraints because if I break free, I am going to snap Alanna's neck.

"Because I'm a doctor." She grins. "And I take my duty of care very seriously."

Bull-fucking-shit.

"But I need her alive. She's your Achilles' heel. She's the one who gives you life."

"You…bitch."

"Funny, that's exactly what she said before I gave her some

283

electric shock therapy."

"No!" I scream, our heart shattering into a million pieces. So it seems fitting when Alanna brings the hammer down onto my knee, breaking it too. The pain is debilitating, but I use it as fuel.

I watch Alanna walk over to Jonathan and hold his hand, and hum along to Beethoven. I almost feel sorry for her. Love makes people do some crazy shit, and I'll do anything to save Luna.

His heart was always meant for me, and I've never felt more protective of it than I do right now.

Most people like Alanna are lovesick. But me, I'm heartsick because this heart will do *anything* to save the one *we* love. Our heart *finally* beats in unison, and like the perfect piece of music, the world applauds this masterpiece that is about to change this fucking world.

Subscribe to my Newsletter:
landing.mailerlite.com/webforms/landing/b4j1v6

Heart Sick Playlist:
tinyurl.com/ahshfb59

Acknowledgements

My author family: Elle and Vi—I love you both very much.

My ever-supporting parents. You guys are the best. I am who I am because of you. I love you. RIP Papa. Gone but never forgotten. You're in my heart. Always.

My agent, Kimberly Brower from Brower Literary & Management. Thank you for your patience and thank you for being an amazing human being.

My editor, Ellie—I FLOVE you! I think I've loved you from the moment we met over ten years ago! My Brother's Editor is the best.

My proofreader—Rumi Khan, you are amazing! Your attention to detail gives me life! At least one of us is organized.

Lori Jackson, this cover is everything and so much more. Thank you for being so patient. You're a true artist.

Michelle—you're magic. This photo gives me life and I love that you took it in our little Vegas villa. And yes, fine, you were right!

Luke Eisner—thanks for being my muse. Now play me the piano please x

My publicists—Danielle Sanchez from Wildfire Marketing Solutions, Sarah Ferguson from Literally Yours PR, and Candi Kane PR—Thank you for all your help. What a bunch of fantastic women I work with! Love you all!

To the endless blogs that have supported me since day

one—You guys rock my world.

My bookstagrammers and TikTokers—Your creativity astounds me. The effort you go to is just amazing. Thank you for the posts, the teasers, the support, the messages, the love, the EVERYTHING! I see what you do, and I am so, so thankful.

My ARC TEAM—You guys are THE BEST! Thanks for all the support.

My reader group—sending you all a big kiss.

MR. J and Michelle Lancaster—My heart is full because of you both.

My beautiful friends—Michelle, Louise, Lisa, Sara, Steve, Chris, Tayla, Isabelle, and Karli; you're my people.

Samantha and Amelia—I love you both so very much.

My fur babies—mamma loves you so much! Dacca, I know you're hanging with Jaggy, Dina, Ninja, and Papa.

To anyone I have missed, I'm sorry. It wasn't intentional!

Last but certainly not least, I want to thank YOU! Thank you for welcoming me into your hearts and homes. My readers are the BEST readers in this entire universe! Love you all!

Oh, and to all the boys I loved—thanks for reminding me of who I am and why I write such kick ass heroines. You're all a lesson learned. Some good. Some bad. But here I am. Hi x

About the Author

Monica James spent her youth devouring the works of Anne Rice, William Shakespeare, and Emily Dickinson.

When she is not writing, Monica is busy running her own business, but she always finds a balance between the two. She enjoys writing honest, heartfelt, and turbulent stories, hoping to leave an imprint on her readers. She draws her inspiration from life.

She is a bestselling author in the U.S.A., Australia, Canada, France, Germany, Israel, and The U.K.

Monica James resides in Melbourne, Australia, with her wonderful family, and menagerie of animals. She is slightly obsessed with cats, chucks, and lip gloss, and secretly wishes she was a ninja on the weekends.

Connect with Monica James

Facebook: facebook.com/authormonicajames
Twitter: twitter.com/monicajames81
Goodreads: goodreads.com/MonicaJames
Instagram: instagram.com/authormonicajames
Website: authormonicajames.com
TikTok: @authormonicajames
BookBub: bookbub.com/authors/monica-james
Amazon: https://amzn.to/2EWZSyS
Join my Reader Group: http://bit.ly/2nUaRyi

CPSIA information can be obtained
at www.ICGtesting.com
Printed in the USA
BVHW042151160223
658724BV00008B/37